Lost in His Silence

Mike Delaney

Contents

Prologue

I stared at my backpack.

There were some clothes inside, a toothbrush, toothpaste, some makeup, my almost empty wallet that comprised two fifty-dollar bills and a hairbrush.

I looked around my room and knew I wouldn't miss a thing about being in this place. The past six years that I'd lived here were nothing worse than a nightmare. I descended the stairs of the house, hoping to put it all behind me.

Nothing in this house was worth remembering, anyway. If it was possible, I wanted to forget everything; starting with my uncle Mark and his son, Ray. The only reason I stayed for as long as I had was only for my aunt, who was ill and passed away last week.

Now, I had no reason to live in this place.

Not a day went by after my aunt's passing that I hadn't planned on escaping.

I tiptoed down the hallway and threw a glance at the living room. Mark sat on the raggedy old couch. A puff of smoke permeated the air, and the ashtray was decorated with cigarette butts. For a forty-five-year-old man, he looked at least ten years older.

He was intently watching something on the TV and chugging a large can of beer when his eyes rested on me and his face contorted into an ugly smile. "Where are you going, honey?" He slurred the words.

I dropped my bag on the floor out of his sight as I answered him, "I'm just going to Perry's house. Forgot my notebook there." I let the lie roll naturally out of my lips.

"Alright, but don't be late. I hate to be kept waiting." He sneered at me before looking back at the television screen.

I masked the look of pure disgust as I pocketed some money lying around on the table. I opened the door to the old rickety house and sniffed the air of freedom as soon as I stepped outside. My Cousin Ray's old beat-up truck was parked out front, but he wasn't anywhere in sight. I assumed he was working on one of his useless cars in the garage.

The trees whooshed as I walked past them. I looked once at the cornfields and tried not to think of all the vile stuff that happened back there.

The scarecrow standing alone in the dark looked like a prop right out of a macabre horror movie, like it was going to follow me.

Cars zoomed past me, some men passed dirty comments, and others offered me a ride. I was dressed appropriately in jeans and a loose fitted tank top. I'd also pulled on a jacket to cover myself so there was nothing scandalous to look at here. I guess it didn't matter just as long as a woman was walking alone on the street; men were going to whistle and cat-call.

Twenty minutes later, I found the bus stop that was going to take me to my final destination. I had to wait for another thirty minutes before a bus pulled up before the station. I climbed in and took the very first seat that was vacant by the door.

Goodbye fucked up past, and hello bright future!

This felt like an adventure, and I tried not to feel depressed about the fact that I wasn't having much cash on me, or that I had lost a permanent home. If I wasn't hired for this job as planned, I was going to be practically homeless.

I opened the app on my phone and checked all the jobs I'd marked important and only one of them was in the same location I was heading towards.

One ad read:

NEEDED FULL-TIME BABYSITTER. Should be beautiful with a curvy body no scars. Interested candidates kindly send your details :)

I rolled my eyes. Why did a babysitter need to have a curvy body? I knew this ad looked very sketchy and there was no doubt in my mind that this man was a perv trying to catch unsuspecting teenage girls. I reported the ad and scrolled through more. A few minutes later, I finally found the one that I was looking for.

The advertisement on the app read:

Looking for a live-in nanny who can work FULL-TIME for a family.

Education: high school degree (At least)

Minimum work experience of two years.

Accommodation and food will be free.

We will allot an extra allowance whenever necessary.

Interested candidates forward your CV at the below email Id.

I'd applied for this job a few weeks ago and was surprised when I'd heard from them. The man said the family wanted to meet me before they gave me the job, and something in the man's voice said that I could indeed get selected.

The signage for Ambervale town came into view and I asked the driver about the address of the house that I was visiting. His brows hit the roof when he read it and asked me if that's really where I planned to stop and when I said yes, he laughed mockingly, which was a little strange. I mean, it's not like I'd asked him to drop me off on Planet Mars or something.

When I inquired what was funny, he shrugged it off like it was no biggie.

It's when he dropped me off the bus that I realized why he seemed to think I was crazy.

In front of me were two huge metal gates with the letter's 'M' on them. I stared at it in awe and into the far distance, my eyes focused on the very large and daunting house, a mansion that looked right out of an Architectural Digest magazine, or a horror movie. You take the pick. The opulence and the grandness of it were nothing like I'd ever seen before.

I decide to call on the number that was provided on the app.

"Hi, this is Millicent. I applied for the job and received a call to come for the interview." I said, a little anxious and shaky, "I just arrived by bus. Is this the right address?"

I heard a deep masculine chuckle on the other end of the line. "I see you, Millicent. Please come inside."

He could see me?

Just then, I noticed the surveillance cameras surrounding the area.

The gates to the house opened smoothly, and I entered them completely unaware of the horrors that awaited me.

* * *

A.N: Hey loves, this is a New Romantic Thriller. I hope to see you all on this exciting journey as I will be making frequent updates. If you enjoyed reading the chapter, please Vote & Comment your thoughts below. Also add the book to your reading lists :)

stay safe x

Chapter 1

Approximately ten minutes later, I was sitting in front of a very intimidating man lounging behind a large cherry-wood desk in an equally impressive office.

The house was exquisite, to say the least. A gothic colonial mansion fit to be called a king's castle with their lawns neatly trimmed, a huge mermaid sculpted fountain in the center, a lake house on the other side of the mansion. The house was built during the early eighteenth century, according to the butler that showed me to Mr. Montgomery's office.

As soon as I'd entered those enormous gates, it was already clear to me that these people were wealthy beyond my imagination and working for them would be like a dream come true.

I was good with kids. In fact, I used to babysit some kids from the neighborhood for extra cash and it worked out well, so I had no doubt I could do this, too.

"Millie," Mr. Montgomery addressed me, pulling me out of my thoughts, "Is it okay if I call you Millie?"

"Yes, that's totally fine."

Devin Montgomery could have told me he worked in Hollywood movies and I wouldn't dare disagree. His rumpled hair was the color of a coffee latte, and eyes so green as if he held an entire amazon jungle there. He was tall and wore a casual white shirt that highlighted his toned body. Men like him usually just appeared in my fantasies and never in real life.

"That's good." He flashed me a grin. "I've read through your resume and you mentioned here that you're pretty great at handling kids."

"That's right," I responded. "There were a lot of kids in my neighborhood, so I'm experienced where they are concerned. Kids love me so you wouldn't have to worry about your son or daughter. I'm also good at engaging them in outdoor and indoor games, although we never had too much outdoor space where I lived, so I think that wouldn't be a problem here."

I was rambling! Sometimes my mouth could run miles without my knowledge.

His smile did not falter as he regarded me with a curious look on his face. "Well, that's a relief, but I'd like to clarify; I'm not married and I don't have kids. It's my brother that I need a caretaker for, and he's not exactly what I'd call a kid. He's...." Devin looked away into the distance trying to come up with the right word, "He's difficult and different."

"I see." I might have been a teeny-tiny bit thrilled by the fact that Devin wasn't married.

How bad could this job be? If his brother was a nasty, disobeying teenager, I was quite certain I could teach him to stay in line. I was guilty of pinching rowdy kids when their parents weren't looking, so this rich Montgomery teen better be nice.

"Are you usually great with kids who throw tantrums and refuse to eat?"

I gave him my most confident smile. "Of course. It's difficult in the beginning, but I can assure you that your brother and I will be best friends in no time."

I was trying to sell this too hard, and I was hoping I wasn't sounding too desperate like a saleslady trying hard to sell the expired cosmetics at a cheap price.

By the looks of it, guess Devin was sold because he said, "Millie, you're hired."

Wow! That was easy...

I couldn't keep the excitement out of my voice. "Awesome! I'd like to meet your brother."

"All in due time," he said, pushing a document towards me, "We have a rule that every person under our employment signs a contract. It states that you'll be keeping this position for at least a year, but before that, you'll be working on a one-month probation period. We'll be monitoring you and we'll have the power to dismiss you when we see fit. It's only because we've had a few caretakers before you who did not treat my brother with the respect he deserves and we were forced to take proper actions. You can go through the entire document, take your time to read it and I'll..."

I choose a pen and signed my name on the document. My desperation had no limits whatsoever. Anything was better than the hellhole that consisted of my uncle and his son. "I want this job, Mr. Montgomery, and I completely understand that you would want to protect your brother from harm. I promise you I won't be that person." While he was talking to me, I scanned a few pages, and it all looked legit. I didn't want to waste more time when he could just decide that I wasn't fit to do this job and hire someone else.

He gave me a pleased smile, his eyes crinkled at the corners, "Call me Devin."

The butler of the house, Mr. Winston, showed me my room, which was on the second story of the mansion. The room seemed comfortable with a double bed, a matching dresser, a wardrobe, and even a flat-screen. A large window overlooked the lake.

It was like looking at a painting and I could certainly get used to this scenery. There wasn't any place I'd rather be.

The walls of the room were covered in baby pink wallpapers with little cherry blossom petals on it, and I was quickly falling in love with this bedroom.

This place was more than what I'd expected and I knew that I'm going to be happy under this employment.

Devin was excessively sweet and his mannerisms screamed 'Gentleman'. He'd mentioned that excluding Castle, (the one they employed me as a nanny for) had two more brothers and a sister, Dayana. I took all the information in as he told me about Theodore, who was seventeen and studying in high school, and then there was the youngest, little Chandler, aged eleven.

Their parents were killed two years ago during a tragic boating accident that took place by the property lake and that had left only their grandfather Hugh Montgomery alive. The man was eighty-five and bound to a wheelchair.

As I listened to Devin reciting the tragic story of his family, I couldn't help but feel sympathy for them.

It was all so depressing and I could feel the sadness creeping into the atmosphere. Devin had to shoulder all the responsibilities of being the only mature man in the family, and my heart went out to him.

The house was easy to get lost in; the passageways were endless and there were so many rooms that I could only cover them all in one week. There was a movie theatre, and a library were my favorite in the house. Devin was quick to tell me I was allowed to use them in my free time.

We stopped in front of a room when he turned to face me, "Millie, just a heads up. About my brother Castle, he may not like you right off the bat and he'll take his time to warm up to you, so I will suggest you learn to be patient with him."

I placed my hand on his. "I will never give you a chance to be disappointed."

He smiled, and then his gaze followed where I touched his hand. I quickly snatched my hand off his shirt sleeve. "I expect you won't." he narrowed his eyes at me, heat radiated from his green eyes. "This is Castle's bedroom. Are you ready to meet him?"

I nodded.

He turned the knob and opened the door. "Castle, look who's here to see you."

The room was empty.

The décor was masculine; the walls painted a deep gray, and the furniture was rich, polished wood, everything in gothic style. It was apparent that they had restored the home in his original unique style from the 1800s.

A toy train moved over the tiny track, puffing out a little smoke, going inside the little tunnel and then zigzagging through mini-mountains and forests.

I stared at the toys, and Devin watched me in amusement. "Castle loves trains. It calms him down to just look at them."

There were other miscellaneous toys sprawled on the floor, along with a drawing book and crayons.

I smiled. "I can't wait to meet him. He sounds lovely."

"He is." Devin agreed proudly.

My eyes then rested over the wooden bedposts by the headboard. There were ropes tied on either side of it. A chill ran down my body, thinking about the reason for the ropes to even be here.

"What are those for?" I inquired, curiously.

Devin followed my gaze, and his smile faltered. "Well, as I mentioned before, Castle can be a little difficult. The ropes are only used for emergency purposes."

Something about his tone told me I wasn't allowed to question him further about the topic.

What exactly were these emergency purposes?

Did his family tie him up? That surely sounded cruel, but I decided not to push it.

He looked at his gold wristwatch. "I'm sure we'll see him downstairs in the dining room, since it's already time to dinner. Join me."

"Thank you," I said.

I couldn't wait to meet Castle.

Chapter 2

The dining table could have easily accommodated twenty people, but I saw only seven seated with me. Eight, if you counted me.

I felt a little nervous when I first entered the room, afraid that I might trip over my own feet and make a complete fool of myself in front of these people. Thankfully, Devin kept his hand on my back as we entered and I felt a little better knowing he was by my side.

All the eyes in the room zeroed in on me like I was the newest species that they couldn't wait to dissect. And if that wasn't enough, I kept worrying about what the family would think of me. I didn't come from wealth; rather quite the contrary and it would be obvious, looking at my outfit, that I didn't belong here.

Devin pulled out a chair for me and I settled down, thanking him. Dayana sat on my left side, and she gave me a welcoming smile. I couldn't believe how strikingly similar she looked with Devin; it was like looking at a female equivalent of him. She was beautiful, with honey blonde hair, sparkling emerald eyes, and dimples that would have any man dancing in her palms. Her style screamed at levels of sophistication.

She was a goddess on earth, literally.

"I'm Dayana. I'm sure Devin told you about me." She said sweetly.

"Yeah, he did."

"Let me introduce you to the rest of us. The grumpy young man sitting directly opposite you is Theodore, but he prefers Theo. He thinks Theodore is kinda old-fashioned and makes him sound like a grandpa."

"Speak for yourself, Vixen!" Theo grumbled.

"Language, Theo! That's not the way to talk to your older sister." Devin scolded in his older brother's tone.

"Whatever." Theo retorted.

He seemed like a typical bratty seventeen-year-old. He'd lost his parents at a very young age, and that must have been hard. I could completely relate to him because I was the same when I was his age.

Just like his older brother and sister, he was also gifted with their good-looks. I bet a lot of girls in his high school swooned when he walked by, and speaking of, I wondered if he played any sport. For a teen, he was built like a bull and probably ate like one too.

"What the hell are you staring at?!"

It took a while for me to realize Theo was talking to me. My face went hot. "N-Nothing," I stuttered, "I'm sorry."

"N-Nothing...s-s-sorry." Theodore imitated me.

"Theodore, I expect you to respect those who are elder to you. That is not the way to talk to Millie. Apologize to her right now."

"Make me!" he threw his napkin onto the plate and pushed it harshly off the table. It went crashing down and shattered on the floor. Maids scurried forward to clean the mess. "And I don't fucking care about dinner. I'm going to order pizza, anyway." He climbed to his feet, snagged up a sandwich from the tray and stormed out of the room.

It felt like I nearly survived a hurricane. That kid needed to learn some manners, and fast. I take back what I said about him being a bratty teenager. More like Satan's spawn. Heck, Damien Thorn was even polite.

"I'm sorry on his behalf, Millie," Devin said softly.

"He's seventeen, but still going through that puberty phase, you know," Dayana interjected. "Teenagers are scary."

"It's okay, really."

"Theo's not been the same since our parents passed away," Dayana mentioned, and the dinner table filled with silence.

"I'm sorry to hear about your parents," I told her. "My parents died when I was little, so I don't remember them much, but I can still feel the loss. I can only imagine what you're going through."

"Thanks." Dayana murmured, giving my hand a little squeeze.

We began with dinner then. I looked at the full plate of meal on the table before me. They served starters in the beginning, some fancy shrimp dish with avocado and cucumber, and deviled eggs, which was followed by duck slices in cherry sauce or something.

I gobbled the food like I was on death row and this was my last meal. I even licked the Cherry sauce off the plate, so much for pretending to be a lady. From the corner of my eye, I noticed how Devin regarded me with interest. The corners of his mouth twitched upward. Between chewing and taking quick bites, I choked on my wine.

Dayana laughed, "Slow down. The food won't disappear."

"She eats like Trixie." A small voice said.

I looked in the voice's direction. I hadn't even noticed the little boy sitting two chairs down from me.

The boy looked identical to his older siblings, and there was a certain sadness in his sea-green eyes, like the kid had seen a lot of unspeakable things, and he was staring at me as if he could look into my soul.

"Who is Trixie?" I asked.

"Our dog, she's a German shepherd."

I coughed, trying not to feel insulted, because clearly, the boy wasn't trying to be disrespectful and only stating what he'd observed. Did all the younger Montgomery's swore that they would slander me as soon as I stepped foot in this house?

"You must be Castle," I pointed out, smiling at him regardless of being called a hungry dog. "I saw the trains in your room."

He looked at me like I'd fallen off the rocker. "Hell naw. I'm Chandler. Castle's over there!" He pointed in the other direction.

I turned towards where his finger pointed and my fork almost slipped out of my hand.

Castle wasn't a kid. Not by a longshot.

Either that or I needed a pair of glasses because this was a man sitting at the end of the table. A freakin' grown man.

He had wavy sable hair neatly combed, and striking aquiline features that consisted of a straight nose and an angular jawline, and eyes the color of Crème brûlée that I was having for dessert.

If Disney Prince's were real, they'd look like Castle. He was probably better looking than Devin, and I wasn't even exaggerating. Devin was all charming and easy to talk to, while Castle appeared to be a complete opposite of his brother in every way. There was a certain darkness masked under his golden features, a mysterious aura.

"Hi Castle," I greeted him and smiled. "It's so nice to meet you finally. I'm going to be taking care of you from here on. I hope we can be friends."

Castle stared at me with a poker face. He didn't even twitch, not so much as a smile, and just continued to gawk at me like I was a Rubik's cube he desperately wanted to solve. I now understood what Devin had warned about his brother being different.

Chandler laughed at my side.

"Castle, say hi to Millie."

He didn't. Instead, he resumed digging in his plate and stuffing the food in his mouth. I noticed the food that was served to Castle was different. He was having biscuits and gravy.

Devin probably noticed my assessment. "Castle has a lot of likes and dislikes for food, so our cook, Susan, makes him special meals."

"I see."

"He likes to dine in his room sometimes, and when he does, I would request you to keep him company."

"Of course," I said and then turned to Dayana on my side, "How old is Castle?"

"Thirty." She answered. "He's our older brother."

Well, I'd signed the contract thinking they hired me to be a nanny for a child or a teenage boy. Being a nanny to a man-child was never the plan.

Guess I didn't have a choice anymore...

The rest of the dinner passed comfortably, and to be honest, I enjoyed being here, becoming a part of a family so classy and wealthy. For someone like me, this was a privilege that I'd never even dreamed about, to sit amidst them and be included in their con- versations. I realized if I was good at this, and did my job perfectly,

Devin won't have a chance to complain and who knows, I might be appointed here permanently.

Before retiring to my bedroom that night, when I decoded to talk to Dayana, "I think Castle doesn't really like me."

She laughed like I was being ridiculous. "That's not true. There were over three-hundred applicants for this job, and he chose you."

He chose me?

"I don't understand." I admitted, "What do you mean, he chose me?"

"Well, he pointed at your picture and told us he wants you as his nanny." She explained. "And Devin thought why not, so he interviewed you over the phone, and Castle listened to the conversation." She patted my shoulder. "It's going to take some time, don't worry. He likes you."

"He can talk, right?"

"Yes, he does. Well, I don't blame you for thinking that he doesn't. Most people who meet him think that way. He just chooses his time to speak."

"Please don't take my enquiring in any wrong way, Dayana. I just wanted to get to know him better. How did he lose his memories?"

"The boating accident." She said, "He hit his head but was lucky to survive. The doctors say that Castle may never regain his memories."

"Oh!"

I felt sorry for Castle. He'd been born into a privileged family with more wealth than he could use in a lifetime, but tragedy had stolen everything from him.

"I have to accompany Devin to a conference early tomorrow morning. I need to go to bed."

"Sure. Sorry to keep you waiting. I've had a long day today."

"No problem, and Goodnight, Sweetie."

"Night," I said.

"Oh, and Millie..."

"Yeah?"

"Lock your bedroom door when you sleep."

She disappeared down to her bedroom, stifling a yawn, and left me there wondering what that was about.

I started climbing the stairs to my room, and since most of the lights were already out; the place was dark with only a few lights left on. Suddenly, I felt a chill running down my body, but I kept walking until I heard something behind me, so I stopped and turned.

Castle stood at the end of the staircase, wearing blue jammies with little turtles on them. His eyes were dead set on me, a grim expression plastered on his face. Something about the way he was looking at me felt so wrong, and I felt my heart drumming against my chest.

I could have sworn I hadn't seen him a few minutes back when I was talking to his sister.

"Do you need anything, Castle?" I addressed him directly.

As I expected, he didn't answer. It took me a few seconds to realize that he was holding something in his hand.

"What's that in your hand?"

Again, there was no response.

"I need you to talk to me, Castle."

He swayed from one foot to another and continued to repeat that. Okayyyyy....

"Good Night," I told him and began making my way upstairs. This time, I didn't look back.

Regardless, I knew he was following me. The loud thumping of his footsteps following me was a good enough reason to make me flee. I sped up and when I reached the floor; I hurried inside my room, shut the door, and locked it.

My heart wanted to leap out of my chest.

He was standing outside. I sat down on the floor and looked at the gap between the door. I noticed some movements there.

I was scared, but I also didn't want to call Devin because I needed to keep this job desperately! He might think I wasn't cut out for it.

There was a knock at the door. I decided not to answer it.

After that, I heard nothing for a while, so I thought he left and almost jumped out of my skin when there was another soft knock.

I was having my doubts about the story that Devin had spun regarding the previous nannies being fired because they hadn't treated Castle well. I could bet that the nannies had left after being harassed by him, and not the other way round.

I counted to five and answered the door to ask him what his problem was, but when I opened it, all I saw was darkness on either side of the hallway, save for the light streaming from the large windows.

"What do you want?" I asked.

There was no sign of him.

I started closing the door when a little toy pickup truck rolled forward and stopped in front of me.

At a distance, I saw the silhouette of a tall figure.

Waiting. Watching.

The truck was radio-controlled and kept bumping against my toe. I looked closely at it and saw a little folded note inside.

I picked the note up and quickly walked inside my room

With shaky hands, I opened it.

The words were scrawled in red crayon.

Hi Millie :)

Chapter 3

The incident that happened last night completely freaked me out and I couldn't sleep the entire night as I kept seeing footsteps outside of my bedroom. It was during dawn that I got some sleep.

When I went downstairs for breakfast, I noticed there was a file left on the table and then I remembered that Devin and Dayana were supposed to go for some conference meeting early in the morning, and Theo and Chandler had already left for school.

That meant I was home alone with Castle.

I tried not to dwell on the fact that being alone with Castle might be a little nerve-wracking since I had to look over my shoulder constantly.

The kitchen was slick and modern, still had a vintage oven, and I knew for a fact that their parents had probably loved and cherished the old designs and kept it. I poured myself a glass of OJ and grabbed two slices of toast as I settled down onto the stool near the island bar and read through the file.

There were pages of Dos and Don'ts, Castle's likes and dislikes and what they expected of me as his Caregiver. A few lines that were highlighted caught my eye; it mentioned that Castle wasn't allowed to roam freely out of the house unattended. He also could not have his meals unsupervised, and from what I could collect from this document was the fact that basically I was supposed to be Castle's guard-dog.

Castle's life seemed gloomy. I made a mental note to get to know him better regardless of how brooding and creepy he was, and I would become his friend if nothing else. His brother was paying me well. It was only natural I took this job very seriously.

"Good Morning, Miss. Millicent. I see that you're up early." Susan, the cook, walked into the kitchen, a bright smile plastered over her face.

"Good Morning, Susan, please call me Millie as everyone else in this house does. And yes, I enjoy waking up early."

"That makes the two of us." She commented, "I hope you had a good night's sleep."

I wondered if this was some kind of trick question, if she knew about Castle prowling around late at night and wanted to see if I spilled, but the more I tried to analyze her, the more I realized I was imagining it. The question was casual.

Susan was a plump woman with a lovely smile; she had the motherly vibe going about it.

"I did." I lied.

I read through the entire file, and couldn't help but think about the caretakers that were hired here before me. What was the reason they fired her?

She served me a very appetizing looking waffle topped with whipped cream and strawberries. I thanked her and knew this was my chance to do some investigating.

"Susan, is it alright if I asked you something about Castle?"

"Go ahead, honey." She said, pouring me a cup of coffee.

"Does Castle normally stay up late until midnight?"

Her bright mood suddenly turned gloomy as she stared into the distance at a memory. "He likes to run free most of the time, so they let him. Mr. Montgomery thinks there's no harm. There was a time when they used to lock him up in his bedroom at night because the Caregiver who was here before you, Tracy suggested that, and she..." Her eyes suddenly turned red, and she snatched a few tissues as she cried, "she harmed the poor boy. Tracy would beat him, and let him scream, and he kept banging on the door, wanting to be out. She was a disgusting woman. The caregivers that came before her weren't any better. I often found wounds on Castle's body inflicted by them."

"That's awful," I said. "I wish I was here sooner."

She took my hand in hers. "Please do the right thing by Castle. He doesn't deserve to be treated like that."

"I will, I promise you. Is there anything else that I should know about him?"

"He won't talk much because he can't remember some words. You need to figure out what he's trying to tell you, dear."

"I'll make a note of doing that. Thanks, Susan, that was helpful."

I left the cook alone after that since I didn't want to upset her more than I already had. It was quite clear the previous caregivers who failed to understand him on a personal level abused Castle.

If I wanted to be his friend like I'd told him before, I knew I had to at least try and make an effort, and for what it's worth, I knew handling Castle would still be a piece of cake compared to living with my uncle where I was treated like an object, and nothing short of a maid.

I closed my eyes and let the memories flood me. I needed to forget that life!

I went upstairs to his room after breakfast, and the door was unlocked, but I still knocked on it. When I didn't hear an answer, I entered inside and found the television blaring, an old rerun of Tom & Jerry was on.

Unlike the last time that I'd been here, all the books and toys were put back into its space. The room was dark, no lights were on and the drapes were closed, so I walked to the French windows and opened them, letting the room bathe in the sunlight. I didn't miss how there were bars on the windows.

I could hear the shower running, and a few minutes later, Castle walked out of the steaming bathroom with a towel hanging over his hips.

He stood frozen on the spot, surprised to find me in his room.

"I...I knocked on the door before entering," I explained stupidly.

His hair was still wet from the shower, and his brown eyes looked almost golden in the sunlight. He had broad shoulders and a body that was sculpted like a Greek God; with a set of lickable abs and a trim waist. There was a faint dusting of light brown hair on his chest that looked so soft; that I wanted to touch, the trail disappeared into dangerous territory.

Castle might be cuckoo, but his body was right as rain.

Oh, God! It was so wrong of me to check out a man who wasn't in his right mind to pay attention to women, and I felt extremely guilty, but that didn't change the fact that he was ridiculously gorgeous.

His dark eyes flashed towards me as if he knew what I was thinking. He looked at the open windows and back at me, his fingers curled and uncurled as he charged forward. I took a few steps back in fear of what he was about to do, but he walked past me, and that gave me time to notice some scars on his body, darker on his wrists and a jagged line across his back.

Castle pulled the drapes almost harshly, bringing the room into darkness. He was facing the other side when the towel slid down and I had a perfect view of his round backside.

Heat crept over my neck, "I'm-I'm...sorry, I'll leave."

"Stay."

I was taken aback.

Castle talked!

And he asked me to stay. It proved that he could comprehend what I said to him.

It was the first time I heard him talk; his voice was soft and hauntingly addictive, and he sounded like he didn't have too much practice with speaking.

I wanted more.

I craved to hear another word from his mouth.

I stayed until he'd dressed up completely in a t-shirt and jeans. I watched him as he took a dry towel and settled down on his bed. The water dripped from his hair.

"May I?" I asked with my hands raised towards him for the towel.

He didn't say a word, so I took that as a yes. I dried his hair with a towel, feeling completely aware of his body heat being so close to mine, the scent of his shampoo made my knees weak, it was a mix of something spicy and blackberries, and maybe you could also throw a little vanilla into the mix.

"Now you're all nice and dry," I said, carrying the wet towel to his bathroom to hang there for drying. I walked out of the bathroom to find him sitting on the floor, cross-legged. "Would you like me to read you a book?"

He shook his head vigorously. "Go...go out."

He was asking me to get out of his room?

I stared back at him, trying to understand what that meant.

"Go out." He repeated, his large golden-brown eyes watching me with interest. "I...I want to go."

"You wanna go out into the courtyard?"

He nodded, slowly looking up at me from the floor, small stealing glances.

"Okay, let's go."

We walked outside the mansion towards the open courtyard, the huge German shepherd named Trixie leading us ahead. It was strange how Castle couldn't communicate much with me, but with Trixie; he had an entirely different language going. The dog knew exactly what her master wanted and she would follow his commands.

Fetch. Down. Wait. Stay.

I bet she was used to following him around even before he lost his memories. Sometimes I wished dogs could talk so they could tell stories. Real. Happy. Ugly. The truth that they'd witnessed.

I sat down on the patio while I watched Castle play with the dog. It was a good thing I'd brought a book with me so I wouldn't get bored, Pride & Prejudice by Jane Austen. I'd read the book before, but since it was so entertaining, I was going to read it again. I'd found it lying around at my breakfast table, so I'd grabbed it.

Trixie barked at something at a distance, barring her teeth out. It had to be a squirrel or birds, or something like that. Castle watched her from the sidelines, not attempting to stop her.

I'd finished reading the first chapter and flipped to the next page when an origami peacock fell to the ground.

I picked it up, and it seemed like there was something written inside it. I quickly opened it.

The words scribbled inside shocked me.

Leave while you still have a chance.

It was the same handwriting as the one I'd received from Castle, so that meant this came from him.

Why was Castle warning me?

Chapter 4

"**M**illie, there's someone outside who wants to see you," Devin informed me one evening, a few days after my arrival at the Montgomery mansion.

I had a slight idea who that was, but I still asked anyway. "Who is it?"

"The man identified himself as your uncle, and there's a younger guy who says he's your cousin. They showed us some pictures for proof as well." He said, "We allow family visitations to our employees, so if you want to see your family, I could arrange for them to sit and chat with you in the spare sitting area."

My blood ran cold. Mark and Ray were both disgusting and worthless people, and I didn't know how they figured out my address. I didn't remember ever letting it slip from my mouth.

I could only think of one reason they would come here.

To extort money from me, and now that they knew where I worked, I was sure they would make things difficult.

"Devin, I don't want to see them. Please make some excuse and tell them to leave."

He nodded, understanding the fear in my undertone. He turned to the house butler. "Winston, tell the gentlemen outside that they have a misunderstanding and Millicent Davis doesn't work here."

They were hardly people you would call gentlemen, but I refused to say anything mostly because once I opened up to Devin about my past, I would have to explain the why, how, and when and I didn't need that right now. I came to this town and took this job because I wanted to start over and talking about my past would just open old wounds.

Besides, the thought of Mark and Ray in this house was like inviting a pair of coyotes. The silver would automatically disappear from the house and no one would even notice.

"Yes, sir." Winston left the room and walked down the hallway towards the main door.

Devin turned to me and placed his hand on my back. "Is there something you want to talk to me about?"

I shook my head. "They aren't good people and I don't consider them as family."

"You're right. Not all blood relatives can be called family. Millie, if you ever need to talk to anyone, I'll always be here for you and I'm sure Dayana would be glad to lend you an ear, too."

"I really appreciate that," I said genuinely.

"And as long as you're under our employment, we will protect you."

That evening, Castle didn't show up at the dinner table, and Dayana was missing as well.

"Where's Castle and Dayana?" I asked.

"He refused to come down to dinner, so I sent one maid to check on him. Dayana has a bit of a headache and said she wants to lie down in her room."

This is where I will be put to test. If I could prove to Devin that I could get Castle to eat without throwing tantrums, they would likely end my probation period and keep me here as Castle's permanent nanny. Well, at least until he doesn't regain his memories.

I stood up from the table. "I'll go see that he eats his dinner."

Devin gave me a grateful smile, "good luck with that." His eyes rested on the plate that I filled with food. "But I would suggest you not to force him if he doesn't want to eat."

Theo sniggered, smiling coyly at me.

I didn't step on his cat, so I didn't understand what this hostility was all about.

And someday I was going to ask him what his problem was.

I carried some of Castle's food on a plate and began climbing the stairs. When I reached his room, I heard someone talking, so I stopped outside of his bedroom, not wanting to pry into the conversation.

"Do you understand what I'm saying? I know you can." The maid's tone was commanding. I recognized her as Barbara. "Don't act smart with me! You tell the nanny something, and I don't need to remind you what happens after that."

I was appalled by what I'd heard and how the maid was talking to Castle.

What didn't she want me to find out?

"Are you going to eat your dinner or not?" she scowled.

I was also horrified by the way she was treating her boss. Even though Castle wasn't exactly in the right state of his mind, it didn't change the fact that he was still the owner and the eldest son of the Montgomerys. Before the boating accident, Castle was the master of this household. I didn't think she would have had any right to speak to him like that if he knew better.

He was reassembling a complicated toy robot; his concentration was on what he was doing as he completely disregarded the fuming maid.

"Fine, suit yourself!" She emptied the plate of food into the bin.

Unable to control myself, I knocked on the door and stepped inside.

"Hey sweetie," I watched as her demeanor changed completely. She sounded nothing like she did a few seconds ago. "Were you standing outside for long?"

She was checking to see how much I'd heard of everything that she'd said before I entered the room.

I shook my head, "I just came here to check on Castle since he didn't show up downstairs for dinner."

She stood up and took the plate filled with food from me. "Castle doesn't want to eat, and I've tried my best to convince him to. Rebellious behavior is punished in this household. He can skip dinner tonight."

"That's not for you to decide, and I'm sure he's hungry. I can get him to eat something."

Barbara's face remained impassive. "If he gives everyone a hard time, he skips dinner. Those are the rules and I hope you would follow them too. You have to be strict with Castle, Miss. Millie; otherwise, he would do as he pleases. Now, if you'll excuse me."

She gave Castle a look filled with vehemence and stormed out of the room, closing the door behind her.

I sat on the bed beside him, but he paid no attention to me. His full concentration was on building the robot from scratch and, by the looks of it, he was doing a good job.

"Castle," I called him to bring his attention to me.

Devin had informed me that if I were to talk to Castle, I needed to address him by his name even if we were alone in the same room because he had a hard time focusing on conversations and because of his memory loss; he didn't understand certain words.

He looked up at me, his golden-brown eyes cut through mine. "Millie," his voice was almost a whisper.

And just then I noticed his bottom lip. It had a little blood on it. There were spots of blood on his lower lip, like someone had tried to force him to eat. I closed my eyes as I felt a wave of ferocious anger build inside of me, momentarily blinded by fresh tears. I quickly wiped them away.

"Castle, sweetie, can you tell me who did this to you?" I touched his cheek and felt the soft bristles on my fingers. I willed him to look at me.

He continued to stare down at his robot, trying to fix it. "Come on, you can trust me with your secret. I won't tell anyone. I promise."

It was no use. He wouldn't talk about it.

Then I was struck by an idea, but I wasn't sure it would work. The file that contained information about Castle mentioned he had a sweet tooth.

I left him alone and went back downstairs. I spent the rest of the evening baking a peanut butter chocolate cake and just before bedtime; I brought it upstairs to him.

I knew he would love the cake because my aunt used to love it, and I baked it for her until the month that she died. I saw a flicker of happiness when Castle saw what I'd brought him. He ate the cake in four bites, not bothering with the fork or the spoon I'd brought him. The icing was smeared all over his mouth, so I dabbed his mouth with a towel.

When he was done with one slice, he reached towards the second one, but I pushed it away from his reach. "If you tell me who hurt you, I'll give you more cake."

He just stared at me like an adorable man-child with shining goo-goo eyes.

"If you tell me the truth, no one will hurt you. I'm your friend, Castle. You need to trust me."

"Friend." He repeated.

"Was it Barbara?"

He stared at me for a full one minute. I'd learned not to feel uncomfortable under his scrutiny.

A few seconds later, he said, "It was...her."

I gave him the plate with the last slice of cake like I promised and left to go to bed.

The next morning, I told Devin everything, and he came upstairs to Castle's room to check the puncture marks on his bottom lip. He seemed disturbed by it, and couldn't believe that Barbara would hurt Castle.

"Castle, is it true what Millie is saying? Did Barbara hurt you?"

"Castle, tell your brother the truth."

He began breathing erratically, gripping his hair tightly and started rocking back and forth repeatedly, screaming bloody murder.

I was frozen in place watching this gorgeous, innocent man going over the edge.

Devin caught my hand and dragged me out of the bedroom and locked it from the outside. He pulled out his phone and called the nurse to come upstairs urgently while I heard things being thrown across the room inside, followed by the sound of loud crashing.

"Winston, I need Barbara removed from this house. RIGHT NOW!" Devin yelled into the phone.

He was shaking when he hung up, and he had fresh tears in his eyes as he leaned his back against the wall. "I'm sorry you had to see him like this. Sometimes he gets ticked off by certain people, so you have to be careful what you say to him."

Hesitantly, I touched his shoulder, and he placed his hand on mine. His emerald eyes were shining with unshed tears. "People told me he was better off in a home, a private facility that gave care to someone like him. But I couldn't do that to him...he's my brother. I wanted him to stay here with people that love and care for him."

I nodded, "I know. You did what you thought was the best for him."

"But he's getting hurt because I trusted the wrong people, Millie."

Devin allowed me to pull him into a hug, and all I wanted to do was take away his pain and suffering. I just rubbed his back in soothing circles. "I promise no one will ever hurt him now."

And I vowed to make that happen.

I heard a noise again that night and when I glanced at the clock; it was past two a.m. In the sitting room below, the grandfather clock chimed, and I heard the faint sounds of it drifting from downstairs. I drank some water and went back to bed.

Just then, there was the sound of footsteps outside of my bedroom.

I sat upright in bed, staring at the door, when there was a brief knock.

My heart thumped in my chest.

"Who's there?" I called out.

I didn't hear any response.

"Castle, if that's you, go back to bed," I said firmly.

Seconds later, there was another knock.

I was just so tired of playing these stupid games. He wouldn't talk to me when I asked him something, but he had the nerve to wake me up at odd hours of the night to scare me half to death.

When the footsteps faded, I opened the door and found something on the floor.

It was an origami rabbit.

And there was something written on the backside. It was scrawled in the same cursive handwriting as the note that I'd received before.

It was Dayana.

Chapter 5

I did some research on the Montgomery family and was honestly surprised about how little information the family had online. It's like someone had done a good job of keeping their family history wiped from the databases.

I found a family picture with the parents that had supposedly died in the boating accident. It was taken when the kids were still very young. I could spot Castle easily in the picture. The sable hair and the golden-brown eyes were unmistakably alluring. He looked no older than seventeen, standing behind his parents, who were seated on a couch with Devin and Dayana on either side of them. Theodore was in his mother's lap, while Chandler wasn't even born.

To an onlooker, they seemed like a happy family that had everything that anyone would ever want: wealth, power, status, a lovely wife and four beautiful children, and yet, things had gone so horribly wrong in the end. It just made me sad looking at the picture, and realizing that nothing lasted for a long time. Good things could be taken away in a snap of a moment.

"Miss. Millie, it's time for Castle's to go outside in the courtyard for a walk." The voice made me jump. I quickly shut the laptop, and I turned to look at the petite figure standing by the door. It was Sally, the quiet maid who liked to keep to herself. She'd rather sweep the non-existent dirt on the floor for hours than engage in the maid's gossip. They had so many staff spread all around the mansion that I was sure I wasn't even introduced to some of them yet.

"I'll be right there," I said, climbing to my feet and walking out of the door.

Castle was already waiting for me in the sitting area, wearing a maroon t-shirt over denim. His usually neatly combed hair was unruly, and for a moment, his gaze briefly met mine before he looked away. He kept his eyes downcast and kept clenching something in his hand.

"Good Evening, Castle. Are you ready to go outside?"

When he didn't respond, I took that as a yes and started walking ahead of him. I knew he was following me. I wore a long-sleeved summer dress and had tied my hair up in a long ponytail. According to the rule book, it mentioned that I was supposed to dress appropriately at all times, seeing as the house was filled mostly with men. They had a few caretakers that tried to entice Devin in exchange for a few favors, but Devin had made it pretty clear that he didn't need such people in his house and more importantly under his employment.

We walked through the mansion gardens; the way paved ahead was surrounded by well-manicured lush green shrubs. Castle trudged behind me slowly, kicking pebbles, and suddenly he raced forward and blocked my way.

I stopped short and kept my distance from him. At five-seven, I was taller than most women, but he was still huge and stood close to me, so close that I could smell the faint scent of soap and something like a hint of raspberry.

Stop thinking about his scent! He's not even capable of reciprocating any type of those feelings. And shouldn't I be feeling guilty to have my heart racing for someone like Castle?

"What is it?" I asked, feeling more nervous now than ever.

What if he hurt all those nannies before me and they were forced to flee? There was no one close here to witness if anything wrong were to happen to me. Castle could wring my neck for "fun" and hang me to dry outside the mansion without breaking a sweat, and his family would probably be like 'here we go again, well, let's just post another ad for an unsuspecting nanny.'

Who am I kidding? The family had tons of money, and good political connections as well. Hiding a murder wouldn't be that difficult.

Castle watched me intently. His brown eyes looked light golden in the sunset. I looked down at what he was holding out in his palm for me. He said softly, "It's for you."

It was an origami flower.

"For me?" I asked stupidly, even though I knew it was. "That's really sweet of you, Castle, thank you."

"Beautiful." He whispered, not taking his eyes off me.

It shocked me to hear the words coming from him. "You think I'm beautiful?"

He gave me a nod.

"You're not trying to flatter me to get your way, are you?" I asked.

When he didn't respond, I assumed I'd said too much, and he had difficulty comprehending a long sentence.

"No," he said.

"Why, thank you, again. You're not bad yourself."

He reached out for my hand and held it, walking beside me. It felt like grade school when Tony gave me a craft plane he made in class and that automatically made him my boyfriend. Well, at least until lunch break was over. By the end of school, he'd given another plane to Lily.

It was a small gesture by Castle, and yet my heart skipped around like a schoolgirl.

The silence between us was comfortable, but I needed him to trust me completely.

"Do you remember anything at all?"

He shook his head.

"Alright," I decided not to push him. "I'll help you remember everything."

"How?" he asked, uncertainty was obvious on his face.

"I can try. I'll speak to your therapist and we'll see what he has to say."

"NO!" He yelled coming to a halt and his breathing intensified. "NO!"

His sudden outburst took aback me.

"Okay, calm down. No therapist." I promised, "Take deep breaths."

He calmed down a few minutes later.

From a distance, I saw Chandler rushing towards us. He threw the ball towards Castle, who caught it in mid-air. Trixie ran forward at full-speed, with her tongue lolling out.

"We're going to play ball. Millie, you're going to join us, right?" Chandler was still wearing his royal blue school uniform from some fancy private school he went to.

"Sure," I said.

We stood at three different corners, and Trixie kept running around the lawn wildly.

"Silly dog," Chandler called after her. He'd loosened his tie and tossed his jacket on the ground. A maid was walking around collecting things that Chandler had discarded.

"I'm going to throw it towards Cas first and then Cas. You're going to throw it in Millie's direction. The first person who drops the ball loses."

Soon the air was filled with laughter, and I was enjoying myself, joking and playing with them. I caught glimpses of Castle's rare smile.

Trixie began barking non-stop staring at the barn, clawing at the door and looking at us with those big brown curious eyes.

Dogs could sense the paranormal. It's not like I believed in all that, but just because I hadn't seen a ghost yet didn't mean I was a skeptic either. The Montgomery's property, even though it was lavish, it dated back to the 1800s. Their ancestors might have done something here, or someone died from their family and their ghost still roamed around the place. On the far end of the property, by the woods, I could see headstones. A family graveyard.

"Trixie! Come back here!" Chandler commanded her.

But the dog wouldn't listen and continued to bark. She ran up towards me and caught the end of my dress in her teeth and pulled me towards it.

"What is it, girl?" I asked as I followed her. "Chandler, wait here with Castle, okay? I'm going to check what's in there."

"I want to come too!" He said. "I don't want to babysit Castle."

"No, you're staying here! I'm going to check first."

Chandler threw the ball on the grass in exaggeration. "I hate everyone in this house!"

The barn was locked tight, and it took all my strength to open it. It was pitch black inside, so I pulled my phone out and switched on the flashlight.

There was no one inside, just haystacks everywhere.

The barking stopped at once and turned into whimpering. She took a few steps back, leaving me standing alone inside the barn.

"What is it, Trixie?"

She continued to whimper.

"Anyone in here?" I called out and hoped to god I didn't get an answer. "Hello."

I shrieked loudly when I saw a white figure swinging towards me until I realized it wasn't a ghost.

The body swung in different directions.

My entire body was shaking, and I was sobbing, but I could see the face.

Barbara was hanging from a noose from the middle of the barn's ceiling.

Chapter 6

The maid's arms and legs had cuts on them; huge, ghastly, and definitely not self-inflicted. I watched her in horror as her body continued to swing from side to side. I needed to compose myself before I walked out of the barn. Chandler and Castle were waiting outside for me, and I needed to report this to Devin.

When I backed out of the barn, my body collided against Castle, who stood at the entrance, staring at the lifeless body stoically as if the scene before him didn't bother him much.

"Castle, come with me," I told him.

He didn't react to what I'd said, so I had to reach out for his hand and pull him out of there. I felt chills all over my arms as the scene kept playing in front of my eyes. I shut the door of the barn door behind me and told Chandler to call Devin immediately.

"Why? What's in there?" He asked. His curious green eyes reminded me so much of Devin. Chandler was like a miniature version of him, and Theo looked similar to Castle.

"Nothing," I answered carefully. I didn't need the child's curiosity to be piqued when he would only see nightmares for the rest of his childhood and adult life.

"I want to see too!" He argued.

"Chandler, I really need you to go inside the mansion and call your brother. Please."

"Well, you can't order me around." He said, and his tone surprised me. "This is my house. And you're just another maid."

"I'm a caretaker, not a maid. There's a difference. And even if I was a maid, that's not the way to speak to someone much older than you."

"I can speak however I want with anybody I want, and what I want right now is to see what's inside that barn!" He screeched like a bratty kid that he was.

I was thankful to be recruited as a nanny for Castle and not Chandler; it was no wonder the boy didn't have a nanny. He probably insulted them left and right.

"Chandler, apologize." Castle said softly.

Chandler's lips were pursed, but there was something in Castle's tone that subdued the ultra-bratty mouth of his.

"Sorry." He said and ran towards the lawn. Trixie followed her little master.

Devin wasn't answering his phone so the only way I could get hold of him was if I summoned a maid and asked her to deliver the message, or I could go to the mansion and look for Devin myself but that meant I needed to leave the area of crime. If I left the barn like this, the killer could come back to tamper with the evidence.

As if on cue, I heard the sound of hooves moving towards us. I turned to see Devin riding a handsome brown horse in our direction, and he looked everything like a knight in shining armor, or a prince living in a castle, one that you read in books about. But this man right here was not imagination but a reality.

When he approached us, the horse came to a halt smoothly and Devin smiled at me, unaware of the horrors inside the barn. "Good Evening, Miss. Davis. You look lovely today." He flirted good-naturedly.

Castle stared at his brother with a scowl on his face. And if I knew better, I'd think he was acting jealous, but that was stupid of me to think like that. How could Castle be jealous? He didn't understand things like attraction or anything related to those matters.

Devin sensed there was something off because he said, "Is everything alright? I saw Chandler running inside the house, being very loud and being on his best disobedient behavior."

"You should check the barn," I suggested.

He dismounted the horse with finesse and handed the reins over to a young man that I hadn't even noticed was here until now.

"Take Tobias back to the stables, Ollie," Devin ordered the man.

"Yessir," Ollie slurred in a heavy accent. He didn't look older than twenty, and was tall and lanky. He had a friendly face, and he was someone you would call cute, with his dirty blond hair and brown eyes.

He glanced at Castle with those lazy-droopy eyes that made you think he'd permanent sleepy eyes, "How are you doing, Mr. Montgomery, sir?" when Castle didn't respond, he looked at me and honestly, I didn't like how his eyes did that bottom to top once over. It gave off a lecherous vibe. "New nanny, right? Lilly, was it?"

"Millie, short for Millicent." I corrected him.

"Right. Nice to meet you, Millie. I'm Oliver, Ollie for most. It's funny how our names match, right? Millie and Ollie. I work in the stables; call me if you need anything. Like anything at all." He emphasized the last part, and I knew exactly what he meant.

But I pretended not to.

"Sure."

"Oliver!" Devin yelled from inside the barn. "Call Winston and Butch. Get rid of what's inside."

I stood there staring, appalled at what he'd just said.

Get rid of what's inside?

He'd spoken about the body like it was a rotten slab of meat.

Ollie walked towards the entrance of the barn and clicked his tongue, "What a shame to see Barbara go. The bitch had it coming, though. Gonna miss those meat pies. Have to ask Susan if she remembers the recipe."

I was further dumbfounded by the stable boy's words. He'd reacted like Barbara wasn't hanging from the barn ceiling, staring at the onlooker with haunted eyes.

"But we need to call the police. This is not a suicide." I said.

Both Devin and Oliver looked at each other and then at me. Oliver had a lopsided smile on his face, like he was mocking me.

"Let's go inside and talk, Millie."

"But Devin..."

"See you in my office in ten minutes."

"Have you gone through your employment contract entirely?" Devin asked me.

We were now seated in his office. Devin looked freshly showered and immaculate. Not someone who'd witnessed a suicide on a part of his property. His body language appeared relaxed.

"Yes, I have."

"Then I'm sure you have read the clause in the contract that clearly states, 'Anything that happens within the Montgomery property stays here."

"I understand, Devin, but a woman died, and she was probably murdered. She had cuts all over her body that show that she might have been tortured before her death."

"By whom?" he asked, his apple-green eyes challenging me.

"I don't know," I said. "But whoever did it could be among your staff or—"

"Think before you utter the next word, Millie, because I won't tolerate you speaking ill about my family and making allegations about murder."

Everything about his demeanor had changed all of a sudden, and I knew at once that Devin was not someone that I could trust.

There was no one in this house I could trust!

His expressions betrayed nothing, yet his distant look was enough to send the message.

"I'm only saying that it needs to be investigated. That's all."

"We had another maid. Her name was Joslyn. She was really bright, like you. Pretty little thing. She enjoyed investigating and poking her nose into matters that didn't concern her."

"What happened?"

"She twisted her ankle on the stairs one night and went tumbling down. Theo noticed her first. She'd landed in quite an ugly shape, with her head on the ground and her arms distorted upwards from two different angles. Grotesque, if you ask me."

I heard the message loud and clear.

"It wasn't anyone's fault because it was an accident. Bringing police into this will only complicate matters more, and I have always believed in dealing with them on my own. Our family has a reputation to maintain and with Castle in the state that he is, I make all the decisions as the head of this family." Devin ran his hand through his hair. "You entered this house and accepted the job with your will, but no one leaves the property unless I say so. I hope we're on the same page, Millie."

"I understand." I said, "Sir."

He smiled, pleased with me. "I hope you do. It's best to put unsavory situations like these behind you. Focus on your job."

I would rather focus on getting out of this place. And fast.

Chapter 7

There wasn't much time. A few days after that incident, in the dead of the night, I packed my duffel quickly. The clothes that I'd been wearing in the house for the past week were all bought by the family, so I couldn't take them with me. Although I was tempted to take the few dresses that I knew I wouldn't be able to afford once I didn't have this job, but I didn't touch those outfits.

I hadn't even been around long enough to get my first paycheck.

I kept telling myself it was alright because my ultimate goal was to live through this. The family was fucking crazy, and I didn't want to be part of this anymore. Devin knew what happened with Barbara was murder, but he'd chosen to stay silent. He was protecting someone, and he was dragging me down with him.

This was some kind of twisted family conspiracy.

Staying on this property for almost two weeks had taught me about most of the exits within the mansion. The servant's quarter's stairs were the easiest way out of here. The only question was how I was going to walk through the courtyard without being seen, and the worst part was going to be convincing the guards to let me through.

Or...I could walk through the woods and find the road. Either way, it was still going to be a challenge.

I was going to be back to square one, and how foolish of me to think this was the best job I ever had. Of course, there was a catch. There's always a catch. It had been too good to be true.

I looked at myself in the mirror once before running my fingers through my dark hair. I didn't even have time to comb them. Then, I tied the laces of my sneakers and I was ready to go, but my feet wouldn't move forward, it's like fear had frozen me in place.

Where would I go from here? What awaited me in the future?

I told myself that I would get through this just as I have for every other situation.

I opened the door of my room and closed it behind me slowly, making sure I wasn't making even the slightest sound. I tiptoed down the hallway and onto the first floor and then made my way to the kitchen. I didn't have much money, but I could at least use some food on my way to nowhere.

I found ham and cheese in the fridge, so I made myself a quick sandwich because a girl's got to keep her priorities straight. I wrapped the sandwich in a saran wrap and dumped Dr. Pepper and a Coke into the bag. Next, I attacked the pantry and threw packets of salted peanuts, pretzels, and potato chips into it. I felt guilty for stealing so much food, but I didn't know how long I was going to be living on the streets with no job and nowhere to go and there was no chance in hell I was going back to my uncle's. I'd rather be homeless than go back to that monster.

Remembering the past disgusted me.

"Hey sweetpea, remember Bruce? He'd like to say hi to you. Now be a good girl and take care of Bruce for me, okay?" Uncle Mark slurred as he barged into my room that night.

I looked up to find Bruce leering at me, and I heard the sounds of his belt jiggling and knew what was coming next. Uncle Mark told him one hour only, and that he was doing him a favor this time. It would be over soon...

I brushed off all those thoughts and walked out of the kitchen. I'd studied the route that the maids usually took when they went into their rooms in a connected outbuilding that was also part of the mansion. I successfully found the stairs I was looking for and I made sure that no one was following me before going forward.

Once I made it outside into the courtyard, I made a run towards the woods. Now I only hoped I could find a road that led me outside of Montgomery's property. I used my phone's flashlight to navigate my way through the thick forest.

And I was in for another surprise.

I walked for about forty minutes, ignoring the eerie sounds coming from deep inside the forest. My legs had turned leaden, but I still ignored the pain and kept going and when I reached the clearing, I couldn't stop the disappointment flooding my emotions.

A lake surrounded the property, and a small villa stood right beside it. I couldn't stop cursing myself for the sheer bad luck that kept weighing me down. There was more vegetation on the other side of the lake. Two small boats and a yacht stood near the pier. The boats seemed to be tied loosely with thick ropes.

I had to untangle one of them if I wanted to use one. It would be difficult for me to row the boats alone using the oars, but I didn't have any other choice. Sure I could go back to the mansion and walk to the main gates which would have led me to the bus station directly, but as Devin had already told me before, no one left the Montgomery property without his permission so there was a chance the guards could stop me, and I couldn't risk that.

I tossed my bag on the ground and began working on the rope tied to the dock when I heard a faint crunching sound behind me, like the snapping sound of a twig.

I spun around quickly, afraid that I was caught, or worse, getting attacked by an animal.

Castle was standing a few feet away from me.

I wondered if he was a figment of my imagination, but that wasn't the case. He was really standing here before me, wearing a t-shirt and sweatpants with disheveled, wavy hair.

"What are you doing here, Castle?" I asked brusquely.

He stared at me with those innocent whiskey eyes.

"Did you follow me the entire way from the mansion?" I tried again. "You're not supposed to be here. I put you to bed."

Castle liked to wander around the mansion at night, and I'd purposely made sure he'd gone to bed and waited for an hour before I'd escaped, but I never thought he would follow me out of the mansion, that meant he'd been carefully tracing my steps until now.

"Millie..." He said in a soft voice.

I trudged back to where he was standing. Castle was huge compared to my size. He could flick my forehead playfully, and I'd likely go rolling into the water.

I reached out and took his large hands into mine.

"Don't leave me," he whispered, and it completely broke me listening to him plead.

He knew I was leaving for good and he'd followed.

"Please, Millie..." his hands wrapped around my waist and he tugged me against him.

I pulled away to look at him, and in the moonlight, his eyes looked dark. "Castle, I can't stay here, sweetie, I need to go or someone will..." I swallowed, but I willed the words to come out. "Or someone will kill me too, just like Barbara. You'll find another nanny."

"You," He said accusingly, shaking his head vigorously. "I want you."

The intensity in his eyes and the deepness in his voice would have suggested something else entirely.

Listening to him asking me to stay, I felt this alien feeling brewing inside me. Nobody had needed me before. I felt guilty doing this; running away without letting him know when I knew that as the days had passed, Castle had become attached to me and I don't mean that in any romantic way, he enjoyed being where I was, and he would follow me around the house and I didn't care as long as he wasn't harming me in any way. He would watch me shyly throughout meals, let me read books to him, take walks together, and that told me he enjoyed my company immensely as a friend, someone who could understand him more than anyone else in his family could so the thought of leaving him was hard, but it was that or get killed.

I cupped his jaw and felt his grip tightening around my waist as his fingers dug into the fabric of my top, clinging to me desperately. "I'll get help from outside and I'll tell someone about you, but I can't stay here in the mansion, Castle."

"I..." He started saying, and the words were clogged up in his throat like he couldn't remember what he wanted to say. "I..."

"You what, sweetie?"

"I'll go with you." He said finally.

I shook my head. "This is your family and your home. You can't come with me."

"NOOOOOOO..." He screamed, and I jumped back a little. "I'll go with you!"

Think Millie, think.

How could I possibly take him with me? If Castle tagged along, Devin would call the cops and there would be a manhunt to find me. Knowing how smart Devin was, he might tell the authorities that I'd kidnapped his brother. Either way, the man could twist the story in a way that he saw fit.

Castle couldn't come with me. End of story.

That also meant I couldn't leave today.

"Let's head back to the house," I suggested, and when he didn't move from the spot, I added. "I won't go anywhere."

He seemed content hearing that.

I picked up my duffel bag and headed back towards the forest. Castle walked close behind me. I guess he didn't trust me not to flee with him, so he kept his gaze trailed on me.

The dark sky was being blanketed with gray clouds as they churned closer, and the sound of thunder resonated within the forest. It was a sign of the impending rainstorm. I picked up speed and jogged ahead through the muddy trail that my shoe prints had left behind, so it was easier for me to know where I was going.

Until...

I dropped to the ground and was screaming at the top of my lungs at the pain that surged through my left leg. Sobbing loudly, I dared to look down and saw that my leg was caught in a trap, the sharp edges sinking into my skin. Castle was on his knees beside me, frantically trying to open the trap with his bare hands, but it made the pain much worse.

From a distance, I heard the familiar voice moving closer.

Devin walked towards us, carrying a hunting rifle, and his expression was downright evil.

Chapter 8

My leg throbbed with the unbearable pain and when I touched my leg, I found blood on my fingers. I had a blurry vision, but I could see Castle hovering over me, trying to help as best as he could. You could tell from his expressions that he was upset with the turn of events and was frantic to help me out. I wanted to scream at him since he was the reason I'd gotten stuck here in the first place. If he hadn't followed me from the mansion, I would have already been across the lake and catching a cab.

Devin had laid the traps here on purpose so any staff that left the property wouldn't be able to cross the forest and I'd fallen right into it. I should have known that escaping from here wouldn't be so easy.

What have I gotten myself into?

What did this twisted family want from me?

"Castle, step aside," Devin ordered him, the rifle slinging against his shoulders. "You're making it worse for her."

"You sick bastard!" I yelled at him.

"There, now Millie. I would suggest you control that smart mouth of yours. I'm your boss and I deserve the respect, besides, you're the one who was trying to break the rules of this house and our contract when I specifically told you that breaking rules have dire consequences." He informed me in a calm tone, "We have traps laid around in the forest for wild animals, and I should apologize that you got caught up in it, unfortunately."

He was lying through his teeth and I knew it. He wasn't sorry about anything.

"Greg, call Dr. Walker, and have him see Miss. Davis in her room."

Greg was another one of the house servants who came forward to pick me up which is when I noticed how he limped a little on his right foot. Devin raised his hand to stop him from approaching me, "I haven't finished talking to her."

Greg stopped where he was and stood there with a solemn expression was on his face like he'd gotten accustomed to seeing employees getting caught in animal traps. It seemed like Greg had seen a lot of other things and learned to be numb to everything.

"Sir, we found her bag," Winston said.

Devin snatched it out of his hand, "Now what do we have here?" he asked teasingly and then opened the duffle bag and emptied the contents of it on the ground.

The sandwiches, the drinks, and snacks fell from it, along with my personal belongings.

Devin laughed, "out of everything that you could steal, this is all you could think of? Millie, the pair of shoes that Dayana gave you the other day alone costs over a thousand dollars. You could have taken those instead." He gave me the boy-next-door smile, the same one that I'd mistaken for charming the first time I'd met him. "But I do love honest people, and that's the reason I hired you that day."

"Please let me go." I cried. "What do you want from me?"

Devin leaned in and tipped my chin upwards to gaze at me, his emerald eyes that I thought were beautiful once, now looked vacant and devoid of humanity. At that moment, I just knew that he was far more capable of worse evils. In a dangerously low tone, he promised, "You'll soon find out what I really want from you, Millie."

My blood ran cold.

He was likely going to use me for something sexual. I was so sure. He was a predator, just like uncle Mark. The only difference between the two was that Mark was poor and doughy around the middle area, and Devin was wealthy and gorgeous.

It's the inside that mattered, and on the inside, both were clearly very ugly.

I take back what I said when I first met him about Devin being a nice person.

He was a monster.

"What do you want me to do with her things, sir?" Winston asked him, addressing me in third person like I didn't even exist.

"Keep the food and get rid of the rest of her stuff. She doesn't need it here."

"I need those things!" I said.

He looked at me once before looking at the butler again, "You know what, she wants the stuff so instead of taking her to her room, just take her to the basement and put that dog collar on her."

"Okay, fine! Throw everything away, but the wallet has my aunt's locket that she gave me before she died. Can I have that at least? Please..." I pleaded even though it was the last thing I wanted to do.

Winston handed my wallet over to Devin who found the locket inside. He inspected it, turning it around on both sides probably thinking it was nothing but a piece of garbage.

"Win, I'm feeling a little generous today, so I'm going to keep the locket with me for safekeeping. Millie, you can consider it as leverage. You'll get it back, of course, when you earn it." He turned to Greg, "Remove the trap from her leg and take her to her room."

Greg used a key to open the jaws that were crushing my leg. Running was out of the question, I couldn't even stand. That was Devin's plan all along. I didn't even know how long it would take for the injury to heal and until that, I would be stuck in this house.

A solid punch landed in Devin's face and he stumbled back a few steps. Castle had landed the blow, and it looked like Devin wasn't surprised by it.

He grinned, wiping the trail of blood with a napkin that Winston handed him. "What was that for, Castle? I thought you wanted Millie to stay with us too, I was just helping you out here buddy, there's no need for violence."

Castle's jaw tightened as he glared at his brother before he leaned forward and put one of his arms around my back and the other one gripped the underside of my thighs, he carried me in his arms with ease and despite everything; I felt safe with him so I held him tightly, clinging to him, burying my face into his chest, trying my best to stay strong.

When we reached upstairs to my room, I felt a little drowsy, and I heard Devin saying that the trap usually had something applied to it to put the victim to sleep.

The last thing I saw was Castle putting me to bed, and I thought that was ironic since I'd put him to bed tonight before all this happened. I knew he whispered something to me, but my mind was so muddled up that his words were coherent.

I drifted to sleep, and the last thing I remembered seeing was Castle's serious brown eyes looking down on me with pity.

I woke up in the morning with a jolt and for a second I couldn't remember where I was until I searched my surroundings and recognized the room. Fragments of yesterday's incident began resurfacing in my mind along and the pain in my leg that felt like someone was stabbing me repeatedly with sharpened knives. The leg was in plaster which was a clear indication that I'd received proper medical attention.

Out of all the people, Theodore was the last one I expected to see in my room. The seventeen-year-old with a serious attitude problem.

He was sitting near my dresser, playing aggressively on one of those fancy gadgets. When he noticed I was awake, he spared me a glance before turning his attention back to the game.

"Don't you have school today?" I asked, sitting up.

"I do, but I don't think that's any of your business. It's Castle you should worry about. Not me." He snapped, pinning me with a sharp look.

"Have I done something to you, Theo? I don't understand what warrants your rude behavior towards me, honestly."

"It's Theodore for you, Millicent. And don't mind me; I always wake up on the wrong side of the bed, honestly."

"Are all Montgomery's crazy like you and your brother?"

He laughed, "Which one? And we're not crazy, maybe a little psychotic, and deranged."

"Same thing," I said.

Theo looked at the closed bedroom door before turning to me, "I've been asked to keep an eye on you, although I don't think you'll be going anywhere with that leg of yours." He lowered his voice down further. "Here's a tip if you want to avoid accidents like these in the future. Stay on Devin's good side, and do what he tells you to."

"Fuck all of you," I said under my breath. "What's his kill count?"

He gave me that slow grin, and he looked so much like Castle. The two were similar in so many ways; well, if you ignored Theo's rude behavior. "That's for me to know and you to find out."

"So if I stayed on Devin's good side, he'll let me go?"

"I won't lie to you, but you're not going anywhere, and it would be best for you to adjust with this life, Millicent."

I suddenly noticed that my good leg had a round black anklet around it. "What is that?" I couldn't keep the fear out of my voice.

"The staff here all wears it. It's a tracker."

"How does it come off?" I asked even though chances were he wouldn't tell me about it.

"It doesn't, that's the point. Unless you die or cut off your foot." He said, deadpan.

Then it just hit me.

"Greg? Why was he limping? Was it because—"

"You're smarter than I thought. Gregory tried to take off several times too and kept getting tracked down so he cut off his foot with a hacksaw. Didn't make it too far, and he would have bled to death anyway but Devin saved his life and now he has a fake foot implant or some shit like that."

"That's pretty fucked up. Devin is the one who put him in that situation, and that's not called saving his life. If he was actually saving lives, he would let Greg go."

"I'm not telling you this to scare you, but I'm hoping you would think before you plan another escape. If you managed to get the tracker off, Devin will still find you, and bring you back here, and the next time around, it'll be worse."

"So I'm not just a nanny in this house."

Theo chuckled, "You're a prisoner." He planted his foot on the bed in front of me. "Just like me."

He was wearing the anklet tracker too.

Chapter 9

I stared at the tracker on his anklet, which was identical to the one I was wearing.

"Why are you wearing that? I thought you said only staff wear it."

"I'm an exception, I guess?" He said, looking at the closed door again. "I have a rebellious streak."

Of course. Rebellious must be Theo's middle name.

"I got into trouble because I tried to bring the Montgomery's secrets out and ended up being imprisoned by my own family," Theo explained. "The only difference is that if I tried to escape, I won't end up dead. As for the staff, I can't say the same thing. I also get to go to school and do my thing."

"That means whoever tries to get out of here dies?"

"You didn't hear that from me." He laughed.

"I heard nothing."

"Think of this as a chess game. Devin, Dayana, and Castle are the key players. The rest of us are pawns. There are things I can't talk to you about, things that Castle can't remember because of his accident, so I would suggest you to not get involved in this mess. The lesser you know, the safer you will be, trust me."

"You just admitted to people dying in his house because they want to get out! How am I supposed to trust anybody after that?" I whispered, "Why should I trust you?"

"Well, I'm not asking you to, but I won't bullshit you, Millicent. I'm not Devin. You've been through enough and the least I could do is give you a heads up." He said simply, picking up his gadget. "My family is craaaayyyy."

"This is kidnapping!" I threw the blanket off my body and tried to climb out of bed when a jolt of unbearable pain stopped me.

"Yeah, the Montgomerys could have a rap sheet if the cops around here weren't so fucking corrupt and actually did their job."

"Wait, the cops know about this?"

Theo gave me a slow smile. His honey-golden eyes were strikingly similar to Castle's. Castle had a serious look most of the time, while Theo's entire demeanor was mischievous.

"The cops know everything, but they choose to look the other way. They don't want to lose their jobs and they also get paid a lot for keeping their mouth shut. We are the most powerful family in the country for nothing." He concluded without taking his eyes off the game he was playing, aggressively punching the gadget.

"So, what do you want me to do? Stay here under captivity and do nothing?" I was fuming. All I wanted was to get away from the mess that was my uncle and get a good job, and start over.

This turned out to be a case of out of the frying pan and into the fire.

"That would keep you alive, at least. I mean, that's something, right?"

"Yeah, sure. Staying alive with a leg that you can't move is the best." I said sarcastically.

"It could have been worse." He reminded me.

"Castle doesn't wear one of these anklets." I pointed out.

"That's because he wouldn't let them. Castle might remember nothing from his past, but he still has that 'dosen't-take-shit-from-anybody' attitude, and if I'm being honest, Devin is a little intimidated by him. Listen, I gotta go, okay? It was nice to chat with you and all." He climbed to his feet, and that's when something fell from his pocket and landed onto the carpeted floor.

"Hey, Theo, you dropped this," I picked up the piece of paper until I realized it wasn't.

"It's Theodore."

It was an origami flower.

I inspected it. The flower was quite similar to the origami rabbit I'd received before.

"It was you. You left that origami for me to find, telling me it was Dayana who hurt Castle."

You could tell from his expressions that he had been the one leaving those notes, not Castle, as I initially believed.

"I have to go," Theo said and stormed out of the door before I could call out to him again.

I spent another week trying to get my legs to work, and by the end of two weeks, I could walk properly even though there was a slight limp, and the doctor told me I'd be fine in a few more days. While they confined me to my room, the maids had taken good care of me and given me proper food, which was something. At least I wouldn't die here out of starvation.

If I could just get this tracker out of my leg, then the only problem would be to find a way to escape this property, but that was next to impossible, so I devised a plan. I was going to do what Theo had told me and try my best to stay on Devin's good side. Take one day at a time, build some trust, and find a way out of here, eventually.

During the days that I'd been recovering from the injury, I noticed how Castle would come to my room at odd hours of the night, and he would stand outside the door for a long time before leaving me alone. My heart would drum against my chest, not that I was terrified of him, but I couldn't get any sleep either, as I would pretend to be asleep instead of confronting him.

The family was leaving tonight for some party and they weren't taking Castle with them, so I was going to be home alone with him. It's after dinner that I lost sight of him and I searched through all the rooms that I thought I would find him in. I heard the thunder rumbling even though all the windows were closed. It would be a problem if Castle wandered out of the mansion. Devin would kill me and feed me to Trixie.

There was no way I could check every room of this Colonial mansion. I'd have to spend the entire night searching for him, and yet, here I was, opening door after door and calling him out. By the time I moved to the fourth floor, I'd almost ran out of energy. I bet babysitting for a ten-year-old would be easier. I halted in front of a room where I heard the sounds of whispering coming from inside. The door was partly open and I know eavesdropping wasn't good, but I couldn't help myself taking a little peek.

An old man was sitting in a wheelchair, and Castle was kneeling right beside him.

That must be the grandfather, Hugh Montgomery. I'd seen his black and white pictures of when he was young, that it had taken me a while to recover.

Hugh coughed and then said, "Has he been giving you trouble again?"

"Not really, sir," Castle answered softly. "If he's troubling you, you come to me, boy." The old man said in his authoritative voice.

"I would." This was the fastest that I'd seen Castle respond to anyone. Usually, he took his time to respond, but with his grandfather; he seemed to answer with enthusiasm, which was a first.

"Chris, you tell that wife of yours that she's not welcome in this house, you understand me?"

"I understand."

Chris? Why was his grandpa calling Castle, Chris, and since when did Castle get married? Or did Devin hide that detail from me, too?

The thought of Castle having a wife that he didn't remember made me ill.

I thought grandma Hugh had fallen completely off the rocker and talking nonsense like some old people would. But what Castle said next shocked me more. "I promise you, gramps. Lorna isn't coming back to this house."

Chapter 10

Castle didn't talk to his grandpa after that and the room continued to bask in comfortable silence until he picked a vinyl and played the vintage gramophone. Soft music drifted from the player. A Himalayan cat I hadn't noticed before was perched on the bed and staring daggers at me. I exited and went back to my room, deciding to give them privacy.

Theo was right; I didn't have any business digging into their family history. My primary aim was survival and to get out of this house alive and for that I needed to find another way out of here that wasn't through the woods. The entire family had left for the party, save for Castle and Senior Montgomery, and an opportunity like this wouldn't present itself again soon.

First, I went to the kitchen and tried to hack the bracelet from my ankle with a cleaver and it didn't work, so getting the tracker off my leg was never going to happen.

I needed to find another way.

I was going to make sure that Castle was asleep this time, so he wouldn't follow me when I tried to leave.

Castle brushed his teeth and changed into his pajamas. That was usually his night routine before bed. He never felt shy about taking off his undergarments in front of me either, but I usually just looked away because that was common decency and I didn't think he would appreciate if I ogled if he was in the right frame of mind. I placed two pills and a glass of water on the nightstand. He usually took them after his meals. I tried to pop one in his mouth but turned his face to the other side, refusing to take them.

"You want to get better, don't you? If you don't take your medicines, you'll remember nothing."

I pushed a sizable portion of brownie in front of him. Sweets always seemed to work for baiting Castle into taking his medication.

"I made this with Susan."

"Cake." He said.

He reached forward to take it when I pushed it away from his reach.

"You'll have the brownie when you take your pills. Those are the rules, Castle."

He huffed and pushed the pills into his mouth forcefully and swallowed it with a glass of water before reaching across me to grab the piece of brownie which he unwrapped and began chomping on it, staring at me in the same unusual way of his. I had to wipe his mouth later with a towel.

Once he got comfortable in his bed, I asked him the question that was bothering me, "Castle, I heard you speak to your grandpa. I was wondering if you started remembering anything."

He had a toy train in his hand, and he spun the wheels of it with his long elegant fingers. His eyes remained downcast, and the dim light in the room highlighted his sharp jawline.

"Who is Chris?" I asked.

He didn't answer, and I gave up on asking him questions until he said, "My father." I placed my finger beneath his chin and forced him to make eye-contact.

"Do you remember him?" The question I really wanted to ask him was 'Are you pretending to lose your memory?'

He shook his head, "No."

"Who is Lorna?" He didn't answer again and started to breathe heavily, his fingers holding the train tightly.

I placed a hand on his shoulders. "Castle."

A gut-wrenching scream pierced through the room as he threw the train across the room and he began rocking back and forth, and continued doing it. I repeatedly asked him to calm down, but he turned more upset. A maid scurried into the room, followed by two other male servants, and one of them was holding a syringe in his hand.

My question had probably triggered something inside him.

"Hold him down." The man said to the other. I watched as they injected him with the fluid. I moved away from the bed when Castle caught the corner of my dress. His brown eyes stayed on me, already losing the spark. I cried when I exited his room.

He was sleeping now, and the maid said he won't wake up until morning. What was disturbing was how the house staff acted casual, like this was a routine and something that they witnessed every day. I'd decided. If I was escaping from this house, I would take Castle with me and think of the consequences later. He was suffering in his own home and I won't let that happen.

On the other side of the mansion, I'd seen a set of steps leading down to a tunnel. It would be scary for me to go through it alone, but it's not like I had any choice. I needed to see where the tunnel led and if there was a way through it, then I could find another opportunity to leave.

It took me several minutes to locate the tunnel and, as expected, it was pitch black inside. In other situations, I would have skipped walking through it, but claustrophobia and ghosts were the least of my concerns.

There was no greater monster than man.

I switched on the flashlight and took slow steps ahead; the ground was muddy and watery, and my shoes were getting caked in the dirt, but I continued to walk forward. The tunnel's ceiling was covered in large pipes and I was following the same route. I thought the pipes had to go somewhere and wherever that it led had to be the way out.

This was a pure gamble again. I knew the risk that I was taking. I could live and get tortured or get killed in the future. And I refused to go down like Barbara did.

I came to a stop when the tunnel split in two different directions. I went with my gut and took the straight road. At this point, I'd spent fifteen minutes walking, and the tunnel seemed to be never-ending. If I found nothing after five more minutes, I would go back through the way I came from. The tracker was blinking a yellow signal; it was usually bright green.

I saw a door ahead, a tiny gray door that had a bolt. I slid the bolt aside and the space inside grew narrower. Stepping in, I saw a staircase leading into nothingness.

I tried to calm my breathing and wondered if finding out what was down there would be worth it. If there was a way out from this dungeon, maybe I could try. There was no way the tracker could show my location as the blinking light was completely gone.

I descended the stairs, my heart in my throat, and expected to see a pile of bodies like the ones you see in movies. But if there were dead bodies down there, wouldn't there be a powerful stench? As I stepped down, I heard whispers and some voices echoing, so I stopped short and hid against the nearest wall.

When I took a peek, I saw four people dressed in dark cloaks huddled close. The small danky place was illuminated by candles and it's when they moved in a circle that I noticed they were standing on a pentagram, chanting something. There was a picture of the diagram but I couldn't see it.

Was this family involved in a cult?

Or was it someone else?

Two more people joined the ritual.

In the center was the head of a dead animal. One figure stood tall between them while the others continued to chant words and kneeled before the figure, who wore a hooded cloak and a mask of an animal with horns. I couldn't tell the person's gender, it could be a man, or even a woman and I noticed the person holding a round bowl with some liquid in it, wearing a ring in his or her index finger that had a black crystal-like gemstone and a chain with a locket. They passed the bowl filled with liquid between the members; each of whom from the circle took sips from it. This felt so unreal, like I'd walked into a twisted episode of The Twilight Zone.

I couldn't believe what I was seeing, and couldn't move an inch. I needed to get out of here. I turned out to leave and in a haste my shoe stumped over the first step and that made the sound of a rustle.

The chanting stopped, and a voice boomed, "Who's there?"

I didn't stop as I climbed the stairs two at a time and when I reached the top; I shut the door and made a mad dash for the path without even bothering to turn on the phone's flashlight.

As I was running, someone said, "Found you!"

And before I could dodge, the person seized my arm, and the next thing I knew something like a rod or a metal bat swung at me and I went down, my body splattering against the slippery floor. I sat up but my head was spinning in circles and kept thinking I needed to get away from here. The sounds of thunder continued to fill the silence in the background, muffling my cries. I was wondering why I was being put through this when I hadn't hurt a soul in my life. All I'd done was help people with whatever little I had. My life so far kept flashing before my eyes, the good and the bad.

"Was she trying to escape again?" That was Devin's voice.

I tried to crawl, to stand again, but it was so difficult to see anything in the darkness.

"Yeah," That sounded like Dayana. "But I'm gonna make sure she thinks a dozen times before she makes that mistake again. You'll remember this, won't you, Millie?"

The next swing came to my legs, followed by the continuous hits and the sounds of my bones cracking.

Chapter 11

The room wasn't familiar this time. It appeared to be the same dungeon or underground area that I'd walked into before. A dim yellow bulb illuminated the place, and I was lying on the concrete floor with nothing but a jug of water left on the side. My legs felt numb and fractured. I couldn't move them an inch even if I tried, but it was covered in plaster so a doctor was allowed to do this, and that meant there were some people working under the Montgomery's who chose to remain silent, maybe they had a family doctor who took care of all the dirty work for a hefty payment.

I ran a hand through my hair and it felt greasy. My stomach growled as I realized I must have starved for a long time. Unfortunately, the room did not even have a window, so it wasn't possible for me to guess if it was daytime or night. Days could have passed as I lay here in this prison. Perhaps I'd slipped into a coma, I couldn't tell.

The pain in my legs was worse than before and even though I hadn't seen Dayana hit me, I was positive I'd heard her voice. She'd hit my legs repeatedly with the bat.

These people were monsters. They had made sure that I couldn't plan an escape for another few weeks. They enjoyed feeding off weakness and fear, and that's the last thing I wanted to give them. I could pretend to obey their orders and strategize my next move.

Just then, I heard the locks turning, so I backed up against the wall.

It was Devin who walked through the door, followed by a maid holding a tray in her hand. She didn't even blink when she saw me on the floor, as if this was a daily occurrence and something that was not worth dwelling upon. The aroma of food entered my nostrils, and it made hunger even worse. I could kill for a morsel of the food on that tray, and that's exactly what they wanted; for me, to be starved and desperate for food that I'd agree to do anything.

He sat down on the floor a few feet away from me, a stoic expression hanging on his face. His apple-green eyes studied me warily. Unlike the few times I'd seen him before, he wore casuals and he looked relatively younger like some attractive man I'd see walking down the street, and not the powerful man in control of a billion-dollar conglomerate that I'd met on the first day.

Devin waved a hand of dismissal at the maid. "You may leave now, Penelope." He said sweetly.

Penelope bowed and walked out of the room, closing the door behind her. He held the tray of food in his hand. I sneaked a peek inside the plate and there was chicken roast indeed, with mashed potatoes and a thick piece of oozing lasagna.

You're fucking kidding me! This was torture, knowing he wouldn't let me have food. He might have just brought it down here to tease me with it.

"You're hungry, aren't you?" Devin asked me in the same voice that dripped of honey.

I glanced away; I couldn't stand looking at it anymore.

I didn't answer him.

"Susan told me you loved lasagna."

"I would have also loved to see you dead." I retorted.

He laughed the way one would laugh at a joke that their best friend cracked. "You're funny, Millie, and I like the fact that you're still strong regardless of the situation you're in. We've had employees crying and begging for their life. I'm glad we took you on board."

"What do you want, Devin?" I asked.

The tray of food careened over to me when he gave it a slight push.

"Eat your chow. We'll talk after that." I stared at the plate of food in front of me.

What if he'd poised it or planned to drug me with it?

Reading my thoughts, he gave me that sly smile again. "If we wanted you dead, you'd be six feet underground by now. The food isn't poisoned." He stated, pulling the plate towards him and sampling a bite of each before setting it down. "See? I haven't dropped dead. If you won't eat your dinner, that's fine. I have people who can force it down your throat. The choice remains yours."

I picked up the plate and began eating it slowly. It was so good; I was going to cry. Devin watched me silently as I ate and after I was done, he handed me a glass of water that I chugged down.

Emotions tightened my throat as I asked him, "You're not going to let me go, are you?" "If you do as I say, you'll be free, Millie." He blinked at me. "You have my word."

"What do you want?" I questioned for the second time.

"Your co-operation," He answered, looking dead in the eye. "I need your help, Millie. That's all I'm asking. In exchange, you're never getting hurt again, or mistreated by any of us. If you show me, I can trust you blindly. I'll even take off the tracker."

"What do you mean by co-operation? What is it you need from me?"

"You'll know soon enough. In the meantime, please take good care of my brother. It appears like he's taken quite a liking to you."

"Can you take me back to my room?" I asked.

Devin laughed again, "It's funny how you appreciate little things in your life when you're put in a situation like this." His eyes twinkled with cruelty. "Like I said, you meed to earn it. If you show me you're a good girl and that you can obey, we'll take you upstairs."

So I was going to be stuck here for a while.

Before leaving, he stopped and turned. "Sorry about what my sister did to you. Don't take it too personally."

When he left, he turned off the lights completely.

By the sixth day, they'd completely broken me, and I don't mean physically. It seemed like my soul had left my body and wandered elsewhere. When I fell asleep, a bucket of cold water was splashed over my body. I was far too numb to notice who was doing it. I ate the food when I got it. A maid would allow me to use the bathroom and bathe me.

The nights were the longest. It was pitch black and sometimes they left the dim light on. It would turn on and off constantly sometimes, and that gave me a headache. I think it was being done on purpose. I was drenched, shivering, hungry, and just someone who was on the brink of insanity. Sometimes, it was hard to even gather thoughts. I wondered if I was dead or living.I heard the lock turning again and I didn't know what day it was. It was probably some maid again. Instead, I saw a tall, enormous figure approaching me.

Devin. This time, he didn't stop a few feet away. He hunched lower to my crouched form and touched my cheek. I screamed and thrashed until he got hold of both of my hands in a firm grip and said something. The voice was so distant, and my head felt so light and my eyes couldn't even see clearly because of tears. But I could recognize the familiar cologne.

"Millie...it's me."

I opened my eyes at once. "Castle!"

I was hysterical, saying some incoherent things that probably weren't even making any sense. I didn't think Castle could even comprehend what I was saying, but the words flowed like a dam.

Castle held me close and caressed my hair. "I'm sorry."

There was someone else standing behind him. It took a few seconds to realize that it was Theo.

Theo gave me a look filled with sympathy. "I thought you died. They wouldn't tell us where you were."

The look on his face was equal measures of disgust and relief. "This is exactly why I don't like getting attached to the house staff. They just end up dying. If they're just going to die in the end, what's the point of me making light conversations with them?"

I felt Castle's stare locked on me. He ignored his little brother's rambling and asked me, "Can you walk?"

I shook my head. "I think my legs are healing, but I can't stand up." I tried to swallow my pleading; I couldn't ask him to take me upstairs. It was quite hard. "Castle, you should go back. I don't want to put you in trouble."

He placed an arm around my shoulders and the other hand to support my legs as he lifted me in his arms. Theo threw him a look. "You're seriously not considering taking her back upstairs."

"She's hurt." Castle said and his hands tightened around my body, "because of me...I'm not leaving her here."

When he said that, it proved two things. One, Castle wasn't as stupid as Devin believed he him to be.

Two, he might know what was going on in the family and keeping silent.

"This is on you, Cas, remember that. I never helped you get the keys." Theo said, "Now let's hurry. I have school tomorrow."

Castle took me up to my room upstairs; his brown eyes looked down at me as he whispered, "I won't let them hurt you anymore."

Chapter 12

I thought Castle would take me back to my room, but I was wrong. Instead, he carried me upstairs to his bedroom and headed straight to the bathroom.

He pulled out a little bathtub stool and made me sit on it. Theo had already left; so I assumed he'd already gone to bed by now and that left me alone with Castle and oddly, I felt safe being close to him. If Castle was with me that other night, I'm sure he would have protected me against his evil pair of siblings.

I'd never been inside Castle's bathroom before. It was big enough to be a bedroom; the tiles were all white marble. A large vintage bathtub sat in the center, transparent sliding doors leading to a shower space. I could see my battered reflection in the enormous masculine sink with matching marble countertop. It was lined up with bottles of shampoo, perfume, and cologne. Everything here was a glimpse into Castle's life before his accident.

I watched Castle as he pulled out the shower heads next to the wall near the bathtub and sprayed some water over his hand to check the temperature before reaching for my dress and lifting it.

He was trying to undress me!

I shook my head; my heart was pounding against my chest. "I'll. ..I'll do it alone."

My body hurt from staying on the concrete floor for over a week, but I wouldn't admit that to him. Castle regarded me with a concerned look in his eyes, and he didn't take his hands off my dress.

"You can wait outside," I whispered.

He stared at me for a long moment and that made me wonder if he was going to refuse to leave but seconds later; he gave me a nod, placed a bottle of body wash next to me, and stepped outside, sliding the door behind him.

Once I made sure that he wasn't going to return, I peeled off my dress and completely stripped down. I tried to avoid getting the water on my plastered legs and let the warm jet of spray soak me entirely. I took some of the body wash liquid into my palm and scrubbed the lather all over my body.

There was a knock at the door.

"I'm not done yet," I called out frantically, thinking he'd enter, not knowing I was naked.

"Miss. Millicent, it's me, Sally. Mr. Montgomery, sent me here to assist you. May I come inside?"

"Oh, I see," I said, relieved it was her. "Yes, come inside."

Sally stepped inside the bathroom carrying a towel and some clothes. I believed Sally was one of the nicer maids. She didn't seem like an emotionless doll, like the rest of the staff, and I always liked that about her.

After the bath, Sally helped me dress up. I couldn't stand up without support, so I couldn't be embarrassed about being naked in front of her. She dried my hair and even combed it for me.

When I glanced into the mirror, I seemed to look fine, but a lot of changes had happened between the naïve Millie who'd joined the employment a few weeks ago and the Millie now who'd endured mental and physical pain. What I'd learned until now is to trust no one, and surely not the ones that seemed "normal."

I was on my own.

I noticed Sally was wearing a similar ankle bracelet, and that made me wonder if she'd been put through hell too or if she'd accepted her faith and remained silent.

"Sally, how long have you been working for the Montgomerys?"

"Five years." She replied.

"Do you like it here?"

I didn't want to ask her any direct questions and get into trouble.

Her dark eyes met mine in the mirror. "Yes, and besides, Mr. Montgomery made sure my mother is getting proper treatment in one of the best hospitals in the country. That's all that matters to me."

I had no doubt she was talking about Devin. They used people's weakness to bind them to this place, and if that didn't work, they used any force necessary.

"I see," I said. "Was Castle married?"

"No, he dated someone for a while." She paused, "but they broke up a few months before he lost his memory."

A wave of relief washed over me, knowing he wasn't married. It was strange. I mean, why should I even care about things like that when I was only his caregiver? I didn't think it would be appropriate to ask Sally questions about their family background. She could recite this entire conversation to Devin and Dayana, and then they would make my life miserable again.

"You're really pretty." She commented without a hint of a smile on her face, and I wondered if it was even a compliment.

"Thanks."

Castle walked into the bathroom a while later and carried me to his bed. I landed on my back on the fluffy pillows, feeling confused as hell.

Why was I being put in Castle's bed?

Sally didn't seem fazed by what he'd done. With a straight face she said, "If you don't need me for anything else, sir, I'll be going to bed."

He dismissed her with one look. She bowed and left the room. I sat upright and straightened the flimsy see-through nightgown. You didn't have to squint to notice the pink lacy bra and the panties underneath. I didn't understand why Sally had chosen this one out of so many other nightgowns, as if this was some kind of honeymoon.

I didn't miss the heated look in Castle's eyes as his gaze moved from the bottom and slowly scanned to the top and his hands curled into a fist. He might have lost his memory, but he was still a grown man with a healthy, able body. Naturally, he experienced urges a normal man would.

I crawled to the headboard, scared of what was to come next. "Castle, please take me to my room." I pleaded, snatching the comforter to cover myself.

He pulled his t-shirt over his head and tossed it onto the floor, never taking his eyes off me. His chest was broad, sporting six-pack abs with a lean waist, a body of a Greek god, and a face that depicted innocence, although I couldn't say his thoughts were exactly as pure. He unzipped his pants and let it fall, which left him standing with only a pair of boxer shorts on.

"Castle..." I said more firmly, "Do you understand what I'm say-ing?" I tried to say each word slowly and clearly. "Take. Me. To. My. Room."

He climbed into bed, and I scooted farther away. I was shaking by the time his gigantic body slipped into the same comforter that I'd taken.

I had flashbacks of when I used to live with my uncle, and I couldn't believe that the same would happen to me right now. Castle could pin me down with just one arm and do with me as he pleased. I wouldn't even be able to move. No one would come to rescue me.

He leaned towards me and I shook my head, "Castle, no."

He gave me a perplexed look before reaching around me and turning off the bedside table lamp.

"Sleep," That's all he said before sleeping on his side of the bed.

What the hell happened?

I stared at his huge muscular body in the dark with tears blurring my vision. Because of my experiences in the past with the men in my life, I was under the impression that every man wanted to hurt me, but to see Castle turning away and giving me space did all kinds of things to my heart. Later that night—or probably in the wee hours of the morning, I woke up distressed and imagining I was back in that dark basement downstairs. Sweat trickled down my body and my throat felt dry. I'd woken up screaming...

"Shhh...I'm here, Millie..." The voice sounded distant.

"Millie..."

Why was he so far away?

"Millicent!"

Castle had a firm grip over my chin as he brought his face close to mine, and I stared into his smoldering whiskey eyes, nestled in his lap, in his bed. He pushed my hair away from my face. His hands were large but his touch was delicate and I was doing my best to not lean into it.

"Castle..." I whispered into the darkness, "I don't want to go back there." He was so close, the heat of his body sent shivers down my body as he continued to stare at me in his usual sensuous way. He didn't prefer speaking with words so much as he liked to convey with his actions. He continued to hold me so I wrapped my arms around him tightly, and buried my face into his hard chest.

"You..." he said, and paused, searching for the right words, his face sinking into my hair, "You smell like me."

It was perfect to have him hold me and I slept peacefully that night, glad that there was at least someone in this house who was kind to me, who cared about me.

The days passed as my legs started healing again; the cast came off, and I was walking slowly without using crutches. Sometimes Castle would carry me from my room to the dining room down-stairs. During the time, I tried my best to avoid any conversations with Devin or Dayana because it was easier to pretend things were normal in this house. They were forcing me to stay here, and the beating was just Dayana trying to prove their point, and I'd received the message loud and clear.

Castle didn't like to make long conversations, but he knew how to get his point across. He chose his words and didn't talk unless it was necessary. He was also an excellent listener. As I'd initially thought that he couldn't understand conversations or what was going on around him, I realized how wrong I'd been. Castle was aware of a lot of things, and I was pretty sure he was hiding something from me, too.

It didn't matter. What did matter right now was the fact that he treated me like an equal and not like I was an employee in this house, but also his friend. I had intentions to keep things that way. I wanted Castle to trust me completely; it was the only way that I could beat Devin and Dayana at their own game.

I was having my evening coffee in Castle's room and he was sitting on the floor watching the trains moving on the tracks. I failed to see what was so fascinating about the toys that he'd stare at them for hours.

There was a soft knock at the door. "Miss. Millicent, it's Lydia."

"Come in," I called out.

The maid walked in with a tray and a glass of water. She placed them on the coffee table. "It's time for Mr. Montgomery's medication."

I smiled at her, "Thanks, Lydia. I'll make sure he takes them."

Lydia bowed and left the room.

I picked up the cup having four pills.

Castle hated taking the meds, and I'd done some research over the pills that were prescribed to him. The prescription was from one of Devin's private doctors, and they were supposed to help Castle cope with his trauma and anxiety.

I emptied the cup into the toilet and flushed them down.

A satisfied smile tugged at my lips.

Castle needed his memories back, and those pills were making sure they didn't.

Devin's medication had to go.

I went back to his room and sat down on the floor beside Castle, watching the trains as they zigzagged. Castle glanced up to me, bewildered about the pills that I hadn't insisted him to take this time.

I casually brushed the dark locks away from his face. "Wanna keep a secret? Just between you and me?"

"What secret?"

"You won't be taking any medications from now on, but if Devin or anyone else in this house asks you about it, we're going to pretend that you are. Okay? It's going to be our little secret."

He grinned, and it was the first time that I'd seen Castle look so happy. I felt like cupid had struck me with a few of his arrows.

"Our secret." He promised.

Chapter 13

Castle stopped taking medications completely.

The maid brought the pills twice a day, but I made sure he didn't take it, and slowly I started noticing some difference in Castle's behavior. The mood swings were getting comparatively lesser; he wasn't drowsy during the day and could form better sentences and appeared happier.

It was like Castle was walking out into the sun from a dull, gloomy day.

All I needed to do now was wait until he regained his memories, and that was okay. I had a lot of time on my hands, considering all I did was sit around and watch Castle playing, eating, and do some more playing.

I couldn't risk trying to find a way out of here, only to be beaten half to death. I had my legs broken before; it wouldn't be too difficult for them to kill me the next time I tried to escape.

My only ticket out of this place was Castle.

And recently I noticed him showing strange behavior whenever I was with him. He would look at me with this heated expression on his face. It wasn't innocent by a long shot. On the contrary, it made me believe he was noticing me as a man, and not someone who didn't understand attraction towards women.

Could I chalk it up as loneliness?

Perhaps, since he'd been without female company for a long time, the basic instinct was making him feel that way towards me. It was very hard to decipher Castle's thoughts and feelings just by looking at him, as he was very good at hiding them well.

I compartmentalized those thoughts and started heading downstairs when I saw Theo heading upstairs to his room. He was carrying a backpack and a bag of Burger King. And he wasn't alone...

An attractive African-American girl was with him. She seemed to be the same age as him and holding two large milkshakes. She was laughing at something that he was saying, and the two seemed to be lost in their world until her eyes met mine and she stopped climbing the stairs. Theo's eyes followed her gaze and rested on me.

"Hey." He said.

"Hi." I smiled at them. To him I said, "Aren't you going to introduce me to your friend?"

Theo flashed me a silent warning, challenging me to say anything about what was going on in this house. But there was also fear shining in those golden-brown eyes, fear of what would happen if I opened my mouth and spill the evil deeds of his siblings.

"This is Madison." He told me. "Maddy, this is Millie. She's my brother's nanny."

"Chandler is a handful. I'm sure you have a tough time with him." She said with humor.

I laughed.

Theo frowned, "Not for Chandler. She's Castle's nanny. Caregiver, actually."

You should have seen her face. "Oh. I see..."

Anyone would be rendered speechless to learn that the oldest brother needed a nanny.

The silence was getting awkward; I could hear the crickets in the background.

"We have burgers and fries; would you like to join us?" She asked me.

Madison seemed like a sweet girl, something that was a breath of fresh air in this house.

Theo gave her the sting-eye and, of course, I noticed the way he subtly kicked her shoe.

I shook my head. "I wouldn't want to intrude and be the third wheel. I'd rather sit in the courtyard and watch Castle count birds."

"Millie has a weird sense of humor. Ignore her." Theo said.

Madison laughed. "It's nice to meet you, Millie. At least someone in this house is interesting. I was pretty sure all the staff around here were androids."

"They're worse. You don't know the half of it." He informed her.

"Don't want to either." She said, "My imagination is wild."

"I would know."

"Wanna test it?"

"Aw. You guys are so adorable." I chimed in.

She had to be his girlfriend. And after this exchange, I had no doubt.

Theo tried to avoid eye-contact. They'd probably forgotten I was standing here until I'd said that.

"We were...we were just going upstairs to study. C'mon, Maddy," He said, running upstairs towards his room.

"I haven't even asked you anything, and be safe, guys. Don't have too much fun." I called out after them.

The door slammed after them.

I located Castle in the horse stables. It was too hot outside, so I'd prepared a jug full of fresh lemonade.

I told him he could have it when he was feeling tired but he ignored me and concentrated on the work at hand, so I placed the tray on an empty crate nearby and settled down on an upturned bucket watching him as he worked on his favorite brown colored horse named Star who had cute silky fringes covering its forehead.

He was shirtless, wearing only a pair of jeans that rode low on his hips. His muscles flexed as he lathered the horse with shampoo, and that was a sight for sore eyes.

I didn't really have a reason to complain.

It was nice to see Castle concentrate on something that he loved doing so much—whether it was trains, or remote control cars or horses.

The sun was beating down harshly; the birds chirped in the trees nearby—it was a lovely day and the mansion looked something right out of a fairytale story. Only, it was anything but. The darkness and horrors inside this mansion were unspeakable.

I tried my best to stop myself from thinking of the negative side and concentrate on the positive, like how Castle's hair had streaks of gold in the sunlight or the way he'd smile when he was doing things he loved.

Drops of sweat trickled down his body, and I stared at him, fascinated.

Stop it, Millie! He might be thirty, but there's no way Castle would even have liked me if he had a choice. He was way out of my league, not to mention, I was employed by his family—More like kidnapped, so what would my attraction towards Castle be called?

Stockholm syndrome?

I didn't think so. Castle was every bit a victim in this family as I was.

"Do you want me to leave?" I asked him.

Castle probably thought I was a hindrance, so I could just walk out here and observe him from far.

He turned to face me. "Stay."

"Well, can I at least help you bathe him?" I asked.

He didn't answer for an entire minute and I thought he was back to ignoring me again when he said, "Okay."

I took a generous amount of shampoo in my palm and began scrubbing the horse. The texture of the horse felt soft under my fingers. "Hmm...this feels relaxing. He's really sweet."

"I helped Star's mother...through labor when he was born." Castle said proudly, like a vet who'd delivered a healthy baby.

Pretty sure this was the longest sentence he'd said to me in a while. I'd noticed since I'd stopped giving him medication, his speech had improved.

"I see. I would love to watch the process someday as well."

Castle shook his head. "You'll be disturbed."

"Trust me. What I've been through so far in this house, I don't think anything else will disturb me for a long time."

Castle froze, his brush stopping mid scrub. He turned to me. "I'm sorry."

I shook my head. "It's not your fault."

Tension filled the atmosphere. And Castle didn't need to feel guilty for Devin and Dayana's sins. Even though he was their brother, he wasn't to blame for what was going on.

To make the situation lighter, I splashed the water from the bucket at him.

Castle stared at me in complete bafflement and for a second I thought he was going to be angry about it, but a moment later, I stood there bewildered until I was sprayed with a water hose.

And the sound of Castle's laughter rang in my ears.

It was one of the nicest laughs I'd ever heard—a rich, deep one that I could never tire of listening to.

I grabbed the pitcher of lemonade and threw it towards him. He walked towards me slowly, the hose still in his hands. I took a few steps back and made a run until I realized I was trapped completely.

Castle's eyes were mischievous as he approached me like a predator hunting for its prey until he grabbed me with his right hand and sprayed more water all over me.

"Oh god," I laughed, "Stop it." I tried to push him, but he wouldn't budge.

I snatched the hose from his hand when I saw the chance and did the same to him, so now he was drenched like me too. I giggled, "Serves you right, mister."

My giggles started fading when he inched closer until I was sandwiched between the wall and him. And I was aware of how the thin fabric of my dress clung to my body, outlining the off-white bra I was wearing underneath, not to mention the dress sticking to my body below the waist and highlighting every shape. By the looks of it, Castle had noticed it too, because his eyes kept darting from my chest to my lips.

He stared at the top button of my dress as if it bothered him.

I was lost in his intense gaze when his lips met mine in a slow caressing kiss. His mouth was insistent over mine as he was silently seeking permission for more. He smelled of something like sunshine, and lemon mixed with the twinge of his male scent that came after a day's hard labor. I moaned, unable to let go or tell him that what we were doing was wrong. He kissed like someone who'd lost practice at it, but knew exactly what he was doing.

I felt myself falling deeper and deeper—like I was being pulled by an ocean current.

My hands went into his soft brown curls, and his grasp over me tightened. His tongue moved desperately inside me.

I pulled away enough to say, "Castle...we can't."

But he was far beyond to listen to what I had to say. He was breathing hard and staring at my lips. He pressed his fingers on my swollen lips. "Tomorrow. Same place."

Chapter 14

I waited in the stables to see if Castle showed up like he said he would.

And true to his word, he was right there, in the middle of the stable, grooming another horse named Lady—the white horse with black patches.

I'd been careful about walking here alone, not wanting to be seen by the other staff. I didn't know what was going on in Castle's mind, or if the kiss yesterday was impulsive or attraction, but when he'd given me that heated look and asked me to meet him here, I couldn't refuse. No matter how much I tried to tell myself that I shouldn't do this, my heart wanted it badly—this connection with Castle.

When I closed my eyes at night, I could only see those hazel brown eyes and I recalled how intense his stares usually were and the way it lit my body on fire and when he'd kissed me last night, I kept replaying it in my mind wondering if I'd imagined it.

When Castle noticed I was here, he smiled, and I loved how his brown eyes would crinkle in the corners and I couldn't stop the butterflies taking flight in my stomach.

Before I had time to say anything to him, he walked over to me, grasped my hand in his and pulled me towards him. I had no choice but to follow him.

And then...

He handed me another brush and showed me how to brush the horse. I stood there like an idiot, thinking he wanted me here for something else.

"Good afternoon, Mr. Montgomery, sir. How nice of you to grace peasants like us with your presence. What can I do for you?" Ollie said, standing just outside the stables. I couldn't tell if he was being sarcastic or real. His clothes were matted with dirt, and I wondered if he was gardening nearby.

Castle didn't respond to him; he acted like he hadn't heard Ollie at all.

Ollie turned his grin towards me. "An excellent conversationalist, isn't he?"

I couldn't believe how rude Ollie was being, and the fact that he was talking shit like this when Castle was standing right next to me. I turned to Castle, "why don't you go outside and wait for me?"

He first glared at Ollie, then looked at me and his expressions softened. He placed the brush on the floor and left us alone.

Ollie watched Castle leave and smiled at me. "I would like to extend all kinds of services to you, ma'am, free of charge. I don't need anything in return from beautiful women such as yourself."

"I will pretend I didn't hear that," I said, turning away from him to leave when he caught my hand in a tight grip.

"Maybe you'll change your mind after you see this." He showed me his phone where he'd captured a picture of Castle and me in the stables yesterday. The shot was zoomed in and showed my hands buried in Castle's hair while his hands holding me to him, and our lips locked in a scandalous kiss.

"You disgusting son of a..." I screeched.

"What? You're going to act too good for me now?" His hold on me only tightened. "You think cozying up with the retard is going to make you mistress of the mansion?" He laughed, "Nannies came to this house and left before you, and the younger ones tried doing what you're doing, that is seducing that idiot. Do you know what happened to them?"

Before I could answer, he went on, his face twisted in a sneer, "they all died strangely. Some of them jumped off the house, others disappeared without a trace, fed to hungry dogs, drowned and the list of atrocities does not end there. Devin Montgomery has a hobby for killing with creativity."

He brought his lips close to my ear, and I could feel his breath fanning over my shoulder. "If you do what I say, I'll delete this photo from my phone."

I tried to push him away. "Let go of my hand!"

It was broad daylight and there no was no one around. I was having all these horrible thoughts about how Ollie was going to do something bad when suddenly, by some miracle, his grip loosened over me, and I looked up to see what had caused it.

Castle stood there, his fingers clenched around a gardening spade, the back of which was now matted with fresh blood.

Ollie was on the ground; a gash had opened up in his head and bright red liquid spilled from the wound.

"Oh No. Oh No. Oh No!" I chanted as I looked at the man who had crumbled and was laying there.

Castle's breathing was labored; his eyes were shining with vengeance.

Ollie coughed and tried to move when a loud splat echoed in the silence of the stables, followed by bone-crunching. Castle had smashed him again. A splatter of warm blood sprayed over my dress.

Ollie's face looked like jam.

The anklet in his leg blinked a blue signal and clicked open.

I was too stunned to move as I stared at the gory mess in front of me. My thoughts were all jumbled up, and I looked over at Castle, who was now shaking and staring at Ollie's smashed face. The menacing look in his expressions had dissolved—he appeared to be absolutely terrified and shocked about what he'd done.

"I-I...didn't mean to..." he said in a regretful voice.

He dropped the spade and took off from the stables. I ran after him to find him crouched on the grass by the tree, heaving his breakfast.

"Millie..." he said, tears trickling down from his face, he looked down at his hands, "He was trying to hurt you...I...I..." he tried to form the words, swallowed and continued, "I couldn't watch..."

I wiped his face with my dress. "We have to let your brother know about this."

"Nooooo...." Castle said loudly, "Devin, he...he would get angry and punish me. He'll give me those awful medicines...please, Mi llie...he killed my previous nannies and tried to blame me...we can't tell Devin about this."

Castle was getting hysterical as he clenched his hair, tears trick-ling down his face. "I...I...didn't mean to..."

The way I saw it, Ollie was a lecherous asshole and reported every single detail to Devin. Castle had saved me from being molested. He'd recused me and brought me back to my room when I was confined in that basement for weeks so talking about this to Devin and getting Castle into trouble wasn't something that I wanted to do.

I cupped his face in my hand. "We won't tell anyone."

Sometimes when I sat alone in the room, I wondered if I would wake up and this would all be just another nightmare. Maybe the Montgomerys were a wonderful family and everything that had happened until now was part of my morbid imagination.

But that wasn't true. I was living the nightmare.

Whenever I tried to close my eyes, all I saw was Ollie's face.

I'd helped someone cover up a murder.

No matter how bad he'd been, no matter what he'd done, murder was still murder.

There were flashes of Castle digging and the two of us lowering an almost headless body of the stable boy into the ground. Castle threw mud over it to cover it up and we buried him deep into the woods.

We also had to get rid of the blood on Castle's shirt, so I sneaked back to the house and washed it in the sink. Everything in Ollie's phone was pulled apart, and I threw it all in the lake. This time I was mindful of any bear traps laid out in the area. I would not fall for that shit again.

Castle and I turned up at the dinner table as if nothing had happened, but when I saw the medium-rare steak on my plate; I had to excuse myself to throw up because my mind couldn't stop conjuring up images of Ollie's face, especially his crushed eyeballs. Castle seemed to do a lot better than I.

Devin asked Winston if he'd seen Ollie and kept muttering under his breath about how he was going to kill the stable boy when he found him. I wanted to tell Devin that we'd done the job for him.

I buried my face in the pillow, muffling my cries.

I'd covered up a murder!

I was startled by a shadow, moving behind me, a silhouette of a person. I sat upright and turned to see a tall figure standing at the door.

How long had he been standing there?

My heart was racing, "You scared me, Castle!"

"Millie..." he whispered.

"Please don't do that again, and you're supposed to knock on the door before entering," I told him.

I probably hadn't locked the door before sleeping because I was too preoccupied with everything that had happened this afternoon.

The time on the clock was one-thirty-six a.m.

I wiped my eyes with the back of my hand. "Come inside."

Castle stepped inside the room and closed the door behind him. It was dark inside the room, so I couldn't see the expressions on his face.

"Do you need something, Castle?" I switched on the beside side lamp.

He approached the bed, and I was more aware of his handsome face now that he was so close. Those brown eyes looked darker in the dim light. His chest was bare, and he was only wearing a pair of sweatpants. He looked even more intimidating in my small room, and his lack of clothing was giving me all the wrong ideas.

He reached into his pocket and pulled out something. "It's...it's for you."

"For me?" I smiled. I'd gotten used to him slipping small things like origami planes in places I would notice.

He placed it into my palm and gasped when I noticed that it was the locket from my aunt that Devin had taken from me.

"This means so much to me, Castle. Thank you."

He nodded, "I...I can't sleep."

"Me either," I admitted.

"Can I sleep here with you?" he asked me, sitting down on the bed and putting his head on my lap.

I couldn't say no, not when he was looking at me like that. If Castle asked me if I could jump off the cliff, I would probably agree to it too. His childlike innocence was something that drew me in.

"I like...I like being close to you, Millie."

I ran my fingers through his soft hair and it felt soothing and so nice.

I was going to say 'me too' when he asked, "Can I kiss you again?"

My breath hitched in my throat.

"We shouldn't," I said.

"Why not?"

"We just can't, okay?!" I snapped at him.

He jerked away from my lap and looked shaken—like I'd slapped him.

"I'm an employee here." I clarified. "We can't kiss."

A while later, he asked, "What about my cheek?"

I smiled. "I guess I could make an exception."

I leaned in and just when my lips were going to touch his cheek; he turned a little, and I was met with his lips instead. Once our lips brushed together, I couldn't seem to stop. When I parted my mouth, his tongue entered my mouth. The kiss was deep, and I wondered if he could even taste my fears and my pain. It was like he was taking it all away from me.

I ended up on the bed and Castle on top of me. He didn't understand the weight he was putting on me because he was too invested in eating me up. His hands moved at the side of my body fervently, and his hand landed on my right breast. I felt kind of electrocuted as he squeezed with his large palm and continued to assault my mouth with his. He was turned on, his hard-on pressed against my pelvic bone, and I could feel the need building inside of me. I needed his hands all over me.

He reached towards the hem of my gown, his fingers tracing my thighs, and I knew what he was going to do, and as much as I loved what he was doing, I needed him to stop. I couldn't let desire take over.

"Castle, no," I whispered.

His hands stopped moving, and he pulled his body away from mine. The sight was glorious, to say the least, and some women might have killed to be in my place.

Truth was that I didn't know if Castle was attracted to me or was just horny because he didn't have female company for a long time since the accident.

I realized I didn't care.

"Sleep?" he asked.

"Yes, let's go to sleep."

He lied down beside me and put his arm over my waist, pulling me to him. I turned around to face him and saw him looking at me and I couldn't help but fall deeper and deeper.

I was falling in love with him.

Chapter 15

It was a late Friday afternoon, which was usually time to read Castle some books. I'm not sure if he understood what was being read because most of his attention was fixated on my breasts, not that I had a problem with that. Reading books for him was part of my job and I enjoyed doing it.

I didn't understand why I was being summoned into Devin's study so suddenly. It was usually the last place I wanted to be.

He sat behind his desk, wearing a beige shirt with a few buttons undone from the top, and emerald eyes that were haunted by horrors of this mansion.

"How are your legs now?" Devin asked me, cheerfully, as if he hadn't witnessed his sister beating the shit outta them and he hadn't just locked me up in the basement after that.

"They are fine." I said, "all thanks to your perfect medical care." I added sarcastically.

Devin laughed, running his hand through his hair. "we take teaching our lessons to the rebels very seriously, but I'm genuinely glad that it worked out, Millie. You seem to have adapted to your life now."

I just smiled in response. If I had a gun, I'd be happy to put a bullet in his handsome face.

"Well, the reason I asked you to come here is because of a party invitation that we received. It's at Beckett's house tomorrow evening." He said, "The Beckett's are an influential family, much similar to ours, and my father used to have a good relationship with them."

"I will stay home with Castle. Don't worry."

Devin shook his head, "the invitation specifically asked all family members to come for the party. They obviously do not want Castle to be left out because he is the oldest son of this family and they knew him since before he lost his memories. He's expected to show up." He continued, "That's where you come in. Winston will deliver a dress and a pair of shoes for you this evening. I need you to wear it tomorrow and look presentable. Penelope can help you with anything else that you may need. Your job at the party would be to keep Castle company. He doesn't do well at parties, especially where there are many people."

"I understand," I said.

"Great." Devin smiled like he was an angel with the halo on his head, but in reality, he was a spawn of Satan.

"I would like to leave, if that's all. Castle is waiting for me in his room, as it's his reading time." I climbed to my feet and made my way towards the door.

I just needed an excuse to get away from Lucifer.

"Wait a minute, Millie," Devin called out to me again.

I stopped short and turned.

"If Castle does any drama at the party, I'm going to hold you responsible for it. Explain to him the kind of behavior that is expected of him during the gathering. Drill it into his brain, if you have to."

"I'll make sure he's on his best behavior," I assured him.

"Oh, and one more thing, Millie."

Now, what asshole?

"I should probably just warn you. If you try to devise any plan for escaping, I'll know. And the consequences of your actions shall be dire."

"I won't try to escape, Devin, because I really want to help you with Castle. I'm taking responsibility as his caregiver very seriously."

Devin looked shocked for a minute. "I'm impressed. Keep that up, Millicent, and I'll give your phone back. Hell, I'll even take off the anklet."

"If that's the case, Devin, I promise you, I won't cause any trouble."

"Good. Off you go then."

I passed him a smile before turning around to leave. The smile turned into a smirk by the time I was out of the study.

It was true that I wanted what was best from Castle and I wanted to help him with his condition. Only, I was playing a double game. Flushing Castle's medications down the toilet would bring his memories back and serve my purpose. I would act docile, follow the twisted rules, and finally get what I want. When Dayana had broken my legs and the time I'd spent locked in the basement down below, I had only one thought that forced me to live through that situation.

I wanted the Montgomerys to pay the price for their sins.

And I wouldn't rest until I'd witnessed it happen.

I tried to remember the last time I'd worn something so beautiful and couldn't recall a single time that I had.

It was a long royal blue velvet dress, off-shoulders with a V neck-line. I didn't have huge breasts, but I had decent curves. I've had men turn around for a second glance at me when I walked down the streets during the time I wasn't a captive employee at the Mont-gomery household and so that proved I was attractive, at least.

A glimmering studded necklace adorned my neck; the sapphire gemstone in the center was beautiful, and it matched my earrings. If I hadn't been their captive, I'd probably be tempted to steal the necklace, but of course, I didn't possess a stealing streak in my body. This necklace would feed a poor family for years. The Montgomerys had far too much wealth. It was old money, passed through gener-ations.

The gown's length swept on the floor of the black limousine as I wondered if Devin had ordered this particular gown for me on purpose, so if I planned to run away during the party, I would likely trip and fall.

Only, I didn't plan on escaping, no matter how badly I was tempt-ed.

Castle sat in the limo facing me. He wore a tailored black tux, his hair ruffled, and his face having a five o'clock shadow. When I'd first went to his room to help him dress up, I couldn't stop thinking about his hands or the innocent way he would keep stealing glances at me with mesmerizing golden-brown eyes. He was drop-dead gorgeous, and I felt a twinge of jealously for any woman he'd been with before his accident. If Castle was normal, I was sure he would have reeked of power. He seemed like the type of man who would be honorable, fair, but also strict when he needed to be. I enjoyed guessing what Castle's real personality would have been before the accident.

The Beckett's mansion was enormous, but if I should admit, the Montgomery's mansion would put this one to shame. Marble floors, beautiful chandeliers and long hallways led us to the ballroom where the party was taking place.

Dayana introduced me to the owners of the mansion, Mr. and Mrs. Beckett, an elderly couple who seemed warm and receiving. I didn't miss how Dayana said I was 'Castle's date' and when I looked at her in confusion; she smiled politely and kicked my foot.

I knew I needed to play along.

The more I stood there looking at all the people, the more I realized I didn't belong with them. My life two months ago was nothing like this, and now I was dropped headfirst into a web of lies, deceit and manipulation. I hated it, but I also hated my old life with my uncle, where my wings were clipped. At least with Devin, I knew where I stood. If I pretended to play by the rules, he wouldn't hurt me.

Castle was settled at a round table with Chandler seated next to him. The two brothers were drinking something.

"Miss. Montgomery?"

I turned to find a handsome gentleman standing near me; a strange look was on his face. He was blond, with blue eyes and sharp features.

"Oh, I'm not related to them." I said quickly, "My name is Millicent Davis."

"My bad. I thought you were Devin's cousin," he chuckled. "I'm Jett."

He offered me his hand. I took it, "Call me Millie." I picked a cup from the table and started pouring a deep orange liquid into it.

"A little warning, Millie, that punch you're about to take. It sucks." He grinned.

I laughed, "Thanks for warning me." I emptied the contents of the cup back into the bowl and poured myself some red wine instead.

"The meatballs suck big time, too. The rest all should be good," Jett said with good humor.

I rolled my eyes. "How do you know so much about the food quality here? Did you do a secret taste test?"

Jett flashed me a grin. "This is my house."

I choked on my wine, laughing, "Jett Beckett?"

"The one and only,"

I couldn't hide my amusement. "I met your grandparents earlier, and they were talking about you, but never mentioned your name. That's why I didn't know who you were."

"I bet they tried to set you up with me." Jett said jokingly, "I wouldn't have any qualms if they had."

Jett was a flirt. A big one. He was the type of guy who was charming and hard to turn down.

"Not really. They knew I came with Castle."

Just then, I felt a little nudge on my back. "Millie..."

Jett's expressions were unreadable as he stared behind me. Castle was standing by my side, brushing his fingers lightly over my elbow. "What is it, Castle?"

Castle glowered at Jett silently, but that quickly faded as he turned to focus on me. "I want to leave."

"But sweetie, we just came to the party," I said, squeezing his hand.

The way Castle seemed upset, something seemed wrong. I leaned in a bit and could get a whiff of liquor on him. Was he drinking alcohol all this time?

"My head...my head feels woozy." He complained, rubbing his head harshly and his breathing turned heavy.

"Are you feeling ill?"

He ran his hand through his hair, "Millie...let's go."

I looked at Jett. "If you'll excuse me, Mr. Beckett. It was nice meeting you."

Before he would answer, Castle got a tight grip over my hand and dragged me out of the ballroom

Chapter 16

We walked out of the ballroom together; Castle's hand was clasped in mine, our fingers entwined. We passed the hallway that led to the ballroom and before we could enter a room, Castle rounded the corner suddenly and pulled me against him.

I gasped as his hands, which were splayed on my waist in a possessive grip, tightened his hold over my body. His touch ignited an inexplicable fire inside me.

"What are you doing, Castle?" I whispered.

He didn't listen to me; his lips attacked my cheek and trailed a path down my jaw and then neck, his teeth grazing softly. The slight bristles over his cheek brushed my skin, making my knees grow weaker. I had to hold on to his shoulders for a better grip, and it was a good thing the high heels were giving me a good advantage here.

He smelled of some expensive scotch or brandy or some other drink, the scent of it mixed with his signature cologne that reminded me of some spice and wood.

He was drunk.

"Castle..." I said, trying to untangle his body from mine for fear of getting caught. "Someone can come here."

He wouldn't listen to me. Instead, his fingers dug into my hair as he tilted my face to claim my mouth in a hot searing kiss.

He kissed me like he was dining on one of the finest delicacies he'd ever have.

And I loved it.

To be showered by so much attention, even if Castle was using me for his pleasures, I couldn't say that I hated it. It was wrong on so many levels to fall for a man that belonged to the family that was keeping me captive and it had more to do with the previous lack of genuine attention that I'd received.

He and I were almost similar. He was bound by his twisted family, forced to do what they asked, and I wasn't any different.

I was hungry for this connection. To be wanted with such passion...

His lips continued the assault, his mouth sucking my tongue. I kissed him back, putting my arms around him. My fingers went into his hair.

I pulled away. "we shouldn't be doing this. Your brother will kill me if he finds out." I said silently.

I wondered if Castle had faked about not feeling well when I was talking to Jett so he could get me away from there.

Somehow, the thought of Castle being jealous over me was enticing.

I closed my eyes and relished the way he groaned into my mouth, pressing his thick arousal against my stomach. I felt the desire inside my core. No one ever had this effect on me. His hands strayed from my hips to the slit at the side of the dress and his palm covered between my thighs. I was breathing hard, but I still managed to say. "No, Castle, not here."

It was obvious that soon he'd want more. He'd want to go forward and if he pushed, I didn't think I had it inside me to deny him what he sought. Suddenly, his moments stopped. He stilled, and I wondered what had frozen him.

In my peripheral vision, I saw why Castle remained immobilized.

Chandler stood a few feet away from us, staring silently. His expressions were unreadable.

He couldn't be trusted!

It wasn't a secret that Chandler, as much as he looked cute as hell he was also a little runt, unlike Theo who appeared to be cold from the outside but cared about people and liked to maintain a distance because he didn't like what his family was doing to innocent people.

Chandler would no doubt spill. I didn't think I could go through another round of 'let's break-Millie's legs' episode.

Castle slowly placed me down. My heels touched the floor.

I walked to where his little brother was standing, her big apple-green eyes watching me as I stepped in front of him.

"Chandler, what you saw here was nothing. Castle and I were only talking to each other."

"With his hands in your panties?" He snapped.

I stood there, shell-shocked. That sounded nasty coming from was an innocent-looking eleven-year-old spoilt rich brat.

"It's not what you think. I promise. Castle wasn't feeling well inside the ballroom, so I brought him here." I explained.

He looked directly at Castle, ignoring what I'd just said. "Devin said we're leaving the party soon. You better eat up your dinner or you're going to be starving when you get home."

"Don't worry. I'll make sure he eats." I assured him.

Chandler frowned. "I wasn't talking to you."

His rudeness was next level. I don't remember hating a kid so much before. Chandler was extremely moody. Sometimes he wanted to play board games with me, and then sometimes he treated me like I was a garden insect.

We returned to the party with Chandler, had our dinner, which was a long buffet of gourmet food, and then Devin told me we were going to leave early.

I was thankful for not getting caught up in any drama.

Three days had passed, and I had heard nothing from Devin. How could Chandler possibly shut his mouth about what he'd witnessed at the party? It was hard for me to assume that this had something to do with luck because I wasn't lucky by a long shot.

I tried to keep Castle's hands off me after being seen at the party, just to be on the safer side, but all I could think of was Castle's mouth on mine and the delicious way his hands would roam all over my body. It was hard to keep myself from fantasizing about what we could be under normal circumstances.

If Castle had been well, would he still desire me? These questions continued to pop up in my mind, refusing to let go.

I sat in the room's darkness with only my thoughts to keep me company.

There was a soft knock on the door.

It was Castle.

I'd successfully avoided his night visitations by not answering the door, but it was proving to be hard when all I wanted to do was to allow him inside. I also had these questions in my mind that preoccupied my mind.

What if Castle had been the same with the caregivers here before me? What if he did the same with them and Devin had killed them for touching his brother?

I'd done some research on the previously employed nannies. Most of them seemed to be in their late thirties or forties. There were only two who were as young as me. Three of which had died tragically. Two others had left the job. Nobody under the Montgomery employment was allowed to quit their jobs. According to what I'd learned, they either ended up dead or stayed on the estate. There were far too many secrets buried within the family, and Devin didn't want it to be leaked outside. After all, they had a reputation to keep. No matter how nice the outside world thought they were, the truth was that they were beyond fucked up. There was something bad going on, but I was yet to find out what.

Another soft knock brought me back to reality.

I asked him to come inside.

Castle stepped into the room. He wasn't wearing a shirt and only a pair of sweatpants on his hips. My eyes glazed over as I took in the vast expanse of his brawny chest, the muscles, and the set of abs that looked almost sculpted.

A wave of lust hit me.

If Castle had tried to do something to the previous caregivers, I'm sure they would have opened their legs for him willingly.

I was going crazy. He was driving me crazy.

"Hey, sweetie..." I whispered, as if the walls could hear us. "What's up?"

He lowered himself onto my bed, the whiff of his familiar scent tinged my nostrils, and if I was shameless enough to admit. I was probably soaking with desire. Despite his silence, he seemed to always find a way to communicate with his eyes, those deep brown-golden eyes that looked almost luminous in the dark. Since I'd stopped giving him the medication, his eyes had a distinct glow about them. They weren't devoid of life like how they used to be when I first came to the mansion.

The fog was slowly lifting from his mind and body. The panic attacks had also minimized.

He placed a paper crane in front of me and smiled. "For you."

If not for Devin, I was sure to die from sugar-coma. Castle was really sweet.

I picked it up, "thank you."

His nose flared as he suddenly reached for my dress and pulled it up.

"Castle, no!" I shrieked in a whisper as loudly as I possibly could allow myself in the night.

I couldn't be mad at him for his indecency with the way he was innocently looking at me.

His hand still stayed on my lap, and he asked, "Why not? You...d on't like me?"

"It's not that." I said, "Devin won't like it."

"But I'm his older brother. He can't...tell me what to do." Castle pointed out.

I smiled. "I know you are, but he's currently in charge of taking care of you." I touched his cheek. "If he finds out about us, he'll destroy me."

"I won't let him..." he stared at me for a few seconds, looking for the right words, "...hurt you...I promise."

I nodded, still smiling. My heart skipped a beat.

He traced the pattern on my nightgown and sneaked a glance at me.

I grinned, "What is it?"

"Millie...you won't ever leave me...would you?"

I was going to cry.

If Castle got his memories back, maybe he wouldn't want me, but that was a risk I was willing to take.

"I'll stay as long as you want me here."

"I'll never stop wanting you." He whispered, his voice was raspy and his fingers now slowly tracing the lace on the hem of my gown. He applied gentle pressure on my thighs. "I feel...like..."

I urged him to go on.

"I feel like I'm myself when I'm around you."

"Me too," I admitted. "I want you to get better Castle, so you can remember everything that happened."

"What if I remember everything....and," he paused, he gave me a pained look, "what if I forget you?"

I laughed, feeling a little melancholic about what Castle not remembering me. "I'll make you remember me again."

He pulled me close, and I wrapped my arms around him, feeling his body relax against mine. There was nothing sexual about the embrace, only a sense of mutual contentment.

And I was falling harder for this broken man.

Castle and I had slept together that night, just holding each other, and I didn't remember ever sleeping so peacefully before. I had to send him back to his room before dawn for fear that a servant would see him leaving my room in the morning and get any wrong ideas. Gossip spread like wildfire in the Montgomery household.

That's the last thing I needed.

After I made sure that Castle had sneaked into his room, I went back to mine and had fallen asleep.

When I finished having my shower and stepped out of the steaming bathroom, I was a little taken aback by two maids standing in the room with a dress laid out on my Queen sized bed. Penelope and Sally looked like two robots operated by batteries. I wondered if they ever laughed or smiled. I wouldn't be surprised if Devin had somehow trained them not to, seeing how sick and twisted he was.

I looked at the dress and then at the two. "What's that for?"

"The dress is for the wedding this evening."

The dress was pearly white, nothing too fancy, but elegant.

"Whose wedding am I attending?"

The two looked at each other in some silent communication.

"You're getting married to Mr. Montgomery."

Chapter 17

This couldn't be happening to me!

The maid's voice continued to ring in my ears as I dumped the dress in the fancy box it had come in and stormed out of there. My legs were taking me to Devin's room, my pulse slamming in my neck with uncontrollable fury.

I rapped on his bedroom door harshly. He did not deserve any polite knocking, not when he'd sprung something like this onto me with no warning.

I wouldn't let this go without a valid explanation.

And there was no way in hell that I would ever marry Devin Montgomery.

I heard a soft command to come inside.

I stepped inside the room and instantly regretted it. Devin was sprawled half-naked on the bed, the other half-covered with a comforter looking like some rare painting hanging in a museum. He had two completely naked women on either side of the massive bed. On his right was a brunette with hair so curly and unruly, it looked like a bird's nest. The woman on his left was a blonde, both of them exceptionally beautiful with curvy bodies. They could have been models or some actresses from Hollywood.

Either way, I didn't care. I was too appalled for words. On many occasions, I'd seen women come and leave the estate as they wished, and I'd been a curious onlooker, wondering if they were Devin's business associates or perhaps some friends. Never had I imagined it was something of this nature.

Not that it was any of my business to be nosy where Devin was concerned, but it was quite clear that this wasn't a onetime thing; it was part of his leisurely routine.

"Good Morning, Millie. What a pleasant surprise, darling. Care to join the party? We have room for one more." He said sheepishly in a lazy drawl, and the insolent bastard had the gall to smirk at me while doing that.

I ignored his teasing and slammed the box on the dresser. "I'm sorry to intrude, Devin. Perhaps I'll come back at another time when you're fully dressed and without company."

He chuckled, "Don't be so formal now, my dear, not when we are about to be family soon."

Anger was bubbling inside my blood like a volcanic eruption. "Can I speak to you for a moment?"

The girls took that as a signal to pick up their discarded clothing from the floor and some draped on the rich looking gold-rimmed chaise by the open doors to the balcony. They didn't seem to mind their nudity in my presence, as if walking around naked in front of strangers was as common as serving guests their coffee.

When the girls were completely dressed, they each kissed Devin on his cheek and he, in return, whispered something in their ears that made them giggle, obviously something raunchy that I didn't even wish to listen to.

"Will see you soon, my loves. Help yourselves to breakfast downstairs." He drawled, and that earned him flying kisses.

"We will." The two said in unison.

I rolled my eyes.

The girls smiled and greeted me before leaving the room and shutting the door behind me.

Devin was still sprawled on the bed between those disgustingly expensive-looking navy blue silk bed sheets. He looked everything like an aristocratic debauched lord of the manor that liked to dabble in liquor and women.

He rang for a maid who came scurrying into the room within minutes of being summoned and wheeled in a breakfast fit for a king.

Must be nice to be so stinkingly wealthy, you could even hire people to keep your slippers by your feet.

Thankfully, he kept the silk sheets draped around his waist as he climbed to his feet to make his way to the bathroom. He turned around to look at me. "I'll be out in a few minutes, and you can have some of this food in the meantime. Georgina always sends breakfast for a dozen."

He dropped the silk sheets before entering his bathroom, giving me a full view of his backside. I looked away instantly. I had reasons to believe Devin did that on purpose. The maid went back to work, making the bed, withdrawing the used sheets and replacing them with fresh ones, all the while ignoring me while I sat there, which suited me just fine considering that I was in no mood for an idle chat.

Devin walked out of the steaming bathroom moments later, dressed in denim jeans, no shirt. Winston walked inside the room and began helping Devin dress up. Only after he was completely dressed (most of the dressing done by the servants, I might add), did he sit down to breakfast.

I showed him the box with the wedding dress inside. "What's this?" I demanded, crossing my arms across my chest.

He sipped his coffee, his emerald eyes dancing with amusement. He found immense pleasure in seeing me in discomfort. "I'm sure you have perfectly capable pair of eyes that can distinguish what's inside the box, or have you turned blind in a matter of hours?"

His sarcasm was getting on my nerves. "Yes, Mr. Montgomery, I have eyes to see what's inside the box, which is what I need your clarification for. Why am I being told that I will be married off to you by evening? I don't remember agreeing to something like that."

He chuckled like he'd heard the best joke ever and picked a bowl of fruit salad. "You should be happy that you'd be living every woman's dream. As you may have realized, you'll be married into our family, bearing our last name, which will bring nothing but privilege to you. You get to live in this mansion, enjoy the luxuries the name brings you, and in return, you are to only play wife. What I don't understand, Millie, is what's all this fuss is about?"

"I did not sign up for this!" I snapped at him. "I will not marry you...you...disgusting piece of—"

"If I were you, I'd watch that mouth before it runs off and causes more damage, damages that you will pay for."

I was shaking and not with fear but my instinct to murder this man and I wanted to scream at him, maybe even take that fork from the tray in front of him and stab him with it. But I did no such thing as I remembered the torment they had put me through, but I'd kill myself before I cry in front of Devin and give him something else to derive sadistic pleasure from.

"Doesn't it matter to you what I want?" I asked.

"It doesn't." He said with indifference. "If you want, I can ask the guards to open the gates for you right now and you'll be out of here, completely free."

"You would?" I asked.

"Yes, you will be out of here in a coffin." He smiled, "On the bright side, your anklet comes off." He laughed, spreading some butter over his toast.

That left me with little choice. Either I could marry Devin or die.

And I refused to die at the hands of this sick family.

He was still smiling as he extended his hand towards me in an invitation. "Come closer."

I shook my head.

His eyebrow was raised in question, like I would dare say no to his request. He grasped my hand and pulled me towards him, and I landed right in his lap. I gasped and tried to get up, but he tightened his hold over my body. Softly, he whispered in a silky voice, "Marrying me wouldn't be so bad. You'd love it, I promise." his fingers caressed my cheek, making my skin crawl. "I'm just thinking of all the things I'd do to you once you're mine." He licked my earlobe.

I just sat there frozen, feeling like this was all a bad dream and hoping I'd wake up. Suddenly, he pushed me off his lap gently and playfully swatted my ass. "Now, if you'll excuse me, my lovely fiancé, so I can go about my duties. I'll be looking forward to this evening."

I'd cried long and hard in the bathroom that afternoon. This felt worse than a nightmare. Devin was a monster that I didn't want to marry, and it didn't help that I kept thinking of the things that he would do to me once I was his wife.

My future consisted of being trapped on this estate surrounded by servants who were trapped or obliged to the family. They would never talk about the atrocities if I found myself in situations where I was being harassed. As my husband, he'd use me in every way possible, would never be faithful to me, and I'd be stuck in a marriage with a man I didn't love.

I went to Castle's room to find him, to see if I could tell him what Devin planned to do and hoped that he'd listen to me and stand against his younger brother, but I couldn't find Castle anywhere. He didn't even have a phone so I could call him, and that killed my last hope. I couldn't ask anything of Theo, not when he was almost in the same position that I was, with the exception that he was trapped by his own family. It was unlikely that Devin would even listen to his seventeen-year-old brother, and I didn't want to give the kid any trouble.

I went back to my room in resignation. Penelope and Sally dressed me up in the wedding gown; they pulled on the back laces tightly, helped with my makeup, and styling my hair like they were pro. I remained numb to everything, my insides screaming at me to run.

Run, but where?

Part of me wondered if I could slit my wrist and end this, but I imagined the heartache that would cause Castle if saw me that way, and I'd promised him I'd make him better, that I'd help him remember his past. Even if I married the devil that was Devin, I wouldn't stop what I started.

I wore my shoes and decided to face the ugly reality. I was looking into the mirror, and although I looked beautiful in the bride's dress, all I felt inside was dread.

Chandler walked into the room a minute later dressed in a tux, holding a bridal bouquet that he handed over to me. "Millie, it's time."

I stood up and stepped out of the room, walking downstairs towards the fate awaited me.

Chapter 18

I walked down the stairs slowly as if prolonging the time would stop the inevitable. I might buy time, but I wouldn't delude myself into thinking the wedding would stop. I knew that wasn't possible. Some fairy godmother wasn't going to appear and stop this wedding. I secretly hoped the place could catch fire or a big hole could appear in the groom's pants that couldn't be fixed in a month or two.

Luck, in my case, was usually nonexistent. I'd lived with facts and tragedies as they continued to pile up throughout my life. This wasn't any better.

I felt so sorry for Castle.

I'd promised him I'd be with him, but if I was going to be married to Devin, I wouldn't be allowed to spend time with Castle as much as I was used to. I would not be his nanny, but Devin's wife—and that was one big tragedy in itself.

Why had he chosen me?

I didn't even belong to a wealthy family like theirs; in fact, my family was dirt poor. If I stole a spoon from the Montgomery's kitchen, it was likely to make me rich and last a year, so why would Devin marry someone so far beneath him?

Unless he had a motive.

Was it lust? Did he think that marrying me would give him the authority to get me in his bed?

Or was I reading too much into it?

Maybe he found out about my brief fling with Castle, well, if you could even call that a fling—the sneaking around the house and exchanging a few passionate kisses. A servant could have seen something and gossiped around, or maybe Chandler notified Devin, so he decided he'd marry me to teach me a lesson.

That could be right.

There was no other explanation for it. None at all. He was marrying me to put a stop to my secretive meetings with Castle, and he thought that was the only way to do it.

Well, he thought wrong.

Even if I married Devin today, I'd do as I pleased.

My mind was going haywire by the time I reached the courtyard, and I tried my hardest not to dwell on the future and live in the present because that's how I was going to get through this—one step at a time, crossing one hurdle after the other.

I noticed just how beautiful the arrangement was. The archway was decorated with flowers. The sun was already setting, leaving yellow and red hue over the mountains, the shades blending perfectly with the green trees that lined the areas. It was like a gorgeous painting that was about to be grotesque by the current events.

Fancy chairs were lined on the side where a few people who I didn't recognize sat with a curious expression on their faces. I assumed they were the family's distant relatives or friends. It was quite obvious the ceremony was private and only a select few people were invited. Their Grandpa, Hugh, was sitting right in the front, and he stared at me in indifference with his glassy eyes. I hardly think he recognized me or, better yet, knew who I was. Dayana sat beside him, looking prim and proper, dressed in a lovely beige dress, her hair in wavy curls. Theo's girlfriend Madison was also there, and her eyes were only reserved for Theo, and she kept passing him flirty glances.

Theo stepped beside me, smiling kindly at me; I guessed it was my final sacrificial smile. "I'm going to walk you down the aisle to the altar. You're going to be my sister, after all!"

I squeezed his hand. "Theo, please stop this. I don't want to marry—"

"If there was anything that I could do to help you, Millie, I would, but my hands are tied down. I'm sorry. And if I should be honest..." his eyes pierced through mine, "I would love to have you in our family."

I didn't know whether to take that as a compliment since the boy had finally taken a liking to me or if I should be angry that he'd rather see me married off to his monster of a brother than set me free.

The Reverend stood at the end of the archway and my husband to be was waiting there for me, dressed in a tailored gray tux. The bastard was so handsome; one would even think they were lucky to be getting married to him until they discovered the evil that lurked behind those uncanny green eyes.

I walked slowly down the path, my throat forming a lump, my mind shutting down.

I didn't want to do this!

And yet I was forced to do absolutely nothing to stop it!

I had no phone to contact any authorities. No way to escape this place. I had nothing. I was completely at Devin's mercy, but I needed to remember the end goal.

I wanted out.

I had to marry him and then stab him in the back.

That was the only way.

Another thought just kept creeping into my mind—more like an image of my wedding night. It was the horrific imagery of getting naked with Devin and consummating the marriage with him. I just couldn't. Maybe I'd just lie down and let him do as he pleased.

Or I could close my eyes and imagine it was Castle.

The thought was disturbing, to say the least.

When I stopped walking and stopped midway, the anxiety was taking over again. Theo looked at me and pressed my hand in reassurance, as if he understood what I was thinking about. I could tell that he pitied me. He had to literally push me forward to walk ahead. With every step that I took forward, I wanted to take two steps backward.

We halted right beside the groom. Devin flashed me a dazzling smile, one that would have charmed the panties off any other woman who wasn't aware of his usual shenanigans.

Theo kissed my cheek and Devin kissed the other cheek as he whispered in my ear, "You look gorgeous, Millie." and he stepped aside.

Castle was standing there beside him, who came to stand next to me. He was hidden from view all along because Devin had been blocking him until now. Theo chuckled as he placed my small hand in Castle's larger one.

I gasped when I noticed what had happened.

Relief hit me so hard, my knees could have buckled. I would have died right there if it wasn't for Castle holding onto my hand.

Tears started spilling out of my eyes. Tears of sheer and utter relief.

I wasn't being married to Devin.

My groom was Castle.

Reverend Philip was at a loss for words, probably having a weakness for women's tears because he began handing me his napkin, telling me it was normal to become emotional on my wedding day.

I looked at Devin, who was standing at the side, and glared at him. The asshole wore a smug expression on his face, having a blast on my account, gloating on the fact that he'd fooled me into thinking I was marrying him.

I ignored him. I wasn't about to let Devin ruin my day. I concentrated on the man standing with me.

I was at a loss for words when I looked at Castle. He looked so incredibly attractive, with his thick sable hair that was styled unruly, giving him the sexy look and brown eyes that seemed almost hazel. His chiseled face and the strong jawline added to his beauty. He wore the tux similar to his brothers, but Castle, in my opinion, looked the best.

He looked sideways at me with the intense way of his and gave me the heart-melting smile. Not only was he sweet, but wanted me as much as I wanted him. I counted my lucky stars for marrying such a man.

Dayana was standing beside me, holding a ring. I tried not to dampen my mood because I would rather prefer eating glass than having this witch as my sister-in-law. If only murder was legal, it would have solved my problem.

The ceremony began, and I couldn't explain my happiness when Rev Philip asked me, "Millicent May Davis, do you take this man, Castle Montgomery, as your lawfully wedded husband?"

"I do."

Later on, there was some dancing, which was followed by dinner. Everything turned out to be amazing the moment I realized I was marrying Castle. The dangerous situation had suddenly turned out to be far better than I expected it to be.

After the party was over, Castle was being held back by some guests, so I made my way back inside the mansion.

I went to my room upstairs to change and suddenly remembered since I was now married to Castle, I could share his bedroom, but all my stuff was still in my room. Everything had happened so suddenly, there was no time to move things. I'd been too disturbed to think about anything since I'd assumed I was marrying Devin.

I took a long bubble bath and changed into my nightgown. Thankfully, they'd bought me some nice ones upon request a few weeks back. A baby pink colored nightie that was short and lacy, not to mention transparent, but I covered the scandalous lingerie with the matching satin robe that came with it. I hoped Castle liked it. I smiled to myself, thinking about him. I felt nervous and excited on equal measures.

I was just combing my hair when suddenly the door burst open.

Castle stood there, panting, and the bow on his neck was tilted. I thought he'd ran upstairs to find me.

He sauntered into the room and gave me a quick once over, his eyes lingering over some parts for longer than necessary.

Then he came towards me and grasped my hand in his, pulling me towards himself. "Let's go to my room."

Chapter 19

It wasn't the first time that Castle had demanded something. Usually, he was shy but never hesitated if he wanted something. This wasn't a subtle request either. There was a possessive glint in his eyes when he grabbed my hand and asked me to go to his room.

I followed him like a good, obedient wife.

A zing of excitement and nervousness rushed through my blood as I wondered what would happen tonight. I was dying a little from anticipation.

A woman like me would have never dreamed of getting married to someone like Castle. If circumstances were different, there was no doubt about it, and even though I had feelings for Castle that ran deep, I wasn't sure if he felt the same way. Even with marriage in the equation, he might never love me. He wanted me; I knew that much, but I'd assumed it was because he'd lacked the love and attention that I gave him. It could be purely sexual attraction, and whatever it was, I would take it.

I hoped that one day he'd learn to love me.

Once inside the room, he turned the lock and my gaze swept around the room.

I spent most of my time here with him as his caregiver, but I never thought that I'd be sharing the bedroom with him. It wasn't decorated like a honeymoon suite, no roses, no scented candles, nothing romantic, and that made me wonder if it was because the family assumed that Castle wasn't capable of the understandings of what really happened on wedding nights.

The look in his eyes clearly said he might not understand what went on, but he was going to be a quick learner.

Castle stood at the door, silent, but his stance was still predatory. His whiskey-colored eyes were blazing as they raked over my body, starting from below and to the top, stopping only briefly to stare at my breasts.

I bit my lip; this was getting awkward very fast.

"Castle, do you...do you..." stop stammering like an idiot, Millie! "Do you know what happens on a wedding night?"

"We fuck?" He asked with a straight face.

I burst out laughing, but Castle wasn't finding this funny. "We make love. That's a better term, don't you think?"

Castle didn't care about the term as long as we were going to get naked and doing it. I could read that on his face.

He took off his jacket and tossed it over the plush chair. I would be kidding if said I wasn't feeling a little on the edge.

"Lose that nightgown." Castle said brusquely.

I reached for the knot on my robe and slid out of it, and that left me wearing only the short camisole.

His eyes were trailed over me, his long lashes lowered.

My heart was beating aggressively against my chest as I stepped towards him and began unbuttoning his shirt. He stood there silently, watching me undress him, and then I felt his callous fingers lingering over my waist before they slid below and cupped my round ass and brought me snugly against his front. I felt his erection through his pants.

I ran my hands over his broad chest and his hardened pecs. He was so strong and his biceps so powerful that he made me feel smaller in comparison. He smelled of some woodsy spicy cologne. Castle was breathing hard as he brought his hand up to hold my face, capturing my mouth in a delicious slow kiss and with his other hand he bunched up my dress in his fist. I took that as my cue to get rid of the cami. His lips got bolder as we kissed deeply, and I moaned into his mouth, my fingers digging into his hair.

We were married now, so we didn't have to hide any longer.

His tongue plunged into my mouth and moved in languid strokes, turning my insides into molten. If it weren't for his powerful hands holding me firmly, I would have sunk to the floor.

He rubbed his fingers over my bra, looking at me heatedly. Softly he said, "Take this off too!"

I reached behind me and unclasped the bra. Now I stood completely naked in front of him, save for the panties. I unzipped his pants, and he stepped out of it. His eyes smothered thick with desire as his hands snaked up my skull to grab my hair in his fist. And honestly, I was noticing a little that Castle liked to dominate when we were alone like this.

I was going to tell him to stop holding my hair so tightly when he picked me up in his arms and brought me into bed, where he kneeled on the mattress with me still clinging to his body and kissed me. He mauled me, his hands covering my breasts as he squeezed and closed his mouth over one and sucked hard, his teeth grazing against the nipples.

I cried, both in pleasure and pain.

"You like that?" Castle rasped, "Millie... how hard... you want me to fuck you?"

Was I hearing correctly?

My innocent Castle was spewing this...

Before I could process it, he pulled his boxer shorts off and his hand snaked around my neck. His hand was firm against my neck as his weight overpowered me. He was a strong man, and I didn't like to be defenseless in bed. I tried to wiggle out of his hold to get into a different position; one that wasn't me flat on the mattress, but I was no match to his power.

His fingers grabbed for my panties as he tore it off swiftly while he kissed me violently, his hand getting tighter like he wanted to choke me.

I had brief flashes of what my uncle used to do to me. Tears blurred my vision. I was shaking all over, paralyzed by fear.

Was he trying to kill me?

"Stop it!" I screeched.

Surprisingly, his grip loosened just a little, I took my chance and sat up. I saw the confused look that crossed his face as I stumbled out of bed and away from him. I was sobbing with relief to be out of his grip and began picking up my robe while Castle was still naked in bed, staring at me in bafflement.

He reached out to grab me again, but I stepped away and out of his reach.

"Millie..." he called me softly, "Why...why are you crying?"

"Stay away!" I said, "I can't do this."

"Millie..." He said in a frustrated voice.

I knotted the robe around my body, feeling the bile rising in my throat. I didn't look at him as I unlocked the door and walked out of our bedroom. I could hear him calling out to me, first calmly, and then his voice was rising with every stride.

I made a run for my old bedroom, opened it, and locked it from the side. I lied down in my old bed.

I heard the knock on the door. "Millie..."

Castle was outside. "Millie, please open the door...I...I can explain..."

Chapter 20

The knocks became incessant and Castle continued to talk me into opening the door. The knob kept turning and his soft voice called out to me from the other side, "Millie, please open the door..."

I was scared of him. I had never thought that Castle would try to hurt me like that.

I avoided Castle for two days straight, and I didn't take my meals in the dining area because I didn't want to face the other members of the family. Castle tried to talk to me when he had the chance, but whenever he was close, I felt intimidated as if he would catch me and try to choke me again so I fled in the other direction.

When I passed Devin in the hallways, I noticed he was wearing a smug expression on his face, like he expected this to happen.

Castle and I were married, and I couldn't keep fending him off. He had every right to demand me to sleep in his bed. Those were his conjugal rights. I refused to believe that Castle was anything like him. While my uncle had always been evil, I'd never seen that negativity when I was with Castle. He was shy, but smart and compassionate. Sometimes he didn't realize what he was doing or what certain gestures meant.

On the third night, I had had enough of the cat-and-mouse game. I sat up in bed and I was going to give Castle a chance to explain his behavior.

I opened the door slowly and found him seated outside on the floor, with his legs pulled to his chest, rocking back and forth. As soon as he saw me, he climbed to his feet; there was the clear pain in his whiskey-colored eyes. "Millie...I'm sorry..."

I tried not to be moved by his tears. Firmly, I said, "Let's go back to your room and talk about this."

I followed him to his room and maintained distance.

Castle stood in the center of the room, shirtless. His hair was a rumbled mess, probably as he stared at me in confusion. He didn't make a move to touch me, so I knew I was safe.

"Did I... do something wrong?"

I closed the door. "You tried to choke me! Why did you do that, Castle?"

"I thought...I thought you would like that..." he wet his lips and looked at me with the most heartbroken expression.

"You were being rough. I thought you were going to kill me," I wiped at the tears that continued to blur my vision. "I was...I'm a rape victim. I don't know if you're aware of this, but I'm not into rough sex. It's also the reason I didn't date anyone in the past. I had deep fear..." my heart rate sped up. "I feared it would happen to me again and then you..." I trailed off. "You're stronger than me, and any man I've known and I don't wish to be treated like that. Are you understanding what I'm saying, Castle?"

He nodded, guiltily he looked up at me, "It's just the video."

"What video?"

He walked to the laptop sitting on the coffee table and fired it up. I watched him as he clicked on an icon on the desktop and a video popped up.

The room filled with loud moans and masculine grunts. A well-built man was choking a woman and passing crude comments while he did it. The clip was an obvious exaggeration, and the acting was bad enough, but I knew what I was looking at. She was screaming but also moaning as he squeezed his hand around her windpipe.

He shut the laptop and met my gaze, "Before the wedding..." he paused, trying to remember the words, "Devin showed me this cli p...and...and...he said you'd enjoy this. He said that's what happens on...the wedding night."

Anger swelled my insides, and I wanted to walk into Devin's room and kill him in his sleep. My face burned with embarrassment. "He lied to you. Well, there are some people who might like it, but I don't."

"I..." He said, obviously confused, "I'm sorry, Millie."

I gave him a small smile, feeling a little relieved that he hadn't meant to do what he'd done and it was Devin's plan for Castle to scare me. He wanted to break me. He expected Castle to do it, and his plan had almost worked.

I walked towards him and wrapped my arms around him. I felt him sigh and his hand came up to my head as he held me close, burying his face in my hair. He seemed relieved. "Just follow my lead, okay?"

I felt him nod against me.

I undressed him and then stripped off my clothes as well. We were both naked in bed when I kissed him slowly, and he mimicked what I was doing. We kissed for a long time and I pushed him to sit against the headboard, straddling his large muscular body. I traced my fingers through the golden-brown dust of light hair over his chest, kissing the side of his neck and then suckling it. He groaned as his breathing turned harsh and his fingers dug into my ass as he brought me closer.

I took his hand in mine and covered my breasts. I taught him what I liked. When his mouth touched my nipple, I arched my back to give him more access. I led his fingers down to my folds and, when I knew I was ready; I positioned him at my entrance and impaled myself.

We both groaned with the intensity of the pleasure that hit me. I met his eyes, cupped his face, and claimed his lips while I began riding him, holding onto his broad shoulders.

"Castle..." I whispered, "You feel so good."

He moaned, and I flipped us over so I was on my back and he was hovering above me.

He took charge, and I didn't have to tell him what to do as instinct took over and he held me close as he thrust in and out of me. He was a fast learner. It was really sweet how he held me as we made love.

"Millie..." he breathed, "Millie..."

The look on his face while he came inside me was something that I would never forget.

It was priceless.

Castle looked tortured and completely awestruck by what had just happened. I took great pride because I was the one to put it there.

The scent of sex and sweat permeated the air. I moaned my release as he collapsed on top of me with a last thrust. I smiled at him when he moved over my body to the side.

"Did you enjoy that?" I asked.

We were both breathless.

He grinned at me, snaking a hand around my waist, pulling me to him, he whispered, "Can we...Millie...can we do it again later?"

I laughed, "Yes."

I kissed his cheek, "I love you." then I kissed his lips, "so much."

"I love you too, Millie."

We stayed like that for a while, just enjoying being together like this. The silence was comfortable.

"Don't listen to what Devin says, okay?" I said, playing with the thick locks of his hair. "Your brother lies to you."

He ran his fingers lightly over my stomach in slow circles. Something crossed his features that I wasn't sure about. "Devin will pay for everything that he's been doing. Pretty soon," He smiled, those wicked dimples kicked in.

I smiled back as I snuggled close to him under the covers, basking in his scent, burying my face in his chest. "Good night, Millicent." He said.

"Night Castle."

My eyes shot open, but I didn't dare move.

A chill ran down my body.

He'd just said an entire sentence without pausing. His demeanor was confident.

He called me Millicent.

Chapter 21

C astle was insatiable.

We made love two more times that night before we fell asleep at dawn in a tangled mess. Castle's left leg was pushed against my body in a possessive way.

That unfamiliar glint in his eyes had faded, and the old Castle had taken charge, and that was the strangest part of the night. I wondered if I'd imagined it.

My brain hadn't conjured up him whispering 'Millicent' in his deep husky voice that it still gave me the tingles and a bunch of butterflies took flight in my stomach as I kept rewinding that moment in my head like a tape.

There was a brief knock on the door and before I could even answer, Penelope entered the room. I was embarrassed by my lack of clothing, and honestly, it was a little uncomfortable about being promoted from employee and thrust headfirst into the seat of the mistress of this household. I used to be one of them, and now I wasn't.

Mrs. Millicent Montgomery.

The name had a nice ring to it.

She didn't even look up as she wheeled the breakfast in, bowed, and left the room.

I guessed that was the routine since the time Castle slept here alone. Now that I was going to share the room, nothing was going to change.

I had to wake him up and force him into the bathroom because he would rather stay naked and in bed than get on with the day's activities.

After his bath, he sat on the bed while I stood between his legs and combed the tangles through his thick, wet hair. Even though I was his wife now, my duties remained the same. I wouldn't let anyone else do this because I loved every second of it. He watched me intently. His light brown eyes glimmered in the sunlight that streamed through the window. There was something so intimate about the moment, in the comfortable silence of companionship.

Castle's hand slipped slowly into my bathrobe and caught one breast in his hand. I laughed, "Can you please stop? I'm trying to concentrate on your hair." But he wasn't listening. He circled my nipple, and with a possessive tug on my waist, he covered his wet, hot mouth over it.

The comb just slipped out of my hand, and my fingers replaced where his comb had been, making a mess of all the tangles I'd just removed. "Castle..."

He lapped and suckled like he'd die if he didn't, and moisture pooled between my legs. I cupped his face and his mouth met mine in a soul-sucking kiss.

We were breathless a few minutes later and staring hard at each other. "What happened to you last night?"

"What happened?" He repeated.

I bit my lip. Should I ask him or should I let it go?

"You called me Millicent," I said.

"I did?" He asked me, his brows furrowed in confusion.

I watched his expressions to see if he was being honest or lying and I could only see sincerity. I wondered if Castle was a talented actor and I was curious to find out.

"Yes." I kissed his cheek.

"What did I say?" He asked, not breaking eye-contact.

I could have sworn I'd seen a glimpse of the old Castle last night, the Castle that had all his memories intact and who knew far more dark secrets than he was letting on. The Castle that was dangerous and calculative, who had been running the Montgomery empire. That man had excited and frightened me in equal measures. While I hoped Castle's memories came back, I was also scared of the consequences. Somewhere deep down, I wondered if I really wanted to awaken the old Castle.

What if the old him was like Devin?

"You have to remember it yourself, Castle. I won't tell you any-thing."

"Millie, I have something for you." He said as he reached across from me towards the bedside table and pulled out his wallet from the drawer. From inside, he took out an Am Ex card and handed it over to me.

"What's this for?" I inquired. The black card had his name in-scribed on it.

Castle Montgomery.

I ran my fingers over his name.

"I remember you told me that..." he paused, "you told me once that you never bought anything nice for yourself because your uncle used to take most of the money. I...I want to give you everything, Millie. Everything. You deserve it. I'll give you this card that I rarely use...you can buy stuff you want."

My eyes were brimming with unshed tears and that made him worry, "why are you crying? Did I say something wrong?"

I sniffled, wiping my face with the back of my hand. "I have what I need. I got what I wanted." I assured him as I pressed the card back into his hand.

"What's that?"

"You."

He liked that answer because I was rewarded with a heart-melting grin. "I was already yours...the day you stepped into the house. Buy something for yourself, Millie."

I sighed, "I can't go out of the house without permission, Castle, and you already know that. Devin wouldn't allow it."

"But I'm your husband!"

I giggled, "That you are, but even if we're married, I don't know if I'm allowed outside and look..." I pointed at the anklet, "If I went far from the property, the sensor will blink and Devin will know where to find me."

Castle stared at me. "I'll tell you a secret. The anklet notifies for only about thirty minutes when you're in town...and...when you drive out of town, it cannot trace the location."

Whoa!

"So you're saying we have to sneak out and hope that Devin doesn't notice until we're far enough?"

He nodded.

I smiled, "I know how you feel, Castle, but I don't want to risk it. Besides, I can let Winston know whatever I need and he will deliver it to me."

He picked my hand and kissed each knuckle. "One of these days...Millie...I'm going to take you out."

Castle couldn't remember what he had said last night, and that made me wonder if he slipped into his old self once in a while.

I needed to keep an eye on him.

Most of the members in the house ignored me, which suited me perfectly. The only person I enjoyed interacting with was Theo. He was different from the rest of his evil siblings. I played board games with Chandler and we had a great time together; he was warming up a little towards me since I was his sister-in-law, but to be honest, I wouldn't trust Chandler with my dog.

I met Susan on the stairs as I made my way towards Castle's room and she told me she'd baked some blueberry muffins that I could pick from the kitchen area downstairs.

Blueberry muffins were Castle's favorite.

I started descending the stairs when I heard the sounds of soft conversation drifting from the hallway.

From Devin's study.

I took off my shoes and walked towards the room. The door wasn't shut completely, but I guessed they were under the illusion that it was closed.

I tried to pick up bits of the conversation.

"Stupid bitch thinks she's smart for flushing down his medications." I heard Devin say.

My heart thundered as I realized who they were talking about.

They knew!

"She's doing all the work for us and she doesn't even know about it." Dayana chimed in.

Devin laughed. "Did you see the smug look on her face? Thought she one-upped us. Now Castle's just gonna fuck her six ways to Sunday. No pun intended."

"Are you sure we should let her keep doing it?"

"Yes. I want Castle wide awake when I go for the kill. I'm a lot of things. Dayana, coward, is not one of them. He will fucking pay!" Devin said angrily, his voice going a notch up.

They planned to kill Castle!

"Devin, do you hear that? Someone's at the door!"

I looked down the hallway. There was no way I could make a run and not be seen. I quickly tiptoed into the room right next to Devin's study and sneaked into the old closet, and shut the door behind me.

Chapter 22

They planned to kill Castle.

Have I heard them correctly? But why would they want their brother dead?

I was missing something here.

I stayed hidden inside the closet while Dayana checked the room. I could see her shiny green pumps from a small opening. She moved around in the room. I could hear the shuffling. I didn't move an inch. My breathing had turned heavy. I pressed my hand to my mouth.

I was married into this family, and even if I'd felt forced to at first, I'd accepted my fate because of Castle, because I loved him, but I didn't have an intention of living my entire life hiding from this family that was supposed to be my family now.

Yeah, I was part of this screwed up family. It was the bitter truth.

Devin followed Dayana into the room and they spoke in hushed voices, looking around in the darkened room.

Just then, my back hit the wooden wall and something behind me moved.

Meeeoowww

The fat Himalayan cat Lulu jumped from a top shelf and went to brush herself against Dayana's legs.

"Aw, so it was you who was making those sounds." Dayana picked the fluffy cat up into her arms. "Are you hungry, baby?" she cooed.

Thankfully, they decided the cat was making the ruckus and left the room, closing the door behind them. I stayed put for a few minutes in case they were still there, listening against the door. I didn't want to get into trouble.

If Devin and Dayana wanted to plot Castle's murder, why would they be so careless and leave the door open? There were a lot of servants in the house who would eavesdrop, and word would certainly get out.

Unless...

They were trying to bait me with it.

I pushed the inner closet paneling a little and noticed a small gap between them. I pushed it harder and the entire thing just fell apart. There was a tunnel ahead of me, much similar to the one that I'd been to before.

This mansion had a lot of secret tunnels and passageways, so it shouldn't have come as a surprise to me, but something about this darkened passage made little sense.

The entry to it was installed through the old closet, which had honestly looked out of place in the vast room. There was old furniture littering around the room, some vintage chairs, tables carved out of expensive wood, and a four-poster bed fit for a king. The room was well maintained as it was being dusted and cleaned by a house staff so if a person stumbled upon this room, they wouldn't guess the inner paneling of the closet led somewhere. It was meant to look like any other old furniture. The secret rooms or passages hid in plain sight.

I stepped from the closet and onto the narrow dingy passage that was pitch black. With shaky hands, I pulled out my phone and used its flashlight to navigate my way through it.

An unsettling feeling crept into my skin. I knew I was making the same huge mistake I'd done before by walking right into dangerous territory. If I was any smarter, I should have turned and walked back like I hadn't noticed this, but I couldn't. Maybe it was the curiosity burning like a flame inside me. I wanted to play Sherlock Holmes. Or maybe it was the thrill to dig deeper into the family's dirty secrets.

The passage turned narrower and narrower, dirt matted the floor. The walls once had some nice wallpaper that was now yellow and peeling. You wouldn't even guess this place was inside the mansion. It was so dank and dirty.

At the end of the way, there was a steep set of stairs. I almost lost my footing. I wondered if one of the Mad Montgomery ancestors who had this built wanted unsuspecting people to run down this passage and fall down these stairs, possibly breaking their necks and end up dead.

When I took the stairs down, it hit a strange dead end. The stairs just ended with a wall, nothing after that. The Montgomery's were sick, but they were also trolls.

I climbed back up and started making my way towards the entrance I'd come from. I needed to get back to Castle before he noticed me gone. He usually wrecked havoc if he didn't find me.

I almost passed through when in my peripheral vision; I saw a tiny hole in the wall. I wouldn't have noticed it in the dark if I hadn't been so vigilant.

I peeped through it.

There were four people in the room, seated on a wooden chair—all of them staring in four different directions, facing the inner circle. I poked the hole in the wall, and the cement began falling off. That's all I needed to get a clearer image.

The people were bound, and the chairs were kept in the middle of large red pentagrams. The walls had similar symbols painted on them, each wall representing the person seated in front of it.

They weren't even people.

These were dead, decaying bodies, preserved like they were still alive.

Each of their foreheads were marked by a symbol. I didn't recognize the other bodies, but I knew one of them—Ollie the stable boy that Castle had killed and I'd helped him to bury.

Someone knew what we'd done and had dug up the body from the ground. The body that had a missing head because Castle had smashed it. Ollie's head was replaced by a goat's head, and it was stitched over the body's torso.

I fought back the urge to hurl up my breakfast. I felt sick to the pit of my stomach, but I continued to watch. Tiny candles were lit in each of the circles.

I needed to leave right now!

I backed away from the wall and sneaked back into the wardrobe. Still shaking, I placed the wooden paneling back, and it clicked right into place.

I couldn't concentrate on anything for the entire day. I kept seeing that horrible imagery of the four dead bodies in a circle, staring blankly ahead.

By dinner time my appetite was completely gone. I couldn't eat the lamb chops without thinking of the goat's head stitched onto Ollie's head. Devin eyed me curiously, but didn't say a word.

It was hard to read his expressions as he'd mastered the art of keeping his expressions poker face. If he knew I'd listened to their conversation, he didn't let it show. Same with Dayana.

They spoke softly about business. Chandler was busy shoveling the food down his throat like he was an escaped prisoner who'd just discovered quality food. Theo, as usual, looked bored and texted under the table.

"What do you think, Millie?" Devin asked me.

"Sorry, I didn't hear what you said."

"I asked if you would be interested in showing up at the next company board meeting? We're launching our new cosmetic brand."

"What would I do at a board meeting?"

Dayana laughed, "You're the oldest son's wife, Millie. You're a Montgomery now. Since Castle wouldn't be able to take part in the board meetings, you can have his seat. If we think you're capable, we'll even consider handing over the brand to you. That's what Castle would have wanted from his wife."

"It must be boring to stay cooped up in the mansion. It's an excellent opportunity for you to learn the operations of the company."

This was a little too much for me to process. They wanted me to join the company board meeting?

"That's a lot of responsibility, but it sounds great."

It sounded too good to be true.

But looking at the two of them, I didn't think they were giving me a choice to refuse their offer. They wanted me on board.

No one in this family was perfect. Devin liked to drown himself in bottles of liquor and brought countless women home. Dayana was as perfect as she appeared to the public eye, only she wasn't. She sneaked in buffed up male escorts into her room, sometimes three at one time, and I'm sure it was a nice big perverted party. I was no one to judge. The siblings had peculiar tastes. The other day, I'd seen one of the other stable boys, the nice looking one called Alan from Texas, who had a southern drawl who was also sweet and respectful, unlike Ollie.

Anyway, one time after midnight, I'd run out of water bottles from the mini-refrigerator so I'd gone downstairs to the kitchen myself.

And regretted it terribly.

There was Dayana and Alan enjoying themselves, fucking each other.

Dayana could fuck the stable boys, the gardeners, or anyone else for all I cared. I know Theo had walked in after me with AirPods in one ear, picked up a bottle of chilled latte, and walked out like what was happening in the pantry was just normal.

Before going to bed, I went to Theo's room. He was the only person in this house that I trusted apart from Castle. And we'd become great friends despite the eight years age difference.

I knocked on his door. "Theo, it's me, Millie."

"Come inside, Millie."

I entered the room.

I rarely visited Theo's bedroom. It was a typical room for a teen boy. He had a floor to ceiling display of action figures, a black guitar was in the corner, posters of heavy metal bands on the wall, and the furniture was dark wood, carved and custom made.

"You can't tell this to anybody," I said.

He closed his book and turned to look at me, "what can't I tell anybody?"

"What I'm about to tell you."

He nodded. "Your secret is safe with me."

I paced around the room.

His brown eyes twinkled as he grinned. "Okay, you need to calm down first and tell me what happened."

I explained to him about what I'd heard Devin saying, that he'd planned to kill Castle, followed by the discovery of the secret passage and the bodies on the pentagram. I left out the part where I realized one body belonged to Ollie because then I would have to explain how Castle had accidentally killed him.

Theo stared at me and then burst out laughing. "That's a nice joke."

"I'm not joking, Theo. I wouldn't have come to your room right now if I was not serious."

"First off, Devin is probably just screwing with you. He wouldn't kill Castle. Second, there's no way they would keep the bodies in the house. Accidents on the property are taken care of. The Montgomery's excel in cover-ups. Our family has the detectives and the police department under their thumbs."

I hated how he said 'our' and included me in the family. I hated I was part of this screwed up family that called murders accidents.

"Devin or Dayana are doing these satanic rituals! I know it!"

Theo shook his head, "that's not possible, Millie! Stop saying that shit!"

"So, how do you explain it? Are you saying that I'm making this all up?"

He ran his hand through his hair, staring into the distance, and then the realization hit him as he froze. There was unadulterated fear clear in his eyes. "Grandpa Hugh." He whispered.

"What about him?" I asked.

"He was the one who used to practise the satanic rituals until he lost his memories. Castle can't remember shit either, Chandler is too young for all of this unless..." he swallowed.

"Unless?"

I knew I would not like the answer to it.

"Unless Grandpa has chosen Devin to carry out what he started, the body count won't stop at four." He tapped his fingers on the desk, and he was visibly shaking. "We will end up dying, Millie. Each one of us."

"How do we stop him?"

Theo stared straight into my eyes. "We can't. Only Castle can stop him, but for that, we need to wake him up first."

Chapter 23

"How do we wake him up?" I asked Theo impatiently.

Theo sat back in his leather seat, thinking hard. "I'm not sure if it will work out, but we need to try. We have to recreate the boating accident."

My eyes went wide. I was positive one of my eyeballs was going to pop out. "You're suggesting that we should create the entire scenario of the day that your parents died so he could get his memories back?

Theo nodded, even though he looked visibly shaken by his idea. "That's exactly what I'm saying."

"That's cruel!" I said. "His psychiatrists have specifically told me not to broach any topics about your parent's death with Castle, especially the boating accident. If we do something that triggered those awful memories, it could make matters worse!"

"You think I don't know that?" He asked, sounding pissed. "It's the only way, Millie. If we somehow don't get him to remember everything, we'll end up dead."

"But why would Hugh kill you? You're his grandson..."

"If Hugh won't, Devin will."

"He is your brother, Theo." I reminded him. "What's wrong with your family? Why is everyone so sick and twisted?!"

"Before Alzheimer's hit grandpa, he used to carry out these vile and atrocious rituals. Innocent people died. His father did it before him, and so on. Our father never agreed to this and wanted it stopped, but Devin was always keen on walking in grandpa's footsteps and he would go to any lengths to make sure the rituals take place. It was all fucked up."

"That still doesn't answer my question, Theo. why would Devin want his own brother dead?"

"Because Devin and Dayana are not related to me by blood!" He confessed and then his face turned ashen.

I guess he hadn't meant for that little information to slip.

He sighed, "Neither are they related to Castle."

My head started spinning. "What do you mean?"

Theo got up from his chair and walked the distance to his vintage dresser. I heard some shuffling. He threw some stuff on the floor and produced a thick black journal from one drawer. He picked it up and brought it to me.

The pages of the journal were yellowed, showing how old it was.

"It talks about the family tree along with certain facts, and deaths of the family members entered into it. Skip the start, and read only the dog-eared pages. There are entries written by my mother, and that's all you need to know."

I hugged the journal to myself. "Thanks, Theo!"

He nodded.

And then there was a knock on the door.

"Quick, hide the fucking journal!" Theo whispered.

I tossed it underneath his bed.

The door opened and Castle peeked inside. "I've been looking.
..all over the house for you. What were you doing here?" His eyes
then went to his brother.

"Theo and I were just talking," I told him.

Castle nodded, "Let's go to bed, Millie."

"Good night, Theo!" I said as I got up from my seat.

"Good night, Millie."

I held eye contact with him, letting him know that I'll be here again
for the journal. He gave me a slight nod, so I walked out of the room
towards Castle.

"You've become...best friends with my brother," Castle noted,
smiling as he closed the door of Theo's room behind us.

I smiled back. "Yeah, I guess so. It's nice to talk to him sometimes."

"You can talk to me too, Millie. I mean...if there's anything. I'm
here for you."

"I know. Thanks for that." I said, pressing the hard muscles of his
biceps.

We went back to our room, and he closed the door behind him.
I brushed my hair and changed into a nightgown getting ready for
bed when I felt Castle's powerful arms going around my waist. His
head was bent to the nape of my neck and he began peppering soft
kisses there.

I touched his face, feeling the stubble on his jaw that gave me
butterflies in my stomach. When it was time for bed, he usually
wanted to make love, which had become a norm. I guess I should
be lucky that he found me attractive enough that he wouldn't be
tempted to look at other women. I'd heard too many stories about
wealthy men having an affair with other women while their wives

played the perfect role at home, but with the way Castle stared at me, his eyes heavy with desire, I didn't think I would ever find myself in that situation.

I felt his hands grope my ass from behind, "I like this." He said in a silky deep voice. "Take off your clothes." His commands were a usual occurrence in the bedroom.

I laughed. "You have your priorities straight." I spun around in his arms, looking up at my towering, extremely gorgeous, and sweet husband. I had to constantly slap myself as a reminder that I was married to him and he wasn't a figment of my imagination.

Castle's golden-brown eyes watched me as I said, "You have to kiss me first."

He smiled, grasping my chin, and bringing me up to meet his mouth. I had to stand up on my heels to reach his towering height. I melted into his arms as he kissed me and then he helped me undress and took off his clothes, too.

It wasn't hard and fast, but slow and languid. I met his thrusts with the same enthusiasm, moaning and writhing under him, whispering his name.

After a while, we were both exhausted and lay in bed together. His muscled arm was draped over me; his thick hair flopped over his forehead, matted in perspiration. I kissed and licked his abs greedily. He kissed my forehead, giving me a satisfied smile.

"I love you, Castle," I said.

He kept playing with my hair and didn't say it back. I swallowed the disappointment.

A while later, when I heard the sounds of his snores, I sat up in bed and made sure he was in deep sleep before walking out of the room and shutting the door behind me.

I walked soundly at first and then picked up the pace. I went to Theo's room and knocked on it.

Theo opened the door, wearing only a pair of boxers, his hair in disarray, and his abs were on display. I couldn't help but notice how he looked like a teenage version of Castle.

"Took you long enough," He said sleepily, stifling a yawn, and then he shoved the journal into my hand. "Do not show this to anyone. After reading it, you need to return the journal back to me."

I nodded, "Got it."

I hid the journal in my robe and tiptoed back to my room.

I walked into the room and my breath hitched in my throat when I saw the silhouette of Castle, who was now seated upright in bed. I couldn't see the expressions on his face in the darkness, but knew he was watching me.

"Where did you go, Millie?" He asked me silently.

"I was just feeling a little sick, so took a walk outside in the hallways." The lie rolled from my tongue.

A few seconds passed before he raised his hand towards me. "Come back to me."

I walked back to him and slipped into bed before quickly retrieving the journal and hiding it near the dresser.

Castle snuggled to my body, "I don't like it when you leave my side." He whispered.

"I'm not going anywhere, baby. I'll always be here with you." I promised.

His hold tightened over my body. The grip was so firm and bruising that I had to ask him to loosen his fingers over me. It was like Castle was making sure I didn't leave the bed again.

I couldn't wait to wake up in the morning and read the journal.

I needed to be completely alone to do it.

Chapter 24

I couldn't get much sleep that night as I kept tossing and turning in bed. My mind was preoccupied with what I would find in the journal that Theo had given me.

Early in the morning, when Castle was still asleep, I climbed out of bed and picked up the journal that I'd kept hidden. The maids wouldn't come to disturb me for at least another hour, and Castle was snoring softly. I knew he wouldn't wake up as long as I stayed beside him. If he found me gone from bed, he would wake up and cause a racket.

I'd gone for an early morning walk in the courtyard last week, making sure that Castle was sleeping, but thirty minutes later when I came back inside the mansion, he was screaming and running around throwing the doors open looking for me.

After that day, I knew not to sneak out. He constantly sought physical contact and finding the bedside empty made him very upset.

He draped his arm over my waist. I traced my fingers over his biceps as I opened the journal to read.

The journal was ancient since being passed down from generations, and the pages in the beginning were filled with entries by different ancestors of their family.

Mostly male.

I realized they were all written by the firstborn member of the family.

Did that mean Castle had written something here too?

Theo had specifically advised me to read the dog-eared pages because he said the other entries were irrelevant. Looking at the first few entries, I realized he wasn't joking when he said it bored the hell outta him. There wasn't anything interesting that the ancestors had written.

I skipped to the middle pages of the journal.

Aster Montgomery.

I tried to recall if I heard that name before.

Was this Castle's mother?

I started reading from the first page, but the pages were all detailing about school life, and college, and other not-so-important events in her life. I skimmed some more pages until I found the juicy parts. The page had a small red star scrawled on it with a pen.

I don't know long I've been in this bed, thinking about ending this madness that runs in my family.

My father wouldn't listen.

Innocent lives have been sacrificed; people have died for some sick rituals. I needed my dad to stop. I needed him to understand that this wasn't how I wanted life to go on.

Sometimes I wish I could just run away far from here. Sometimes I sit by the lake and stare into the water, wishing I had the guts to jump into it. The blue, serene water calms me down somehow. It feels like a soothing balm to my loneliness.

If I jumped into the lake, it would all end then, wouldn't it?

The pain and the sufferings would be gone.

But I was a coward and couldn't bring myself to commit suicide.

Dad wanted me to get married soon as I was turning twenty-five, but I didn't want to as I knew the man that my father had chosen to marry me.

Terrance Briggs was nice, sweet, intelligent, and kind. He made me smile, and his family was as influential as mine. I went on a few dates with Terrance, just to make my father happy. I liked Terrance, but that spark was missing.

He didn't make my insides turn to molten; he didn't make me laugh until I had tears in my eyes, and he wasn't as handsome as a movie star.

Christopher was all those things. And more.

It's too bad Christopher was born on the wrong side of the blanket.

The wrong side of the town.

He was a stable boy on the Montgomery estate.

The sounds of loud thumping of footsteps made me shut the journal quickly and hide it beneath my pillow. A soft knock on the door broke into the silence.

"Come inside."

Penelope stepped inside the room. She bowed, her eyes never straying to Castle's half-naked form on the bed or his hand holding me, crushing me possessively against him. I bet she was used to walking into far more compromising situations of her other Masters, so she wasn't bothered with a married couple still in bed.

"Good Morning, Ms. Millicent. Master Devin has asked for you and Master Castle to be ready in twenty-minutes. He said you were going with him to the head office."

I sighed. I'd completely forgotten about the board meeting he wanted me to join.

I gave her a nod. "Tell him we'll be ready. Also, please send in the breakfast."

She bowed once again and left.

I wasn't interested in going for this stupid board meeting. I'd rather be cooped up in this bedroom and read the journal. There were so many secrets still waiting to be uncovered, so many lies that the family had spewed. I needed every bit of information. Knowledge is power after all, and I was going to dig deeper and find out what was going on, starting from the family history.

I turned to Castle and kissed his collar-bone. "Time to wake up, baby."

He squeezed my body towards him, mumbling something in his sleep.

I traced the back of his face with my fingers. "Castle, baby, we need to get ready."

Devin drove us to their office in his black BMW. Castle rode shotgun, and I sat in the backseat.

The trees rolled past us. I watched as the iron gates slowly shut and the mansion turned smaller as the car moved farther away. It was the second time I was allowed to be outside the mansion. Throughout the entire fifteen minute drive, I kept imagining Devin stopping the car somewhere and throwing me out. Blame it on my trust issues over the family; I couldn't predict what would happen in the very next second.

Despite everything, he chatted with me like we were old friends, as if I hadn't been forced into marrying into his family. Let's not forget the time he'd broken my legs or when he'd threatened me with a hunting rifle.

He was such an amazing brother-in-law.

My ass.

I smiled while he talked to me about the company. I'd chosen a simple beige blouse over a pair of skinny slacks, matching them with cream-colored pumps and a Chanel bag. My ears were adorned with a pair of diamond earrings that Theo had given me as a wedding gift that had belonged to his mother, and I should have them. I'd been too emotional to say anything. Being given his mom's jewelry meant Theo had completely accepted me into his family.

I'd kept my attire casual and formal, looking every bit like the wife of a wealthy businessman. I didn't want Castle to be shamed for my upbringing; I would never do that to him. So even though this new wealthy Millie wasn't part of who I used to be, I was ready to do what I needed to in order to belong to his world.

Castle was dressed immaculately in a white button-down shirt and khaki slacks that were snug over his delicious thighs and his ass looked perfect in it. I didn't think I would ever stop lusting over my husband. Sensing that I had my eyes on him, he glanced at me from the front passenger seat and gave me that killer smile.

The car rolled to a stop in front of a tall building. I was just admiring the glassy design of it when the door opened. I stepped outside. Devin tossed the keys to the valet and placed a hand on my back as he led me inside the building.

"Good Morning, Mr. Montgomery. Mrs. Montgomery." A beautiful brunette greeted us at the reception. "It's so nice to see you here today. I'm so glad you could grace us with your presence and—

"Piper," Devin cut in between, "Tone down the ass-kissing. We're going to the fifth floor of the board meeting. See that no one interrupts us. Hold all my calls. You know the drill."

"Yes, sir." She was still smiling, no traces of embarrassment whatsoever.

I guess she was used to Devin's barrage of insults. The man could charm your pants off and still threaten to kill you. He was ruthless in every sense, and if Devin didn't want Castle to wake up, it meant that Castle had him under control until he lost his memories and things went haywire.

We rode in the elevator together. Several employees smiled and greeted me politely as we made our way towards the board meeting room.

Devin leaned towards me and whispered, "Keep Castle in line, you know how to do that."

"You don't have to worry. He won't be upset as long as I'm with him." I assured him.

I was close behind Devin as he opened the door of the boardroom for me. The members all stood up and gave me a polite smile. I made my way towards one of the empty leather chairs in the corner since I'd assumed I would take notes today, but Devin waved me towards the second seat near the head chair.

"Gentlemen, please meet the new co-chairperson of Montgomery Enterprise, my sister-in-law, Millicent Montgomery."

Chapter 25

I don't think there was a time in my life that I was truly shocked.

When my aunt died of cancer, it was inevitable. I knew it was coming eventually, and when she finally died, I felt relief because that meant her sufferings had ended.

Devin declaring me as Co-chairperson of Montgomery Enterprise had my jaw on the floor.

It was the last thing I expected to hear when I'd entered the room filled with the board members. Their eyes bore into me like a group of vultures ready to tear their prey. I didn't think I had ever felt this intimidated in my life.

I remember feeling the blood drain from my face as the unexpected news had befallen me. Despite my shock and worries, I'd thanked everyone who had congratulated me on the board.

Devin told them that in case of his absence, I was the one who could make decisions and sign documents as the new co-chairperson in his place.

The meeting started after the brief introductions, and when it was over an hour later, I pulled Devin out of the room to have a private chat.

"I do not have the qualifications to become a co-chairperson of a billion-dollar conglomerate." I had told him.

He smirked and pulled out a file from a briefcase that he handed to me.

"What's this?" I asked.

"Read."

I opened the file and my eyes popped out. "I'm not...I'm not..."

"Yes, you are. A Harvard graduate in Business management."

"These are fake certificates!" I silently screamed, controlling myself before I flew into a rage. This asshole was up to something. "I'm going to tell everyone the truth!"

"And who will believe you?"

"What do you want from me, Devin? Why are you doing this?"

He smiled sweetly, as if he hadn't just fed a bunch of lies to his employees. "I just need your co-operation, Millie." He slung his arm around my shoulder and laughed animatedly. To the onlookers, it seemed like I had an amazing relationship with my brother-in-law. Close to my ear, he whispered, "I used to be co-chairman but since Castle hasn't been in the state of mind to take important decisions, I had to assume the role of Chairman and CEO. The board needed someone to fill my former place."

"What about Dayana?"

He shrugged. "Dayana isn't exactly interested in business."

Right. She was more interested in fucking the house help.

"But it doesn't have to be me!" I said.

He pointed towards the pantry across from us. A man who was probably in his mid-thirties stood on the other side of the transparent glass wall, dressed in a navy suit, making coffee.

"That's Samuel Hall," Devin told me.

I'd met Samuel briefly during the board meeting, and it had appeared as if he'd been sizing me up. I wasn't sure why he'd been friendly enough that I had paid little attention.

"If it's not for you who will take over the place, he will," Devin told me. "Sam's got all the qualifications needed and if Castle was on board, I'm sure he would be his choice."

"So give Samuel the position!"

Devin clicked his tongue. "I want it to stay in the family. An outsider can't make decisions for us."

I narrowed my eyes at him. There were a lot of things that Devin was hiding. He wouldn't take such a huge step without having an ulterior motive.

The Co-chairperson title was for show.

I was a puppet, Devin the puppeteer.

I wish I had the power to stop whatever that was happening. I wish I could just take Castle away from all this.

"Castle's signed the papers too. He wants you to do it." Devin said.

Castle was being manipulated. He didn't know what he was doing. If Castle hadn't lost his memories, I didn't think he would have approved of what Devin had done by putting me in the Co-chairperson's seat. Heck, I don't think he would have even agreed to marry a nobody like me.

I briefly spoke with Castle's old secretary, a nice young lady named Julia, who was sweet and welcoming. In the back of my mind, I wondered if he ever had a fling with her. She was cute enough that I would have to worry, but I let the thought go. If he ever had something with her, it was in the past. He wasn't the same man anymore.

Julia talked a lot about Castle, and how he would take her out on lunches if they were stuck in a long outdoor meeting. She said he was a caring boss. I tried to look for some hidden meaning but couldn't find one.

Mentally, I kicked myself for being jealous.

I needed a new strategy get Castle to remember his past. The chances of the boating accident recreation working were unlikely, even though Theo was quite adamant about us trying it.

Castle was playing late-night arcade games with Theo and Chandler in the gaming room on the fourth floor. It was Theo's idea to keep him busy while I read some of the family journal.

I sat down on the chaise and opened it from where I'd left off.

Aster Montgomery.

I know Christopher is the one for me. I have seen how his eyes followed me around when I went for a horse ride.

I'm going to be engaged to Terrance in two months, but I just can't seem to feel anything for my fiancé. I know I should be honest with him, but Terrance hardly has time for me. He's busy with work and making preparations for the wedding. He doesn't look at me the way Christopher does.

And I know for a fact that if I married Terrance, I'd just be another wife of a wealthy man tucked away in the corner, taking care of his children while he did whatever he wanted outside of the house.

I don't want that life!

I don't want to marry Terrance!

I closed the journal for a moment, wondering who exactly was Aster.

Have I heard that name before? Is this the entry Theo wanted me to read?

I opened the journal again and started reading it.

Christopher and I spent a lot of time together, whether it was for horse riding or just reading books together. I'm always with him.

His smile makes my heart melt. I love him with all my heart and I know he loves me, too.

June 3rd

Tonight I sneaked out of my room and went to the other wing. It was pretty late. Christopher lives in the servant's quarters of the mansion. His room was bare save for one bed and a table that held a nightstand. Some of his clothes hung in the small closet next to it.

He didn't have much, but he could give me what I wanted.

And that was love.

I visited him often in the servant's rooms.

I turned the pages because it droned on and on about how Christopher looked, even his outfits were mentioned, along with every visit and their talks about the weather. I wasn't interested in learning about the weather. I needed the juicy bits of their past. Turns out Theo thought the same too; the pages with repetitive passages about Christopher's physical description weren't dog-eared.

It was pretty clear Aster had like a massive crush on Christopher. I bet he was hot back in the day.

I stopped flipping pages when I found the page marked for reading.

June 10th

We are exchanging kisses when no is around. It is thrilling yet amazing. I like how my heart keeps fluttering with him around.

Today when my family had gone out, we made love.

And then I was snuggled up in his arms when I told Chris that my family would never agree to our marriage, especially my father.

So I told him an alternative.

July 29th

I'm pregnant.

When Dad found out, he had no choice but to accept me and Christopher.

I told Terrance the truth. I couldn't hide anything from him any longer and he was upset at first, but he told me it was for the best. He liked me, but he wasn't in love, and I would not settle for anything less.

Father put one condition before I got married and I hated him for it.

I had never wanted his wealth, the power, the legacy that came with the Montgomery name.

He told me that my husband would have to marry into our family and bear the Montgomery name. If there was no male heir, the women in our family may take over, and that meant the husband would be a Montgomery and live in the mansion.

Those are the rules.

Christopher agreed because he loves me and didn't care about anything else.

Christopher Gates is now Christopher Montgomery.

My amazing, gorgeous husband Chris.

It is the start of my new happy ending. I never thought I would be able to get what I want, but here it is—a handsome, loving husband and a baby on its way.

Somehow, I have a feeling the baby is going to be a boy.

If he's a boy, I'm going to name him Castle.

Chapter 26

I kept the journal hidden at all times and would only read it late at night or when I was alone in the room. I couldn't risk Castle reading it because the contents in the diary could affect him.

I wasn't sure what other vile family secrets were in here, but I was going to find out.

After dinner, I was taking a stroll outside. Castle was being moody and sitting on the floor watching the trains move. He was upset because of the argument we had yesterday.

"Well, why didn't you ask me before?" I'd asked Castle when I came home after being told that I was co-chairperson by Devin.

Castle stared at me incredulously. "Told you what?"

"Castle, do you realize that I'm not qualified to become a co-chairperson of your company? Why did you sign those papers without asking me first?"

"You're my wife, and you'll...take decisions for me when I can't. What's so hard to understand?"

"You say I'm your wife, but you never ask me anything, not even when the decisions are directly affecting me."

"Fuck, Millie. I don't know...what the hell you want." He said, frustrated. "Why don't you just fucking say it?"

"What I want is for people in this house to stop deciding for me! That includes you too! And for god's sake, don't listen to your brother..."

He was sitting on the floor now, clearly upset by my outburst, and rocking back and forth, mumbling to himself.

The trains moved through the tracks, zigzagging, blowing smoke and whistle, moving through the tunnel in the hill.

"Don't talk to me like that!" He was breathing erratically.

I sighed, realizing my mistake. I started walking towards him, "Castle...I'm sorry...I was just..."

"I said don't talk to me! Leave." He screamed, swiping his hand over the moving trains and toppling them over. The engine lay on the ground on the side with its wheels turning.

I snapped back to reality. Castle has never been upset with me before, never screamed at me, so right now my heart ached with the thought that I was the reason he was feeling like shit. I shouldn't have said anything...I should have just let it go.

I was walking alone in the gardens; the mansion loomed at a distance, and the fog surrounding it was giving it an eerie look. I could hear the sounds of the water fountain. It was peaceful everywhere, the calm of the dead, and I was used to it. Nothing scared me more than people anymore.

I turned a corner and almost bumped into Theo.

He stood against the finely trimmed shrubs, holding a cigarette between his fingers.

"What the hell, Theo?" I stood there, dumbfounded. "You're just seventeen!"

He looked like he'd been caught doing a robbery. He took a long drag and puffed the smoke like a pro, which told me this wasn't the first time he was smoking.

"It's just a fucking smoke! Don't tell Devin or anyone about this."

"Drop it!" I ordered.

"Come on, Millie."

"I said drop the cigarette."

I guess it was my authoritative voice that made him drop it on the ground and crush it with his foot. He was still wearing the uniform from his private school.

I raised my hand towards him.

He rolled his eyes, fished out the packet of cigarettes, and handed it to me. "You know I can buy another packet, right?"

"You won't." I said, "Because if you do, I'll tell Devin. I don't care about anything else anymore."

"What's the big deal?"

"Technically, you're still a child."

His brows arched up.

"I'm seventeen." He said as if I didn't know it and as if seventeen was the new twenty-seven or something.

The kid lacked manners, and I had Devin to blame for that. I could bet Castle used to be the one to keep him in line. I also felt bad for him. He was at this age where he wasn't a child neither an adult, stuck somewhere in-between.

"A child," I said. "A bratty child with too much money and far too much time on his hands."

"You on your periods or something? A cactus gotten up your ass, maybe?" He snapped, "I'm not stupid. I know you had some fight with Castle too."

"That's none of your business."

"Listen, did you read the marked pages of the journal?" He asked. His tone was soft, secretive.

"No, I haven't."

"Well, by the time you finish it, Chandler is going to get married and have his kids. You're at a snail's pace and we don't have time for you to finish it."

I let the sarcastic comments slide. "What do you mean, we don't have time?"

Theo's light brown eyes met with mine. It always seemed to catch me off-guard and reminded me of a teen version of Castle. "Tomorrow we will recreate the day of the boating accident."

Fear splintered inside my heart. "How are we going to do that?"

"Leave that to me. Make sure you bring him to the lake. We recreate this without the other players. Devin and Dayana shouldn't know. The same goes for the little runt. Do not underestimate Chandler for his age; he knows more than he should."

I had a bad feeling about this.

"Is this going to be safe, Theo? I don't know what you have planned."

"And it's best you don't. Just do what I've said, Millie. We don't have any other choice. Castle needs his wits about him. His memories will only get triggered if he's exactly in the same situation."

"I'm worried about him."

"Me too, but if we don't want to end up buried in the family cemetery, we have to take this risk."

"Where are we going, Millie?" Castle asked me innocently as I buttoned up his shirt.

"For a little picnic with Theo by the lake. It would be nice to get a breather. You're spending too much time in your room." I tried to be as vague as possible and felt extremely guilty for doing this.

He didn't look too happy. "I don't...I don't like being near the lake too much."

I ran my fingers over his cheek. "I know, baby. This will remove that fear from your head, I promise."

He stared at me. A pause later, he said, "I trust you, Millie."

I felt a stab in my chest. I was going to betray his trust in me.

"And guess what? I made your favorite food. There's deviled eggs, chicken lasagna, and mini pizzas. All of them are my recipes. I told Isabelle not to worry about the cooking, and I also made lemonade and lemon tarts for dessert."

"I'm so lucky to have you in my life... I wish I'd known you sooner..."

"Now you have me."

He pulled me close, wrapping his arms around me and covering his mouth with mine in a long sizzling fervent kiss that made me weak in the knees. His lips moved eagerly against mine, his tongue sucking mine as his strong hands tilted my face to get better access. I moaned.

"I love you," I whispered between kisses.

As usual, he didn't answer me.

When he didn't say it back, the disappointment settled in, but I didn't let it show.

"Let's go, Castle," I said and turned around to leave.

I walked to the door when I heard it.

"Love you too, Millie."

I turned around, tears blurring my vision, as I saw a genuine smile on his face.

I walked back into the room. "Thank you..." the fat tears rolled down my cheeks. Do you even say thank you to someone who said they loved you back? I guess not, but no one had ever loved me, let alone said it. "Thank you so much...I can't tell you how much that means to me."

He pushed a lock of my hair behind my ear. "You're a very simple girl." He laughed.

What if he completely forgot about me after he regained his memories? What if he refused to acknowledge me as his wife? What if he knew I was far below his league and wanted a divorce?

Then you'd be free.

There would be no more crazy in-laws trying to mess with my life, Castle would take charge and change things around here.

I would be happy for him if he got his memories back, but it came at a price. He could forget me.

I took his hands in mine. "Whatever happens...know that I'll always love you, okay?" I told him.

His expressions were perplexed. "I don't understand."

I wiped my tears, shaking my head, and plastering a fake smile. "Let's go. Theo is waiting."

Chapter 27

F ew Hours Earlier.

I opened the diary again to read it. Castle was still in bed, and I was taking a bubble bath in the tub. No one was going to disturb me right now, and the door was locked. Castle wouldn't wake up for another hour and I needed to do a pep talk before this evening. I had to convince Castle to go to the yacht with me.

I picked up reading where I left off. The next dog-eared page was four years later.

Aster's Journal

January 10th

Castle is such a lovely boy. My boy has dark hair and golden-brown eyes that look like glimmering imperial topaz. He's a gem indeed, my Castle. He's such a smart kid, even at four, I know Castle is special.

I named him Castle because it suits him. He's nothing less than a prince. Everyone in the house adores him. Dad is always buying him gifts and taking him out for walks. He is completely spoilt. I mean, who has a room filled with toys? He merely points at something and he gets it.

I think it's safe to say that things have changed for the better.

The madness has finally ended.

Dad has changed too. He's not doing those crazy rituals in the house, and I'm sure about this because I don't see bodies in the house anymore and that gives me hope.

I think meeting his grandson has made him undergo a change of heart.

While I was curious to read the rest of the pages, I noticed a thick amount of omitted pages in between. Whatever happened after these chapters had to be the turning point. I skipped directly to the next marked page by Theo.

Aster's Journal

17th Oct

I feel bad for these kids. They aren't too older than Castle. While my Castle is twelve, Devin and Dayana are ten.

I think the poor kids have an abusive alcoholic father, and the mother Lorna works in the mansion gardens to support the family. She's a sweet woman, and since the kids are young, I let them play with Castle.

You can tell by the way the kids eat hungrily at the table that they don't get enough food. Devin eats with both hands. Devin doesn't look ten either, more like six years old. The girl is healthier than the boy and it makes me sad for the children.

The kids don't go to school, so I have taken upon myself to put them in schools. I don't want them to grow up without proper education and I know for a fact that their mom can't afford it. It gives me immense pleasure to do good after all the bad that has followed my family. After all the blood that's on our hands, the fucked up ancestors.

I will not let history repeat itself.

It's time to change things around here.

Christopher is a loving husband, and it's wonderful to see how our son is growing up to look like him.

I sat there dumbfounded by the revelation in the journal.

Devin and Dayana were not related to the Montgomery family by blood. They weren't even Castle's real siblings. I wanted to solve this mystery desperately, so I leafed through the pages to get to the other marked passages.

I noticed how there was a time-skip now. Aster didn't write the journal daily. It was an occasional occurrence when she thought some moments were important enough to pen down.

Aster's Journal

13th August

Dad gave Castle a Lamborghini on his sixteenth birthday. I told daddy it was a little too much and that Castle shouldn't be so spoilt because it would make him think he was invincible.

When kids were younger, it was so much easier to forgive them for the mistakes they used to make. But now he's old enough to understand everything and I'm not sure what to believe.

Devin and Dayana keep complaining that Castle bullies them at school, that he shows them he is superior. Personally, I don't believe them. Castle has never been a vile kid. He's everything that a future Montgomery heir would be which is kind, understanding, thoughtful, and smart.

He's my son, and he is growing into a man that I know I will be proud of.

I think Castle didn't want me and his dad to adopt Devin and Dayana into the family. He's still a kid, and although the kids played since childhood and I'd never differentiated between them, he knows and understands that they are kids of Lorna, the house help.

I also think after Theo's birth, there's been tension between the children. Theo is a baby, and he has taken a liking to Dayana.

I think Castle doesn't like that and I often see them arguing for the baby's attention.

I'm not sure how Christopher and I are going to make this work, but we promised their mother that they were our responsibility. Dad doesn't approve of it, but I know I have done the right thing by adopting these kids.

Yet, I'm under this constant fear I might not be doing a good job of raising them all.

But I don't regret it. I have excepted Devin and Dayana into our family. They are Montgomerys, and Castle will understand that with time.

I see a beautiful dream where all the siblings sit together at the table and laugh and bicker the way true siblings should.

I want this dream to become a reality.

"Millie, maybe we should just do this at the patio in the court-yard." Castle suggested. His forehead had worry lines etched in them.

"Trust me, this will be fun," I assured him as I dragged him towards the lake by his arm.

It was a yacht with the name Phantom'on it.

Castle was frozen on the spot as he stared at the yacht. "I'm not sure why...but I don't like being on boats anymore. I can't remember why...I don't like it at all."

I went up on my toes and kissed his cheek, "do it for me. It would be fun."

You're a nasty bitch, Millicent! And you're probably going to hell for this.

He put one of his arms around my waist. "I'll do anything for you."

I smiled, "let's go."

Theo was on the deck, looking like a rare gemstone dug out of the most dangerous mines, and he was wearing a military green bomber jacket, tousled hair with denim jeans. If Castle looked exactly like Theo when he was a teen, I could bet he had panties showering over him whenever he walked the school hallways.

I kind of felt jealous. Why hadn't I known Castle when he was younger?

It was stupid how I was having these thoughts.

He hopped on board and then extended his hand for me to take. His gaze held so much trust, I didn't know how he would react when this was done.

Honestly, I was having second thoughts. Maybe this is a terrible idea...

Theo took me around to show the luxuriously furnished yacht. Plush sofas were against the side windows, a staircase leading to two bedrooms upstairs and one below. There was a small kitchen with a stocked mini-refrigerator and a gaming parlor. The topmost deck had a nice patio for chilling.

A stocky middle-aged man waved at us from the small cabin there. Theo introduced him as the Yacht's captain.

He took Castle's hand in a firm handshake. "So glad to see you here again, sir." He had a heavy accent, "Thought I would never have an opportunity again to sail this beauty...you know, after the..."

Theo coughed loudly, and that caused a distraction. "Ronald, what's that thing over there that's throwing lights around?"

"Young master Theo, that's a lighthouse. Thought you would know that...a high school going lad like you."

"Well, I tend to forget things these days. And we're not sailing too far." He quickly steered the conversation away. "What do you think, Millie? Does my ship have your approval?"

I laughed, "yours, huh? And it's not a ship." I teased him.

"It's a ship, and Castle said it's mine when I'm old enough to buy drinks."

"I don't remember saying anything like that." Castle said.

"Of course you wouldn't, but I'm sure you'll remember everything soon enough," Theo said confidently.

I gave him a look. What the hell was he doing?

"I love this yacht," I said. "I wish I could stay here forever."

"You might reconsider your words a while later."

"What? Why?"

"Come on, I'll show you the bottom outer deck." He offered.

I followed him downstairs. Castle said he wanted to sit at the top for a little more time.

The yacht roared to life, and I watched as we started moving farther and farther away from the pier and towards the darkness of the lake.

"If you think this one is beautiful, you haven't been to our other boat. We own a ship, the size of a Queen Mary."

"You're kidding?" I laughed.

"Okay, not Queen Mary, I exaggerated, but we own a ship and you married a rich man. Deal with it."

I rolled my eyes.

He pointed at the lower deck, that was equally stunning with golden and ivory seats. It was all custom-made, and so breathtaking. I could live in this boat forever.

And then my gaze shifted to the railings.

Something red and dried up.

"Dad was standing right here when he slipped and toppled. His head hit the railing here and there was a loud crack...the sound of his skull breaking and I was sitting here..." he pointed at the leather seat near to where I was standing. "And I saw everything. He fell into the water...and we saw it, Millie...we heard it...clear as day..." his breathing turned erratic and his brown eyes turned a shade darker. The anger and frustration were shining in them. "We heard the boat's fan running through his body...and the blood...god there was so much blood just spreading through the water..." he gripped the railing of the boat until his knuckles turned white. There was a distant look in his eyes, and I knew he was remembering the gruesome details. I didn't have the heart to ask him about their mother; it would be like opening more wounds.

I placed my hand on his shoulder and gave it a reassuring squeeze. "I'm so sorry."

"The cleaners came in and tried to scrub the blood from the railings, but it wouldn't go. No matter how much they tried, it stayed as a grim reminder of that day and we never got it replaced or repainted."

"When I close my eyes at night..." he continued, "I remember everything. Every single detail and it keeps playing in my head. I want this fucking nightmare to end."

He stopped talking when we heard the sounds of footsteps descending.

Castle was standing there. "Why did you guys stop talking?"

"It was nothing." Theo said, "Got emotional. There's champagne in the fridge."

The mansion wasn't visible, and we were in the middle of the lake, darkness surrounding us from all sides. We hadn't gone far, Devin wouldn't even allow it and the anklets would have sent out warning signals.

The yacht was anchored and since the boat was now stable; we had our snacks while we played cards. Theo was pro at it, and I had a burning suspicion he was good at cheating. So far, he hadn't told me what he planned on doing and that just continued to stress me.

After an hour, he stood up. "I'm going out to get some fresh air. You guys wanna come with?"

He was so laid back; I wondered if he'd changed his plan. I was kind of hoping that was the case. The brothers were talking while we stood there watching the serene lake. The moon hung low behind the trees and the light illuminated the water.

A lovely night...

Then there was a loud splash.

Theo had pushed Castle out of the yacht.

I couldn't believe what he'd done.

"Theo!" I screamed.

Castle was nowhere in view and my heart pounded as fear stole my ability to think. "Why did you do that? You told me he would be safe! This was not in the plan. Castle...Castle!"

I stared at the dark waters and I was ready to jump after him when Castle's head bobbed above the surface.

"You little shit!" Castle appeared to be angry. "What was that for?"

Theo laughed, "Lose up a little. Be a sport, Cas."

Castle reached the step and moved up. Theo offered him his hand. "You can throw me in when you're up here, I promise." He said jokingly.

"You're an immature kid."

He started pulling him up, but then something changed...he caught Castle at a disadvantage and shoved him down into the water again.

"I hope you'll forgive me, Cas."

"Theo, Stop!" I yelled at him as I tried to push him away, but he was powerful. He knocked me into the corner.

I watched in horror as Theo continued to push Castle's head into the water and my husband struggled to come up for air, struggled to breathe...the water splashing as he thrashed his arms to survive but whatever had possessed Theo, his desperate need to succeed surpassed everything else. Theo was on a mission. He wouldn't fail. I didn't miss the dangerous glint in Theo's eyes, menacing and downright scary.

I'd made a grave mistake.

A seventeen-year-old boy, Castle's very own brother, was trying to kill him.

Chapter 28

"Theo, please stop! That's your brother...how could you do this to him?" I screeched at him.

I watched Castle's head getting immersed underwater and his body submerged into the dark water.

"Nooooooo...."

My brother-in-law had just drowned my husband in front of my eyes.

I pushed past Theo and stepped over the yacht railing. I was a sobbing mess, ready to jump into the lake to save him. "Castle!"

"Millie, wait!" Theo called out.

"I need to go."

I started jumping off when Theo grabbed my arm and pulled me onto the yacht.

"Stay here." He said before going over the ledge and diving into the lake.

A few minutes later, Theo pulled Castle out. By then I'd called the Captain for help.

"What in the heavens happened here?" He asked.

Before I could answer, Theo beat me to it. "He fell out of the yacht."

I had a sudden urge to throw Theo into the lake and drown him the same way he'd done to Castle.

He put Castle on the floor. His eyes were closed, and he appeared to be unresponsive. My heart was in my throat, my chest tightening as I feared for his life.

If Castle died, I'd have to take responsibility.

I'd be alone and I would have to kill the family myself.

Theo was pumping his chest relentlessly, trying to get Theo to puke the water. If Theo had wanted him dead, then why would he try to revive Castle? It didn't make sense.

Theo opened Castle's mouth and conducted CPR, but he remained unresponsive. A feeling of dread settled over me. I didn't even know that I'd started crying uncontrollably.

He'd removed as much water as he could from his system, but Castle wasn't waking up.

"You told me everything would be fine! Drowning him was never an option! How could you do this without letting me know about it first?"

"I didn't tell you because I knew you wouldn't agree."

"How dare you? That's my husband!" I shrieked, "If something happens to him, Theo, I'm going to toss you into the lake and I don't care that I'll be charged for the murder."

"Shut up and let me think!" He snapped.

He brought Castle's head in my lap and brushed the wet hair away from his face. "Wake up, please wake up, baby."

Theo picked up his hand and I could see he was on the verge of tears. "I can't find his pulse."

"Try the CPR again. Better yet, let me try."

I tried giving CPR, but nothing was working. Tears blurred my vision as another soul-shattering sob erupted from within me. Theo sat with his back against his yacht, horror plastered over his face.

"I'm calling 911." He said.

I was crying ugly, and my sounds were muffled because I buried my face in Castle's wet shirt front.

Suddenly, there was movement.

It almost felt like a miracle.

Castle coughed out the lake water and sat up. Hacking, he pointed his finger accusingly at Theo, "You tried to kill me!"

The silence in the yacht was deafening.

Who was this?

The Castle with amnesia or the Castle who remembers the past?

I wasn't the only one who was confused. Theo looked scared and curious on equal measures.

Had it worked?

Ronald brought a towel that he used to dry Castle's hair.

"I'm very sorry." Theo said, "I was desperate for you to remember everything, so I tried to recreate the day of the boating accident. I swear I wasn't planning to kill you."

Castle didn't look convinced. "Millie, I want to go back to the mansion."

He called me Millie.

Theo noticed it too.

It hadn't worked.

"I'm so glad you're okay," I said, helping him out of his wet shirt. He changed into some dry clothes that were available in the master bedroom upstairs.

"Were you in on this, too? Drowning me?" He asked me, his brown eyes shining with betrayal. It hurt to see that he would think I was capable of doing this to him.

"Of course not."

"I told you I didn't want to be on the boat, but you insisted, and I trusted you." He said, "You had this planned with Theodore!"

"I swear, I didn't know what he was about to do. Castle...baby..." I started touching his head when he slapped my hand away.

"I don't want you anywhere near my sight. Leave me alone."

"Alright," I said, deciding to give him some space. He would talk to me again tomorrow morning.

Truthfully, if the roles were reversed and if my husband had tried to drown me with my sister, I'd be pissed too, so I couldn't blame him.

I went back outside, where Theo had changed into a pair of clean clothes. He looked at me regretfully before staring out into the dark.

"I owe you an apology." He whispered. "I really thought it would work and I don't know why I assumed that if we recreated that day, he would remember. I thought if he drowned again...

"Again? You mean he drowned before?"

Theo nodded. "We thought he was dead. No one could find his body, so a few days later we were having a funeral for Castle. Arrangements were made, people had gathered, mostly distant relatives who never called him when he was alive. The reverend gave his speech and then Devin went to the podium to give his eulogy. He'd made it to the middle part of it. I remember sitting in the front row, feeling numb to everything, wishing I could run away, and then the door bursts open..." He continued, "He was standing right there, dressed in some old borrowed clothes. There were shrieks and confused mummers as everyone saw Castle walking into his own funeral. It felt like a ghost, to be honest."

He smiled at the memory. "Best fucking day of my life. The irony of it, though. Until he walked into the funeral home, I wished I'd died with him."

"How did he survive?"

"Castle was a Gold medalist swimmer in school. He could hold his breath underwater for a long time and he'd won national competitions so when he drowned that day, he survived somehow. I'm guessing it has to do with his swimmer instincts. He told us he woke up in a fisherman's boat surrounded by strangers who looked worried about him. He said he remembered nothing else."

"I'm beyond pissed, Theo. He could have died just now. You pushed him too hard."

"His memories are suppressed. We needed to do something to bring him back."

"That's enough. I won't tolerate this again and I won't let you jeopardize Castle's life. I don't care if he gets his memories back or not. Do you understand what I'm saying?"

Theo nodded. "I understand. It was a mistake."

Ronald sailed the yacht back to the mansion. Castle gave us the silent treatment the entire way, and he refused to look at me. Theo had told me everything, but he hadn't mentioned exactly how Castle had drowned that day when his parents died.

Did he slip? Was he pushed deliberately? By whom?

Devin was lounging in the guests receiving area, talking to someone. He was dressed in a black shirt, over slack pants, and sat in the velvet chair looking like a king of some country ready to give orders to his army and cause destruction. Knowing the contents of the journal, and Devin's history, I couldn't imagine that a man yielding so much power could have been a poor little malnourished kid.

I almost felt bad for him.

Devin looked at us when we walked in. There was another man seated beside him whom I recognized as Anthony Marshall from the head office. As far as what I knew, he was the company's legal attorney.

Anthony stood up and gave me a polite nod. "Mrs. Montgomery."

"How was the day out?" Devin asked.

Before I could answer, Theo said, "A fucking blockbuster."

"Language, Theo, how many times have I told you that F-bombs and other verbal abuses will not be tolerated in this house?"

"And how many times have I fucking said that I don't give two shits about your stupid house rules?" The rebellion that Theo was, he continued talking mockingly, "I'm going to fucking abuse as much as I fucking want." He marched into the room and grabbed a bunch of cupcakes from the tower of assortments on the three-tier glass pastry stand. "Excuse me, Anthony, pardon my intrusion."

"Don't look so surprised, Tony, this is a usual occurrence in our household. Theodore is yet to cross puberty. He gets moody some-times. It's completely normal."

Anthony looked like he wanted to flee from this house.

"What's this meeting about?" Theo asked.

"It's none of your concern. Go to your room, Theodore." Devin said, waving his hand dismissively, the way you would shoo a fly.

Theo glared before walking out of the room. He made his way towards the grand staircase. Castle had left for bed early because he'd rather sleep than talk to me.

"I'll have to see that Castle doesn't sleep before his medication." I made up an excuse to get out of there. "It's nice to see you, Anthony."

I started walking out when Devin called out to me, "Wait, Millie! We need you here. Castle's medications can wait."

Dayana walked into the room at the same moment.

I looked between the three of them. "What do you need me for?"

It's not like they asked me to make any important decisions about the company, even though I was appointed the company's co-chairperson. The title was in name only.

Devin pointed towards the couch. Having no other choice, I sat down.

Anthony handed me a few papers and a pen.

I took the papers and pen in my lap and gave each of them a questioning look. "What's this?"

Dayana maintained the same icy exterior that was hard to decipher. She was very similar to her cold-hearted brother.

She smiled in fake candor. "It's nothing for you to worry about. Sign the papers."

I leafed through the pages, scanning the contents of the documents. As each letter, each sentence starting sinking in, my blood boiled like a volcano.

"You've got to be kidding me!"

They looked at me like I was the crazy one.

"Just sign the goddamn papers, Millicent. We haven't got all night."

"These papers are a testament that I have somehow laundered money from Montgomery Enterprises and used the company assets for personal gain. What kind of sick game is this? You know as well as I do that, I do not have such authority!"

"You and I know it, but the people in the company don't." Devin pointed out.

Dayana was busy inspecting her new manicure.

"You're framing me for something that I did not do!" I said and then turned to Anthony, "Why are you letting this happen?"

"I work for Mr. Montgomery, ma'am. I have his orders."

"And he's four million dollars richer." Devin smiled, "Now, I'm busy man, sign the papers, Millie."

"I won't," I said, standing up and walking towards the exit.

Dayana jumped up and locked the door before grabbing me and forcing me into a chair.

I struggled to be free, but the siblings were towering over me. Devin placed the papers and the pen on the table.

His emerald eyes leveled with mine. "I'll give you two choices. Sign the papers or die."

"I choose death," I said, looking him straight in the eye.

Chapter 29

<hr>

Devin smirked at my answer. He leaned in and whispered into my ear, "You'll beg for death."

They forced me into a chair and slammed the papers on the table.

"Sign." He commanded.

"I won't. No matter what you threaten me with. I won't sign it. You can kill me."

"Very well, you've made your decision," Devin said as a ghost of a smile spread across his lips. He raised his hand out towards the maid standing to his right. "The tool, please, Penelope."

From the corner of my eye, I noticed a trolley with a stainless steel plate and torture tools laid out on it; it glimmered under the crystal chandelier lights. As if Penelope was an assistant surgeon in an important operation, she handed Devin a plier.

I stiffened.

Don't let them see you're scared, Millie. They will feed off your fear. They want you to grovel and beg for mercy.

Don't give them the satisfaction!

I kept a straight face, numb to what was about to happen to me.

You've been through worse, you'll get through this, too.

Horrified about what was about to happen, I watched Devin wedge the plier into the nail of my index finger.

"One last chance." He said sweetly.

"The answer is still no," I told him, trying my best to not showcase the fear crawling deep inside my bones.

I was doing this for Castle, for freedom that I wanted for the both of us. As I was someone who was initially appointed to care for him and to protect him, I would do my job until I drew my last breath.

A second later, a horrified wail filled the silence and pain so potent speared through me. I wished I'd signed the papers and be done with it so I wouldn't be subjected to this torture.

My finger was soaking in blood, dripping, and devoid of a nail. The smudges stained the beautiful carpet below.

That was ironic. A beautiful home like this one held nothing but years of pain, sufferings, lies, and deceit. There was no love found between these four walls, only a hunger for power and the title that came with it, and somehow I'd been part of all this madness.

He wedged the plier into my thumb. "Don't make this hard on yourself."

I kept a straight face, even though my insides were screaming hell-fire. "Do it." I challenged him. "Do your worst, you sick bastard, but I won't sign the papers!"

Devin passed me the same charming smile from the first day I'd met him, "with pleasure, my love."

I screamed loud enough to shatter the glass windows of the entire mansion.

The nail on my thumb was gone, too.

"The blood is staining the carpet." Dayana pointed out, inspecting the expensive Turkish carpet. "I think we should stop, Devin. She won't talk even if you pluck all her nails, and it's not worth ruining a carpet worth three million dollars that was won from an auction. It's vintage and handmade."

Devin seemed to think Dayana had a point. The carpet was getting ruined after all.

Well, thanks to the expensive carpet, my torture was halted.

"Penelope, clean Mrs. Montgomery's wounds."

Penelope had come equipped with a first-aid kit. How very convenient.

Why did I have a feeling these two devils incarnates did this casually to people and got away with it? The housekeeper, Winston, had lost an entire leg, for god's sake! He seemed to do well with a replaced fake one.

The door had loud knocks on them. "Millie...is Millie there? I heard a loud noise." Castle's voice drifted from the other side.

I started calling him out, getting out of the chair, when Dayana scrunched up a ball of cloth and shoved it into my mouth to shut me up.

"She's not here, Castle." Devin said in his casual tone, "I heard her say she was going outside for a walk in the courtyard."

"Okay."

Then I heard the sounds of the retreating footsteps. I slumped back into the chair.

Penelope cleaned my wounds with some alcohol and covered my fingers with a bandaid.

Dayana brought a pen and forced it between my fingers. She had brought the document, the contract papers of when I was hired as an employee. The papers had my signature on them.

Dayana held my hand in hers with the pen and forced a signature on the paper. It was scrawly, but she'd managed to put Millicent Montgomery.

"It's done," she said happily, looking proudly at the papers. "The writing is a little funny, but I think no one would care though to check."

Devin looked at the paper, "you're right. As long as we got her signature."

I didn't know what problems were going to come over me, and I knew nothing would prepare me for what they had planned. I wasn't sure why they were being so cruel.

Castle's parents, especially his mother Aster, had taken in two unfortunate children and given them a roof over their heads, wealth, education, and everything else that kids born in the family would have gotten. They were biting the hand that fed them.

Their greed knew no bounds.

The door opened, and I climbed to my feet, spitting out the cloth from my mouth. "Karma is going to come for you soon, Devin, and when it does, I'm going to be there to see it happen."

He grinned, "Can't wait."

"Millie, my head hurts," Castle complained when I went upstairs to our bedroom. He was holding his head between his hands, his face contorted with pain.

"what's happening to you?"

"I...I don't know." He was breathing hard. He grabbed my hand. "I need my medication! It's throbbing...the pain's unbearable..."

"The meds are not good for your health."

His eyes shifted to my fingers. "What's wrong with your hand?"

"It's nothing. I cut myself on the cutting board." I lied to him. "I'll see if I can find some mild pills for your pain, okay?"

I found some pills in the drawer that I handed him. These weren't prescribed to him, but they were normal pain meds and then I changed into my nightgown, aware of his watchful eyes following me.

"You're lying." He said.

"What?"

"You're lying about your hand." He said, "what...what happened to you, Millie? Who did this to you? Don't lie to me."

I couldn't control myself. If he wanted the truth, he would get it. "Your family is evil. Your brother and sister are monsters! And they plan to do vile things to us, Castle!"

He was on the edge now. I had his attention. "What vile things?"

I made sure the door was properly locked. "They want to kill you and frame me for it."

"No." He said almost as if his denial would be enough to prove me wrong.

"It's true! They are making me out to be a gold-digger who laundered money from your company when I have done no such thing. They are creating this scenario so that it would be easier for them to kill you and make me a scapegoat."

"Devin wouldn't do that," Castle whispered. "I...I handed over the company to him after my accident because I couldn't remember my past...much less how to run a corporation. It was voluntarily...so why would he kill me?"

"Because they are afraid you would remember!" I whispered, screamed at him. I close to him, holding his face in my hands, "They are afraid you would remember each and everything about the accident and whatever happened before that. Devin and Dayana want you out of the picture."

"They are...they are going to kill me?"

"Baby, I won't let them touch a hair on your head. You have my word." I said, hugging his head to my chest, "But you have to remember...

His light brown eyes filled with confused tears. "It's all hazy and unclear. I can't remember anything after the day I turned up at the funeral."

I wiped his tear with the pad of my thumb, "You have to try harder, baby. That's the only way we can stop them."

"Or what happens?" He asked.

I knew hiding the truth from him was of no use. We didn't have the liberty to keep information from him that could only cause him harm.

"If they succeed, then you'll be dead and I'll be in jail convicted for your murder."

Time was running out.

I had to read the journal to find out the truth before things went down. I skipped to the next set of marked pages.

Aster Montgomery's Journal

12th September

I'm not usually a suspicious person. I don't doubt anyone unless I have a reason to. I have wondered if Dad is secretly still doing those devil-worshipping rituals and I've been wrong with my assumptions so far. I'm happy to be wrong about this.

But then Christopher is acting strange. He would come home late at night, sometimes he would be out for days due to the business.

I suspect him. My father isn't the type who would give up on what he started and it is likely possible that he somehow influenced Chris into being part of the rituals.

I hope not.

I've been late to enter the diary because I'm not in the right state of mind. Last night I was gone for a charity function and told Chris that I would return late at night, but luckily the event was wrapped up early and so I got home earlier than usual.

I planned to surprise Chris because he complained I wasn't giving him enough time. With four kids, it was sometimes impossible to spend time with him. I bought him a set of cuff links. I knew how much he loves collecting them.

When I climbed the stairs to our bedroom, I saw the door was slightly ajar and the sounds of someone speaking in hushed whispers drifted from the gap.

My heart thundered. I stopped dead in my tracks, listening.

'What if the kids see us together?' The female voice asked.

'They won't. Castle, Devin, and Dayana are out for some friend's party. They won't be here until midnight. Theo is asleep and as for Aster, she won't be home until mid-night as well. It's just you and me until then.' That was Chris's voice.

My Christopher.

There were sounds of kissing, followed by a moan. 'Stop it.' She giggled.

Lorna. The house help. Devin and Dayana's biological mother.

'Will our kids ever know?' She asked him silently.

At that moment, I wondered what they were talking about. I was tearful and I couldn't believe my ears. I wanted this to be a nightmare.

'They are better off not knowing.' Chris replied. 'With this baby on our way, we have to act fast. You know we can't let Aster find out. The kids adore her.'

'But I'm their mother.'

'Hush.'

'I'm scared Chris. Sometimes I think you love her more.'

'No. Never. I've always loved you, Lorna. Aster was only a means for us to get all this wealth. You're my real wife. Just a few more days and then it's all ours.'

I should have known. I'm crying...NO...I'm sobbing while writing this. There are smudges on these pages, but I don't care. I need to pour everything out.

Christopher Gates is a swindler, a fucking thief! Dad was always right, but I was blinded by love. Chris had known Lorna before he knew me, and he'd been having two families secretly. He had children with two women.

How hadn't I noticed?

Devin and Dayana had Chris's features. They had Lorna's green eyes, so I hadn't realized...I was a fool.

Nobody gets away with fucking up a Montgomery.

I going to ruin him.

Chapter 30

Aster Montgomery's Journal

17th September

I want to ruin Christopher's life, but you know...when you're in love with someone for so many years, it's hard to comprehend the fact that your husband never loved you.

I gave him a choice and had a little talk, which turned out ugly.

'You've been having an affair with Lorna for so long! How could you do that to me, Christopher?'

He received my outburst with shocking calmness, as if he expected me to find out about it soon. "I'm sorry, Aster, I wanted to tell you since a long time back. I don't love Lorna, but she's very hard to get rid of...I don't know what happened to me...' he said.

'You have two children with her and a third one on the way. How many lies are you going to tell me?'

'Aster, I love you. I had to pretend with her.'

I held up my hand for him to stop talking. 'I want you to pack your stuff and leave. You can take Devin and Dayana with you if you want since they are yours and Lorna's...'

It had hurt me to say this because over the years I had loved and cared for both of them as much as I had for Castle and Theo; it shattered me to do this but there was no way out of this.

I picked a checkbook and signed a hefty amount. 'Take this money and don't show your face here again.'

Christopher looked broken, and I tried not to let it affect me and yet it was difficult to not feel anything at all. He'd cheated on me, married another woman while being married to me, yet in a small deep corner of my heart, I wanted him to leave Lorna and come back to me.

'Sweetheart, please, don't do this!' He begged. 'I'm Castle and Theo's father too.'

'I don't care and I don't need you in their lives.'

'I'll divorce her.' He said, 'I'll break off the marriage with her and be with you.'

'No. I want you out of my life and in this house. I will not change my decision.'

'What decision?' Castle stood at the door. He looked so much like Chris. I knew it would break my heart every time I look at him in the future. He looked between his father and me, clearly picking on the tension. He had a basketball spinning on his finger.

'Nothing. Go back to your room, Cas.' I told him.

'Mom, Devin is being an asshole again. Can I throw him in the garbage or better yet, ship his ass off to some isolated island?'

'How many times have I told you to watch your mouth, son?' Chris asked him, obviously feeling threatened and taking the joke seriously.

'Don't talk about your brother like that, Cas. Now leave and close the door on your way.'

He made a face before closing the door.

'Did you see the way he talks about Devin? He thinks he is entitled to everything.'

'But isn't he?' I asked. 'Castle is my heir, Chris, and it will always be that way. If not for Castle, it will be Theodore.'

Chris laughed, 'you're taking revenge on those poor kids.'

'Those poor kids are the ones you forced into the house by lying to me. Castle and Theo are my blood! After the divorce, Devin and Dayana will go with you, and they won't have any more share into my will. I will pass whatever assets that you possess onto them.'

He loved Devin and Dayana more. When he talked to them, he had a different spark in his eyes and over the years I'd ignored it, as I always thought Chris treated them like his own out of the goodness of his heart.

But that was never the case. My children, Castle and Theo were born out of greed for my money. Devin and Dayana were born out of love.

'This is unfair.' He seethed.

'You can tell that to my attorney.'

'You're a heartless bitch, Aster.'

Those were my husband's last words to me. He called me a heartless bitch when all these years I had been feeding his kids. He'd lied to me time and time again while enjoying the luxury that my family name offered him.

I flipped the pages in the journal looking for more entries, but there was nothing.

Blank pages.

That was strange.

The journal was left at an unsatisfying ending. It was kind of like reading a thriller novel and getting the most unsatisfying cliffhanger ending, only this was reality. This had been someone's life.

I joined Theo and Castle in the gaming room upstairs that evening. Chandler was with us too, but he was busy playing the Pac-Man arcade game. Some of these arcade games were vintage, straight-up. Why go to the malls to play these games when you can bring the arcade room home?

The family came from old money. They never had to worry about anything and the evil siblings had shown how ungrateful they were to what Aster had given them.

"What's wrong with your fingers?" Theo asked me, inspecting them.

"It's nothing."

"The tabloids are talking shit about you." He told me, joining me on the leather seats.

"Tell me about it. I was a nobody until a few months ago. Now everyone knows my name for a completely different reason."

"Have you read the news?"

I shook my head. "I don't want to."

Theo didn't take a hint and started telling me about the lies the newspapers and broadcast were saying, "they are calling you a gold-digger, a nobody who married into our family for money."

"Oh please, no one would be interested in being part of a psychotic family, regardless of how much money they had."

"Ouch." Theo chuckled. "They know you never went to Harvard. They also know that you forged the documents. I'm sure Devin had something to do with this. That would explain why the media circus is tearing you out like a bunch of vultures."

I was tired of this.

I was tired of constantly living in fear and knowing there was no way out unless Castle regained his memories. I wanted a normal life. That's the only thing I hoped and longed for, and getting to that dream meant making a sacrifice on the way. There was a likely chance of a divorce, but I'd get the freedom and the empire would have their original heir.

Theo followed my gaze, "When mom was alive, we used to travel a lot. I don't remember a lot since I was too little, but we have the pictures to prove it. Castle enjoyed playing in the arcades and sometimes he would become this annoying kid who wanted to buy the arcades and take them home."

I laughed, "And he got what he wanted, didn't he?"

"He was mom's favorite, so they ended up buying the gaming machines for him."

I watched Castle and Chandler as they moved from the Pacman game to the Super Mario one. The familiar game sounds drifted from the arcade machine.

"You share a father," I said.

Theo's brown eyes burned into mine. "You've been reading the journal."

"Yes, I have. So I'm a little confused. The entry that I read proves your father was already having an affair with Lorna before he married your mother. Does that mean Devin and Dayana were born later?"

Theo nodded. "You need to understand something, Millie. My father, Christopher, was a con artist. He and Lorna were a team that lived off of by tricking other wealthy people. Dad took employment in the Montgomery household after a lot of planning and plotting, but Mom got pregnant before Lorna did. It would make sense that Dad kept the two families away from each other, and a few years later after Devin and Dayana were born, Lorna took up the job in the mansion, and she fed some horse-shit to my mother about an alcoholic husband. My mother believed her and that made it easier for Dad to manage two families, having all his children under one roof while he deceived our mother as she invited snakes into our home."

"The journal is not complete. Where is the rest of it?" I asked.

"There's a separate one. I'll give you that journal tonight."

"I've been wondering, Theo, is it possible that Castle knew something more about what's going on?"

Theo nodded. "Castle had secrets of his own."

"I don't understand."

Theo looked at Castle, who was now playing bowling with Chandler. "He and Devin knew things I did not. I don't know what happened exactly but before the boating accident, I talked to Castle and he said, I quote 'you're better off not knowing anything.' I'm not sure what it means."

"Did Aster kill Lorna and Chris?"

Theo stiffened with that question. "I'm going to let you read the second journal."

The second journal was delivered to me after midnight.

Chapter 31

A ster Montgomery's Journal 2

29th September

I'm heartbroken. Completely shattered.

I tried to kill Lorna. I can't imagine how low I would stoop. I was about to kill a human being out of jealously!

What if my children find out the truth? They would think I'm a monster! But I'm not. Loving your husband is not a crime.

I wanted to extract revenge from them. Suddenly, I'd become this evil person who would do anything to make sure the two won't be happy. I want to destroy them.

If I can't have Chris, neither can Lorna.

1st October

I poisoned her coffee.

I shouldn't have done that, but I did.

And Lorna survived. She didn't drink the coffee and gave it to the other maid instead, who died.

They know I did it. They know I tried to kill her and she's threatened to call the media because she knows the police department would brush this underneath the carpet. She knew no one in town would dare touch a Montgomery. We are invincible. We have immense power.

4th October

I have to leave. I have to disappear before she takes the news to the media and destroys me.

Dad would understand. Castle and Theo would know the truth. They are wonderful children and I guess I will have to accept my losses.

Lorna will be a good mother to them. I know I said she was evil, but really...I think when I see her now and how much I've caused her pain, I think I'm the evil one.All this while as I was plotting her demise, trying to poison her, she's been calm and looked hurt. She apologized to me and asked for mercy.

She says we could co-exist. She would never take Chris's affections for herself and she wants to continue the arrangement the way that it was. Chris would continue to live in the mansion with me, Devin and Dayana would still be my children, but Chris would also visit her occasionally.

She wants to share.

She wants to share the man I thought was only mine. I'm beyond hurt. I'm dying inside.

I can't take this anymore and so I'm going to leave. I want my children to know that I love them with everything that I have. Castle and Theodore would grow up to be handsome, powerful men. They would live up to the Montgomery name. And as for Devin and Dayana, I wish them well, too. I want them to succeed.

It's too bad I won't be here to see it.

This will be my last journal entry. I loved you, Chris, and forgive me for all the pain that I have given you.

I can't do this anymore.

I turned pages, but there was nothing else written in the journal after that, which was a sign that she'd given up on Chris and left the family.

Not only her husband, but she'd abandoned her children too?

Was that the truth or was there something else that I wasn't reading clearly into this?

Did she commit suicide or did Chris had perhaps gotten her killed?

My mind was boggled with all the possibilities to the point where I couldn't sleep at night.

I was obsessed with solving this. I wanted nothing but to understand what had happened in the family. If I were to get to the bottom of this, I needed to know everything, including the secrets of the past.

"Millie..."

"Millie!"

Castle was staring at me with eyes filled with desire. "I said...I want you to come and sit on my lap."

"Okay." I climbed into bed, smiling, "What are you going to...ouch! Heyyy..."

He grabbed my hips and pulled me into his lap like he couldn't wait another minute to do what he'd planned.

He started kissing me with wild passion, his lips pressing against mine urgently, his tongue moving inside my mouth in urgent strokes. I turned molten every time his hands worked the magic on my body and his expert tongue continued to stroke. I moaned.

He buried his face into my hair and nibbled softly over my neck, his fingers working deftly over the strings of my dress. "Take this off."

A few minutes later we were both completely naked, his whiskey brown eyes watched me intently as he sank inside me and started moving. I held onto his powerful biceps as he continued to reward me with hard and fast thrusts.

"Yes...Oh god, Castle..." I whispered.

"You like this, Millie?"

I kissed him hard as an answer to his question.

When we were done, we were sweaty, and I felt like my soul had officially left my body, but that was usually what happened when we made love. He was propped over one arm, looking down at me with what seemed like obvious devotion.

I raised my hand to his face, staring adoringly at him. And maybe I was a little lovesick too. "What are you looking at?" I asked him, shyly.

"You're so beautiful." He said, his fingers grazing over my stomach.

I giggled, snuggling closer to him. He kissed me slowly this time like we had all the time in the world to be in each other's arms. He nuzzled my neck. "What do you think about...having a baby?"

I smiled up at him. "I would love that."

He curled and uncurled a loose lock of my hair. "Our kid would have everything in this world...I'll make sure of it."

I nodded, "I'm sure you'll be a great dad."

A few seconds passed between us, and then I asked him, "Do you remember anything about your mother?"

He shook his head. "I just know what they've told me. Theo says our mom left us about ten years ago. Apart from that...well...I don't recall anything. When I look at her picture, I don't remember her. ..which is cruel because who would want to forget the woman who gave birth to you?"

"I'm sorry. Do you remember anything at all? Even the smallest detail would matter."

"Why..." His hands began shaking, his face contorted in pain. "Why are we talking about this?!" He demanded angrily, "I told you I don't want to...god...my head's hurting again. I'm having these flashes...it's suffocating! I woke up the other day with..." He lost it.

He howled aloud in agony.

"Castle, calm down!" I told him softly, trying to touch him, but he slapped my hand away.

He was holding his head in pain, his eyes tight shut, living some kind of nightmare.

There were loud bangs on the door, and Winston's voice drifted from there. "Is everything alright?"

"Please come in."

I pulled on a robe and made sure Castle's lower half body was covered before I let Winston come inside the room. "Do you have some aspirin for the headache?" I asked him.

The maids standing at the door hurried, one was pouring water into a glass, another busy doing something else.

And then Castle stopped screaming. He looked at the empty doorway, his eyes red-rimmed. "I will ruin your lives! Mark my words!" He barked those words in an authoritative voice that I did not even recognize.

That was followed by deafening silence.

He stopped screaming and then looked around. Everyone had stopped doing whatever they'd been doing. They were staring at

Castle in sheer horror. Even Winston's eyes had popped out of its sockets, but he refused to say a word.

He wouldn't even step closer.

And then something changed in Castle's eyes, he was tear-soaked, "Why are you..." he sniffled, "why is everyone looking at me like that?!" He clenched his hair in his fists, "I'm tired...I'm going to bed."

With a shaky hand, I ran my fingers soothingly through his hair. "I didn't mean to cause you distress. Goodnight. We'll talk tomorrow."

He ignored me and turned in bed to face the other side.

Whatever had happened just now wasn't normal.

And by the looks on everyone else's faces, it looked like they'd just witnessed a dead man come to life.

Chapter 32

"You're telling me she didn't run away or commit suicide?" I asked Theo the next evening.

"Nope. Mom was a strong person, and she would never do something like that. She cared too much about us to abandon us like that. I mean...I was very young, but I remember how kind and caring she was. She never mistreated the servants the way Devin and Dayana have been doing."

"But the journal indicates she left, Theo!"

"Yes, I know. It's her handwriting, but I don't believe it. I don't know what happened..." He whispered the next words, "But Castle did. He knew stuff that he was hiding from us."

"The journal is strange," I admitted. "It doesn't make sense. If she wanted revenge, why would she decide to leave everything behind, especially her children?"

"Exactly my point."

"Is Chandler?..."

"He's Lorna's son. We're half-siblings."

"I see. So, after your mother disappeared, Lorna took over your house?"

"Yes. Castle wasn't at a legal age to inherit the company; he didn't have that kind of power. After mom left, Lorna moved into the master bedroom that was my mother's... "It was fucking torture...watching this sleazy woman...a thief walking into our home, wearing my mother's things and trying to take her place. It was disgusting and by that time, grandpa had already lost some of his marbles. I was sent to boarding school; and Castle went to college."

I listened to him silently. "He came back a few years later, and good for us, Mom already had paperwork done stating that when Castle was of a certain age, he was to inherit everything. Devin and Dayana had no right over the estate or the money, not even a single piece of the fucking furniture and when the lawyer announced this...you should have seen their faces."

"And since then, Castle has been taking care of everything like he should be. This house is ours. They are nobody, and the only reason they got you married to him is because they wanted to shame him. No offense to you, Millie."

"None taken."

"They thought since Castle was helpless and couldn't remember a thing, they would hire a help with no family background or wealth and get her married to him because they think Castle in his right mind would have never stooped so low as to marry a nanny. You get what I'm saying?"

I nodded. They wanted to embarrass him. A business tycoon getting married to a nobody...yeah, they'd basically tarnished his name.

"We have to get to the bottom of this." Theo said. "Make Castle remember...keep asking him to remember..."

"I can't do that! He gets upset, and he gets these headaches."

"What headaches?"

"If he tries to remember his past, his head hurts, and his body trembles."

"I don't care. He needs to fucking remember before we're slaughtered!"

"Did I hear about slaughtering?" Devin walked into the room with his easy swagger, "you know who gets slaughtered? Pigs...are you a pig, Teddy?"

"I don't talk to stinky assholes."

Devin ignored his brother and turned to me, tossing an envelope on the coffee table. "I realized you and Castle could use a quick getaway, a honeymoon, since you never got a chance before."

"A honeymoon?" I asked.

"Yes. The maids have already packed Castle's stuff. I've instructed them to pack yours as well. You're flying to Paris on a private jet. The car will be here in an hour exactly. Sorry, this might be a little sudden, but Castle was subdued this morning because of his recently frequent episodes. It's not a good sign. I think a change of scenery would do him good ."

"Yes, but..."

"Prepare for the trip. Off you go." He pointed towards the staircase.

I sat down in the car. Castle was seated right next to me, and our luggage was placed in the trunk.

It was not uncommon for the Montgomery's taking international trips on a whim, Devin and Dayana sometimes flew to different countries just to shop for a pair of shoes. To them, it was like taking a trip to the mall.

Trixie stood on the lawn looking at us. The German shepherd was trying to hop into the car, barking incessantly, pulling on her leash to get to Castle.

Castle opened the door of the car, noticing the dog's obvious distress, and raised his hand towards her. The servant holding the dog's leash let go, and the dog came to Castle, scratching his paw on his leg and licking his face.

Castle laughed, "You're a good girl, Trixie. I'll be back before you know it."

Chandler came running towards us and started getting inside the car. "I want to go on this trip with Castle and Millie."

"Chandler, they wouldn't have time for you. Come here."

"But I want to go to Paris!"

"Chandler! I told you to come here."

Huffing, he climbed out of the car and walked towards Devin. "Get me a box of macarons. All different colors."

"Okay, Buddy," Castle promised.

Devin got hold of Trixie's collar and pulled her back. "Down, girl."

Trixie wouldn't listen. She was still barking, trying to get out of the leash. "I said, Down!"

The dog whined and sat down, looking at Devin nervously.

Devin came to my window and looked inside, "Millie...I hope this trip with Castle gives you time to ponder on the things that have happened so far. I know I've been cruel and disgusting, but I did what I had to do to make sure this estate and the company remain in my hands. I'm utterly selfish, but I want you to see it from my standpoint and find it in your heart to forgive me."

"I don't understand what you're saying. But I'd you are really looking for forgiveness, then you would give me and Castle what we want."

"And that is?" He asked.

"Set us free. Remove my anklet and give me the freedom that I deserve as his wife. Let Castle and me be in peace."

Devin gave me a warm smile, "consider it done. When you're back, we'll get the anklet removed. It's a promise."

Did Devin have a change of heart? Maybe he decided he didn't want to torment us anymore? Maybe he's had enough of it all, too.

As if that wasn't enough, he leaned in and kissed my forehead. "I'm sorry for everything that I have done."

I only smiled back because forgiveness he wasn't getting.

We said our goodbyes. The car moved forward, taking us farther and farther away from the large Colonial mansion.

I had dreamed of this, of driving away from the mansion one day in good spirits. I guess this little honeymoon would be nice for us.

Devin knew for certain that being in the house was causing Castle to remember things, he was smart enough to know that it was harmful to him to remember and so Devin hatched this plan of getting a change of scenery so Castle would be distracted.

Trixie ran towards us, galloping like a horse. I laughed at her, waving. "We'll see you soon, sweet girl."

The car drove through the gates, which closed behind us, trapping Trixie on the other side. The 'M' emblems on the gates glinted in the moonlight. She pawed at the gate.

I turned to face the front and placed my head on Castle's shoulder, my arm linked around his. "Your brother is strange, you know."

"Which one?"

I laughed. We laced our fingers together and then interlocked them.

"I had the most bizarre thought. If I say it, you wouldn't think of me as stupid, right?"

"Nothing you say is stupid," Castle promised me.

"What if we took this trip and disappeared?" I asked.

He looked at me in confusion. "I don't...I don't understand, Millie."

I drew circles over his pants with my finger. "I mean...we go land in Paris and then..." I looked at the chauffeur in the front and lowered my voice down, "and we could book another flight...somewhere far...another country where no one can find us."

Castle kissed my cheek, "I would have liked that...very much. But...we can't leave Theo there alone."

My heart sank. How could I have forgotten about him?

"Yes, you're right. It was foolish of me to think that."

Foolish and selfish.

A few minutes passed, and I noticed he'd taken another exit on the Freeway, the exit that wasn't supposed to take us to the airport.

"Isn't this the wrong way?" I asked the chauffeur, Austin.

He didn't answer me. I turned to Castle, "Do these Private planes owned by your family have a different airport?"

Castle shook his head. "It's the usual one. We just have an....an exclusive route of boarding the plane, no queues or other rules and...and they check the baggage and we only have to board. Se rvants...they take care of everything else."

Castle stared at the front seat, "Austin, that's not the way...where are you taking us?"

"I apologize Mr. Montgomery. I have orders from your brother." He said, "He told me he'd make sure my children would go to the best universities. He's going to give my family a lot of money...the kind that I can never earn even I were to be born ten more times. I'm truly sorry, sir..." the man sobbed, "I can't afford to be fired."

The car zoomed forward onto the road in a dangerous speed. The road was narrow surrounded by thick woodlands. He'd brought us here on purpose.

"Stop the car!" I yelled at him.

"I'm not doing anything, Mrs. Montgomery." He took his foot off the accelerator, showing me that the brakes weren't working anymore. "The car has a timer. It will blow up at the right time."

We weren't going to Paris.

Devin was sending us to our coffins.

'Let Castle and me be at peace.' I recalled telling him.

'Consider it done. When you're back, we'll get the anklet removed. It's a promise.'

We were going to be at peace, maybe somewhere in heaven, he'd meant, and of course, I was going to have my anklet removed.

A dead body didn't need a tracker.

I was hyperventilating, my chest tightened with unadulterated fear, my blood running cold.

We were about to die. Austin was paid to commit a murder-suicide. We were going to die in cold-blood, and then they'd do the same to Theo. He wouldn't be foolish enough to keep any Montgomery heirs.

Castle's eyes registered what was going to happen. He pulled me closer into his body as if to say 'let's be together in death too.'

"No!" I yelled.

The grim reaper was standing right there, knocking. He was about to take us away.

I refused to let death fuck up our plans! I refused to die before I found out the truth!

I got hold of Castle's shoulders. The car was moving straight ahead, and I knew it would stop only when we'd get blown to bits.

"Listen to me carefully..." tears streaked my face, but I quickly wiped it. "We cannot die here! We won't! Your mother's dream was for you to become strong and succeed."

He nodded earnestly, sobbing, "Yes."

"Then that's what we need to do. We cannot die!"

The car jerked forward with the bumps. "Do you trust me, Castle?"

"Yes."

"On the count of three, open the door and jump out. We need to roll on our bodies. Do you understand what I'm saying? You can't screw this baby, okay? Promise me!"

He nodded. "I promise."

I kissed his hand one last time. "You need to live, and if I don't make it..." I gave out a humorless laugh, "just don't bury me in the Montgomery cemetery."

"Don't say that, Millie!" He tightened his hold over my hand.

"I love you," I said one last time. We had only a few seconds. Something was beeping inside the car.

"On the count of three, Castle..."

Few seconds later, I was lying on the ground, injured. Castle had rolled down the hill. A blast had erupted only a second after we'd jumped. I scrambled on the dirt, crawling to the other side of the road, my body screaming in pain. I wanted to find my husband.

"Castle..." I called out.

An ongoing car flashed its lights and was speeding on the road towards me.

Chapter 33

You know sometimes when you're in that depressive phase and you think about death, and how you would die, well I always wondered, if I would grow old and die in my sleep, or if it would be tragic, gruesome, and painful.

Well, now I knew I was going to die being crushed by a car.

I closed my eyes.

I hope Castle is safe.

The car screeched to a halt.

I opened my eyes, only to be blinded by a pair of headlights. Car doors opened and slammed shut.

A worried young man walked out of the car. "Shit! What happened? Are you okay? Were you hit by a car?"

"I had an accident..." I began explaining.

There was a woman with him too who I assumed was his wife. She passed him a look before I heard her whispering, "Maybe it's a trap to rob us. We shouldn't get involved in this."

"Please..." I pleaded, "My husband was in the accident too. He might be injured. Help me get him to the hospital. At least let me call the emergency."

"Let's go, honey." She insisted, grabbing his hand and trying to pull him back inside the car.

The man looked torn between listening to his wife and doing what was right.

"Please." I had nothing to lose. If they refused to help me, I'd die anyway.

"Fuck it." He walked around the car and put one arm around me and the other below my knees as he lifted me.

"Wait! You have to help me look for my husband first," I told him. "He must be here somewhere."

The man looked at his wife. "Call the emergency. She's having wounds. I'm going to go look for her husband."

"You can't be serious, Shaun!" she shrieked.

"She clearly needs our help, Chelsea! Don't be such a cruel bitch."

"wow, I'm a cruel bitch now, do I have to remind you all the times that you—"

My head felt heavy, and I was losing consciousness. My vision was turning blurry, and they were going in and out of focus. I didn't have the luxury to be unconscious. I needed to make sure Castle was safe. I reached out towards them. My mind and body battling against each other while they continued to argue.

"Castle..." I choked out.

And then there was darkness surrounding me.

I opened my eyes to a hospital room. My arm was attached to an IV and there was no one around.

Who was I? I wondered.

Then it came to me. Oh, yes, I'm Millicent Davis and I live with my worthless perv uncle.

No, that's not right!

My breathing started picking up as I thought harder, racking my brain. Why was I in the hospital and what led me here?

I'm Millicent Montgomery.

That led me to question: Where's Castle?

I panicked and started scrambling out of bed when a nurse barged into the room and told me to calm down.

"But my husband..." I sniffed, "He was in the accident too. Where is he right now?"

"Lie down Mrs. Carter."

Mrs. Carter?

"Your husband is fine, but he's still unconscious. The doctors are doing their best."

"What day is it?" I asked.

"Tuesday."

The accident happened on Sunday. That means I'd been out for about forty-eight hours.

"Do you have any other close family that I could call?"

Did I have any close family?

Theo!

"Yes," I said. "But can I please make the call? It will only take two minutes."

She looked at me with pity, and I didn't care if I was being pitiful as long as I got what I wanted. After giving it some thought, she nodded and led me outside to the public phone.

My entire body hurt, but I had to do this. I dialed Theo's cellphone number, thank goodness for my good memory that I could remember the digits. A few minutes ago, I had a hard time remembering who I was.

He answered on the second ring, "Hello."

"Theo."

He went completely silent for a moment, and then I heard soft sobs filling the other end of the line. "Millie...?"

"Yes, it's me." I said.

"Oh god, Millie...you're alive." He sobbed for a minute longer and then composed himself. I never knew Theo could cry. I'd never seen him cry, not during the months that I had lived with the family. Warmth filled my chest.

"Are you alone?" I asked.

"Yeah. I'm in my room. Is Castle alright?" I could hear the worry in his voice. It seemed like he would rather not learn the truth if Castle didn't make it.

"Yes. I'm yet to see him, but the nurse said he's fine."

"You are on the news, Millie. They are showing us a badly crushed car. This is breaking news that every channel is covering. Austin didn't make it so we assumed..."

"Devin did it."

"What?"

"Don't say a word, just listen to me. Do not tell anyone that we are alive, Theo, do you understand what I'm saying?"

"Yes."

"Devin sent us on this trip to get us killed. The car had a bomb attached inside, the brakes weren't working! We are supposed to be dead, but we survived since we jumped off the speeding car."

"But Austin..."

"Austin was on a murder-suicide mission. His family is getting money and his kids are going to some Ivy League college." I told him, and then turned around to find the nurse hovering over me, "I need your help."

"Anything."

"I need money."

"How much?" He asked without hesitation.

"Twenty thousand dollars."

My request was met with silence and then he whisper-shouted, "Are you insane? I can't give you that much! It's not that I don't have it, I have plenty, but Devin checks my debit card statements. I wouldn't be able to explain where I spent that much money."

He had a point. He sighed. "What are you planning to do with the money?"

"Disappear with Castle. Start a new life, anything, until he gets his memories back."

"I can give you five thousand for now." He offered.

"I'll take it, and I'll return it as soon as I can," I promised him. "Also, I think you'll need to pay for the hospital bills anonymously."

"Done. Tell me where and how. It's going to be difficult, but I'll figure it out."

"Thank you and please be very careful. I'm worried about you, too."

After I hung up on the call, I went back to my room. I wanted to see Castle, and I was desperate. I had to insist a lot on the nurse to let me see him because I wanted to make sure he was okay. It took tons of arguing on my part, and some tears to gain sympathy, and then finally she agreed.

Castle's eyes were closed, and he appeared to be sleeping peacefully. There was a large gauze wrapped around his bare chest but he was breathing easily. Not wanting to disturb his rest, I let the nurse guide me to my room.

On my way back, I noticed the chaos that surrounded me. A young man was brought in for a drug overdose, an unsuccessful surgery which led to the death of a woman, and the loud ear-piercing wail of the woman's mother. These melancholic feelings were taking a toll on me.

"Mrs. Carter, your husband is awake!" The nurse announced the next afternoon.

I rushed out of my room, almost running, galloping towards where Castle was kept.

He's okay. We're fine! We survived. My mind continued to scream.

This is all I wanted for now. For Castle to be safe.

A tall man was standing outside of Castle's room. He wore a long black trench-coat, and a hat concealed his face. I passed him as I walked inside Castle's room.

That was strange. Who was this man?

Castle was eating his meal slowly, the same thing that I'd eaten, or rather, forced down my throat. There was chicken noodle soup, some potato salad, and pudding for dessert. His thick long lashes were casting a shadow over his defined cheekbones. He gave up on soup and picked up the dessert. He didn't look happy for whatever reason.

I smiled at the familiarity in his behavior.

"Castle."

He looked up at me.

"I was so worried about you," I said, going to sit beside him. "How are you feeling?"

"Millie...I didn't know where you were...I kept asking them how you were doing."

"I'm here now." I kissed the top of his head. "Get well soon so we can leave this place."

"Where are we going?" Castle asked like we were going on another adventure.

That was the million-dollar question.

Where would we go?

Chapter 34

Time at the hospital felt like a vacation. I was kind of liking it, i.e. laying in bed, having the nurses bring the food (even though it was crappy), getting fussed over, and talking to the old granny, the one with the Alzheimer's who thought her son was still in preschool, and not having to constantly worry about how I was going to be tortured to death.

It was a good feeling.

But as they say, all good things come to an end and my fun little six day vacation in the hospital was over too. Time was running out and as much as I would have loved to sleep on this depressing but nice bed and sip on my non-existent Piña colada, we needed to move our asses out of here and besides; we were okay. There was no need for medical attention anymore.

I had bought a few burner phones from a nearby departmental store, which I'd been using to contact Theo. Our cellphones had already turned to dust in the crash, and if I wanted to play dead, it was convenient to not use our cellphones.

I told Theo where I wanted the cash to be delivered because getting a wire transfer was out of question. I also didn't need his cards to be traced, which would only cause more problems and give away our location.

Devin was smart, and I would be stupid to underestimate him. He'd done well making sure we didn't survive, and if it weren't for my decision to jump off a speeding car, Devin would have gotten what he wanted.

I made sure the nurse was nowhere in view and passed Castle some clothes that I had bought from the store. It wasn't his usual expensive designer stuff. This was a cheap t-shirt, and jeans the type you would get in a bargain sale, but he needed to make do with this. We didn't have the luxury to play Richie Rich, definitely not when I needed the money if we planned to drag the days with the five thousand dollars that I had.

I must mention though, Castle looked extremely hot in a hospital gown, it was loose yet I could see outlines of the hard ridges and the defined abs underneath.

I shook away from the cloud of lust that was trying to blind me as I watched him undress and then put on the clothes in front of me. I changed into a dress. It wasn't flattering, to say the least, but I wasn't exactly trying to impress anybody.

I placed a baseball cap on Castle's head and pulled it low. Looking up into his sexy golden eyes, I told him, "We have to be discreet about this as much as possible. We can't get caught, okay?"

Suddenly, I wanted that vacation to France to be real. How nice it would have been to sit in some café in Paris and stuff my face with éclairs. I didn't even have a passport until a few days ago, and I was about to die without having a stamp on it. It's hilarious how far Devin had gone to make this vacation ruse seem believable.

Castle nodded, and I loved that about him. He trusted me completely. I went up on my tiptoes and kissed him once before giving him a heads up as to what we were supposed to do.

He listened to me intently and allowed me to make decisions.

"Why are they calling us Mr...." he pondered for a moment, "Mr. and Mrs. Carter?" He asked.

"I have no idea. When I woke up, that's what they were calling us, Mike and Shelly Carter, and I didn't correct them because I realized it was best we take an alias. If we go by..." I looked outside, making sure no one was under earshot, and lowered my voice, "if we go by Montgomery, we'll easily get traced and we can't let that happen."

The name held power and it would be a lot messy if someone put two and two together and we were discovered.

"Where are we going, Millie?"

"I don't know, but we're taking the bus." I told him.

He didn't look so sure. I interlaced our fingers. "We'll figure this out, I promise."

I remembered my previous conversation with Theo, and what he'd told me.

"Do not go to the police. The department might have moles, and as soon as you report the complaint, Devin will know and he will turn this against you. Be careful, Millie. With the way Castle is right now, he might not be able to help you. You're in this alone."

We sneaked out of the back staircase, but we still had to pass by the main reception. There was no way around it.

"Okay, stay calm and walk normally. If they ask us something, we'll tell them we've been discharged from the hospital."

"Are we?" Castle asked me innocently.

"No, but we're going to tell them that."

"Why can't we stay here...for a little while longer?"

Because your half-brother is a fucking psychopath and wants to kill you.

"We can't." I said. He just kept looking at me in that usual way of his. I knew he had something on his mind that he wanted to say.

"What is it?"

"Millie..." he started, "you regret this, don't you?"

"Regret what?"

"Taking up this job..." he looked close to losing it, "getting married to me...being forced to...I wish so much that things were different..."

"That's not true." I said, "It's not something I wanted, but I don't regret marrying you. I'm actually glad I did."

Your family is sick, and they don't deserve you.

"Let's go." I said, hooking my arm with his and trying to sprint out of the hospital reception without being noticed. We'll have to figure out how to pay the bill later.

"Mr and Mrs. Carter, wait!"

Shit! Shit! Shit!

I stopped and turned around, plastering a smile. "Yes?"

She looked between me and Castle, "where are you going?"

"Just going for a walk outside. I changed for that reason." I pointed at my dress. I was completely bull-shitting, but I hoped my acting skills were good enough. This was our only chance. "We were coming back real quick."

"You have a phone call." She said. Her tag read 'Rachel.'

"Who's calling?"

"Your brother-in-law." She told me the receiver was at the side. "I was just about to connect the phone to the office upstairs. Good thing I found you here."

Why was Theo calling now? I'd promised him I would call once things were okay, and we had contacted each other only during emergencies.

I went to the desk to answer the call. "Theo."

"Hi Millie."

That voice.

Fear hit me like a bucket of ice water.

"You seem a little tongue tied." He chuckled, "trying to act a little smart, are we?"

"You tried to kill us! You expect me to say howdy?"

"Theo here thought he was being very sneaky, but the walls have ears." Devin said, "Now, listen carefully. I want you to take a cab and come home. Am I understood?"

"Go to hell." I said, biting back a few other choice words.

"You want to make this difficult for both of us, I see. Well, how about this..." I heard a loud scream coming from somewhere on the side. They were hurting Theo.

"Don't touch him!" I yelled into the phone.

"If you don't take the cab home right now, you will hear about Teddy's drowning accident on TV. I'll give you three hours. After that, I'll gather the media and tell them how you planned to murder my poor brother and when it didn't work out, you kidnapped him for a ransom. You're smart, my love, but I'm smarter." That said, he hung up.

How did he find out about the hospital? I didn't think Theo would give out the address. He wouldn't, unless Devin had done some sweeping, taken a wild guess about the hospital that was nearest to the location of the accident.

That could be possible.

"Is everything alright?" The receptionist seemed genuinely concerned.

"Yes, we're fine."

Not really. We're about to ride a cab to our deaths.

I could run, but run where? And could I stomach having something happen to Theo on my conscience? I was selfish to think Castle and I could just pack and drive into the sunset.

He would find us, and we would still end up dead.

We walked out of the hospital and I hailed down a cab. A woman was standing at the door, she was middle-aged, and well-dressed. When I looked at her, she gave me an eerie smile.

A cab stopped in front of me, and we settled inside it. I told the driver the address while my thoughts started scattering about, my mind was running through all the possibilities and how Castle and I could get out of this situation unharmed.

I didn't like the answer.

I think I was blank for the entire two hours that took us to get to the mansion because there was nothing I could do. We'd been so close to earning freedom...

Winston opened the car door, and I walked inside the mansion like I was a robot set up to do so.

Devin was in the den, Theo was nowhere in view. "Welcome home. I hope you had a great trip." The sides of his mouth turned in mock humor.

I sat down on the plush couch, and then I tuned him out because he was going on and on about how I had tried to escape his clutches.

Am I going to give up so soon?

Castle walked to the end on my opposite side and sat down on the single velvet chair. It always reminded me of a throne with its gliding golden frame and a tiger face carved into it.

I watched as he slowly crossed his legs, right to left. His arms resting on the sides, his fingers picked the crystal pyramid, and he swirled it between his fingers in deft, skillful motions. His expressions remained schooled, but there was a dangerous aura that was emanating from him.

And then his gaze met mine, and we remained transfixed. Something flashed in his golden eyes. It was all clear to me.

The playful innocent glint was missing, the softness no more.

He didn't recognize me anymore.

My Castle was gone!

For good this time and replaced by this man who was driven by vengeance.

Devin didn't see it since he was facing me.

But I did.

And god help me because I was absolutely terrified.

Chapter 35

I had always wondered what it would be like when Castle regained his memories. Many scenarios played in my mind and my answers to every conversation that we would have, but the reality was completely different. Nothing had prepared me for this.

Devin had lectured me about following his rules, but my eyes were trailed on my newly awaked husband. Castle had sat through the grilling without a word, and Devin had assumed this to be one of Castle's usual oblivious behaviors. Then, I'd gone straight to our bedroom, and I was thinking of what I was supposed to do now that he was back.

I was quite certain that he had regained his memories unless I'd imagined what had happened downstairs and it was all in my head. His face had morphed completely, like he finally knew what was happening around him and I would be lying if I said I wasn't remotely intimidated.

I was in my bedroom, over-analyzing everything that had happened during the car ride. I'd zoned out, and Castle had been silent throughout the way home.

And then I heard it, the footsteps coming closer to the bedroom.

Cold-sweat broke over my neck as I felt his presence behind me. I knew he was standing there.

What if he wanted a divorce?

It would completely shatter my heart, but it was a possibility that I couldn't deny. As much as I loved the innocent, caring, sweet Castle, I knew the real version of him was a different man. He was a man of a high social standing, rich, powerful, and I did not even compare to that. Devin had gotten me married to Castle as some twisted revenge, and if not for that, I'd just be another employee in this house.

So if Castle told me he wanted a divorce, I would give it to him.

But I would first tell him about my feelings. I loved him whole-heartedly, and I was ready to accept the new man that he was. The money didn't matter to me. I wanted him safe and loved.

I owed it to the old Castle, the one I'd fallen in love with.

Suddenly, I wished I'd worn something better. The Castle that I knew didn't care what I wearing, but I wasn't so sure about this one.

Oh, stop it, Millie. There are no two people.

I was standing by the window, looking outside, when he stepped inside the room and I looked up. He closed the door behind him.

"Millicent." He spoke, looking directly at me.

"Castle."

He smiled knowingly while reaching out to inspect the train on the mantel. His demeanor screamed for control. "You know, I was single when I had the accident and when I woke up, it turns out I'm married." He chuckled, "It's fucking hilarious. How long has it been?"

"You've lost your memories since a year, but we married four months ago," I told him.

This is the moment he says 'yeah, but I didn't even remember marrying you. Let me pull out those divorce papers.'

He gave me a nod. "I'd like to thank you for everything that you have done for me so far. The marriage, the torture, the escape plan. None of it was included in the Caregiver's contract when you signed it, was it? Or did Devin make amends?"

I stared at him foolishly until he started laughing. The sound of it was a deep timber, like dark chocolate. He'd switched personalities. I'd never known this playful side of him.

"I...I...didn't know..."

"Are you afraid of me, Millicent? You sound very afraid." He noted.

"No, sir."

His brow arched up.

My face burned up, and I kicked myself. This wasn't my boss, for god's sake! He's my husband. He's my Castle...only...he wasn't.

"I mean, no."

He just had this aura that was making me a mumbling mess.

Before Castle could open his smart mouth again, I said, "Listen, Castle...I understand that this is not what you expected, but Devin forced this marriage on us."

"I know." He said.

I continued, "But I accepted it wholeheartedly," because I love you. "This wasn't just an obligation from my side, neither was it from yours. I'm not sure how much you remember, but it would be very unfair of me to expect you to love me the way I love you." I had to lay it all out and be honest with him.

His whiskey eyes leveled with mine; I felt the weight of his scrutinizing stare. I sighed. I kept my head held high when I said it. "I may not be of your social standing; I was only an employee looking after you, but took my duty as your wife very seriously. If you want a divorce, I completely understand." The tears almost blinded me, filling my eyes to the brim. I swiped them quickly, embarrassed that I'd let him see them.

Castle said nothing for a few seconds and then he was walking towards me in those same confident strides. He stopped in front of me and took my hands in his. He brought them to his lips and kissed my knuckles, his fingers tracing over the small ring. "Is this all I could give you? This ring is a shame. Devin is an asshole. For that fall you took from the speeding car, you deserve an eight-carat diamond emerald."

My Castle had humor. I laughed as I let the tears fall freely. They weren't lying. He was charming.

I looked up at him as he swiped the tears with the pad of his thumb.

"Do you remember everything? I don't mean just your memories, but the time that we spent together. I mean...do you remember me?"

"It's coming to me. Piece by piece, one memory after the other. I remembered when I first woke up in the hospital, but it wasn't quite there. When we were in the car, it was a tsunami of memories flooding through my mind. When I looked at you, I couldn't recall who you were until it slowly made sense."

He pushed some loose tendrils behind my ear. "Judging by the way you're looking at me, and shaking like a leaf," he grinned, "I'm guessing you thought I was some kind of monster like Devin. Regardless, I have two choices for you. One, you can have the divorce on grounds of irreconcilable differences, I'll take the blame for it and I'll give you the house in Beverly Hills which belonged to my mother and a hefty settlement that will let you live the rest of your life without having to work. This also means you'll be far from this mess; you wouldn't need to worry about anything regarding me or the family."

It was an option I would have taken happily if I hadn't fallen in love with him.

"Castle—" I started.

He raised his hand, cutting me off. "Let me finish. My second option is for you to continue to live with me as my wife, but in doing so, you would be exposed to any amount of danger my family poses in the unforeseen future. While I promise to protect you from them, I know they will continue to target you to get to me." He said, "I can't have you become my weakness, Millie. I don't want anyone to hold leverage against me."

"I want to stay with you, fight with you, and I promise not to come between whatever you're planning. This is what I want, to continue to be your wife and support you."

He gave me a nod, pleased with what he'd heard.

"What do you want, Castle?"

"I want you here with me." He said simply, caressing my cheek.

A weight seemed to have lifted from my shoulders. All those days that I had spent thinking about how we could get out of this situation unscathed, I hadn't been able to sleep at nights as I had been constantly worried about Devin's next move and how I could protect Castle.

The Castle right now didn't need any protection. This time, he would protect me.

There were so many things I wanted to ask him, so many questions that needed answers to. His family history, the mysterious death of his parents, and if he remembered who drowned him that night during the boating accident.

He pulled me into a hug, and I buried my face in his chest, so relieved he was here. His touch was tender, and the heat of his fingers burned through my skin. "This will all be over very soon." His fingers thread through my hair. "We're a team."

There was a knock on the door.

"Millie, are you here?" Theo's voice drifted from the other side.

"Yes, Theo, come inside."

"Mills...did you..." Theo started saying and then he looked at Castle.

Castle pulled away from our embrace and turned his attention to his brother. He dug his hands in his pockets.

The posture. The stance. It was a dead giveaway.

"How have you been holding up, Little Booger?"

I thought Theo had stopped breathing for a moment.

He kicked the door shut with his foot and exclaimed, "Fuck!"

And for the first time, I saw the strong, foul-mouthed Theo, who had far too much pride to show tears was sobbing uncontrollably without caring that I was standing right there. He ran into Castle's arms, who wrapped him in an affectionate brotherly hug, more like squeezing the life out of him.

"I never thought I'd get such a warm welcome."

"Fuck you! You took too long." Theo said. "You almost fucking died!"

Castle looked at the both of us. His expression was now serious. "Not a word about this to them, alright? I'll handle the rest."

"So good to have you back," Theo said, wiping his snot on his t-shirt sleeve.

"Now," Castle said, his face read Game on. "I want you two to listen to me very carefully."

Chapter 36

The plan was for me and Theo to do nothing.

Yeah, you heard me. Castle did not want us to be involved while he did whatever that he had planned to do, and so Theo and I didn't know what was going to happen. He said it was best this way. Devin wouldn't suspect anything and there were zero chances of a fuck-up.

I felt bad for Castle. It's been like a few hours that he regained his memories and he was pushed head-first into these responsibilities of trying to save himself from being killed while also protecting me and his brother. He didn't have the luxury to be relaxed. He needed to be on his toes every second of every minute.

The dinner table had the most epic silence. Castle didn't take his position at his usual place; he was seated at the head table where he could analyze everyone from his seat. I wasn't stressed any longer. I was content with this new controlled version of my husband. He was someone literally out of a fairy tale story. I'd assumed my position beside him.

His eyes met mine, and he caught me staring. I looked away at once, color rising to my cheeks. He leaned in and I got a whiff of his intoxicating perfume. "I don't mind if you keep staring at me."

I laughed, "I'm sorry. It's just...I'm still trying to get used to you being like this."

Castle nodded in understanding.

Chandler was texting on his phone; I didn't really understand why an eleven-year-old kid was having more liberties than I did. I sneaked a peek at the screen and saw him typing a text to someone under the table.

Love you too.

I stared at him with my mouth hanging open. Chandler had a girlfriend in school. I wondered what they did as a couple exactly? Compare their Candy Crush scores? Collect bugs together?

When Devin entered the room, he looked at Castle and something flickered in his green eyes.

A slow grin formed on Devin's face as he looked at his brother. "Well, I'll be damned!" He seemed happy to see his brother. "I don't believe this. Look at you..."

"I do." Castle said with a chuckle, "I keep looking at myself in the mirror and thanking my good fate that I was born better looking than you."

"Fuck off!" Devin said and then he realized Chandler was there with us so he said, "I mean buzz off!"

He made his way towards us in a few strides and enveloped Castle in a hug, and patted his back with a few hard thumps. "It's been difficult without you around, Cas. I was barely hanging on, you know, with everything, the company, and the family...I'm so goddamn happy you're back, brother."

It sure looked like he wasn't faking it, and if he was, that was some good acting. An award-worthy performance.

And then Dayana strutted in, dressed for dinner like she was going for a party. She looked at Castle and then at Devin. Her bitchy demeanor changed all of a sudden. "Is this really happening?"

"Castle..." she sniffled. "Do you know me?"

"yes, you're the giraffe who escaped from the zoo and kept loitering into my backyard. I can never forget you."

"Oh god, it's really you." Dayana cried harder, laughing at the same time as Castle raised his hand towards her. She made a dead run towards Castle and into his arms. "I missed you so much. We've been waiting." She cupped his head in her hands and kissed his cheek, crying uncontrollably. "Cassy..."

My eyes almost bulged out of their sockets. She called him Cassy, and I felt like I'd walked into another dimension, one in which we were all part of this slice of life movie where the hero regains his memories and the family members are shocked out of their socks but also super supportive and lovely. Kind of like a modern Jane Austen book. Happily ever after. The end.

This looked more like an episode from The Twilight Zone.

I wish my life was simple.

Castle kissed the top of her head in return like a caring brother would. I'd expected surprise, yelling, and a lot of mayhem, but not this...

Devin and Dayana acting all jolly about Castle getting his memories back.

They went back to their seats. Devin raised his glass of wine, "To Castle. For regaining his memories and to his good health."

"To Castle," Dayana said, raising her glass.

I couldn't decipher what Castle was thinking by expressions. He had a smile on his face, like he accepted the love and affection his family was sprinkling all over him.

Theo stormed into the room while the staff served dinner.

"Sorry, I'm late." He said, taking his seat opposite from me and then gave me a wink.

"Chandler, put your phone down," Castle ordered. "It's my first dinner since I'm back, so I'm gonna go a little easy on everyone, but I need all of you to be at the table at seven-thirty. Phones will be left outside of the dining area."

Chandler sighed and put his phone away. That was new, especially since Chandler didn't even listen to Devin when he yelled at him. I guess Chandler had only known Castle as the authoritative figure after the death of their parents, and he was much more successful in keeping the brat in line.

It gave me an impression that Castle didn't need to raise his voice to get things done here. One icy look from him did it.

Devin was looking directly at Castle; he hadn't taken his eyes off him like he expected Castle to pull a knife in the middle of dinner.

The two brothers started talking about their company and what was going on. I was tempted to intervene and call out to Devin about how he'd almost framed me for Castle's murder.

How could he sit there, laugh and joke like he hadn't done those vile things?

"I need a detailed report from all the department heads, starting with finance. We need to know what happened to the five-hundred thousand dollars..." Castle said, cutting into his steak. He raised it to his mouth and then stopped, "Unless one of you could enlighten me."

"You want all the reports?" Devin asked.

"Did I stutter?"

Theo laughed.

Devin shot him a glare, but he was feeling threatened. It seemed like it was a hard pill to swallow for Devin, since he wasn't going to run the show here anymore.

"Okay. I'll get them to you on Wednesday."

"I need them tomorrow." Castle said, "You tell everyone that. I won't be in the office, but I'll want the reports. Look, Devin, I don't know how things used to run here when I wasn't around, but you best believe it's going to change."

"Does that mean you remember how you drowned, Cas?" Chandler asked, with a mouthful of food.

"I remember, yes. Every single detail."

"Well, I saw—"

"Chandler, take your dinner upstairs to your room," Dayana told him.

"I'm not going anywhere!"

"Winston, take Chandler's food upstairs to his bedroom. He's not needed here." Devin interjected.

Winston obeyed without a word. Chandler did not throw a fit, but exited the room in a huff. He pushed a plate down from the table, which I think wasn't by accident.

"Millie, you can go upstairs too."

Castle grabbed my hand. "Millicent stays here. She's not a kid. She'll listen to everything that you've got to say."

"Fine."

The staff exited the dining area, leaving the five of us alone in the room. So far, I hadn't said a single word.

"I'll be honest." Castle started saying. "I think you should cut it out, this exaggerated display of affection, acting all fine and dandy. I'm fucking done pretending that everything is okay."

"Well, what do you want us to say, Cas?" Devin demanded, throwing his knife and fork down on the table. "That we are sorry? What the fuck would I be sorry for? You know as well as I do the things that you did to land yourself in that mess. I'm not responsible, neither is Daya, nor anyone else. It was you. Your fucking mistake."

Theo scoffed.

Devin's eyes met mine and then he turned to Castle, "Cas, why don't you tell your wife here what exactly you did..."

Castle's gaze turned sharp. He turned to Winston who was the only staff member allowed to stay in the room. "I need Millicent and Theo's anklet trackers removed. Tonight."

"Sir." Winston bowed and left the room.

"What? You won't tell her?" Devin laughed, a maniac glint in his eyes.

"Tell me what?" I asked.

"Shut up, Devin!" That was Theo. "Don't take the bait, Millie."

But it was difficult not to. There were a lot of things that I wasn't aware of.

Devin ignored him. "Tell her, Castle." He kept taunting. "Your wife needs to know all your secrets. Don't make us out to be some villains when you're not a fucking saint. You know, I was going to let this go because we're family after all, but since you want to start this shit-storm, I won't stop you." He tugged off the napkin and tossed it on the table.

"You want Millie to stay and listen, so she fucking listens," Devin said, exploding with rage.

Castle regarded him coolly, not uttering a word, keeping his glacial exterior intact. His jaw was set hard.

"Don't listen to him, Millie," Theo said desperately.

Devin looked straight at me, and he wasn't in a mood for jokes. He seemed dead-serious. "He's not any better."

My appetite was already dead. I didn't dare sneak a glance at my husband.

"Castle killed our parents in cold-blood."

Chapter 37

Devin thought I didn't know about their parents. I'd read Aster's journals, I knew how Devin and Dayana had been adopted into the family even though they were Montgomery's by name only, but if I mentioned I knew their history, I would have to tell them about the journal, and then Theo would get into trouble.

Devin was still looking at me, waiting for me to say something.

"I'm sorry your parents died, but what else do you expect me to say? I cannot trust you, neither believe anything that you're telling me because you've been nothing but cruel to me. I almost died because of you. Castle would have been dead if we hadn't jumped off a speeding car. We looked out for each other, so if this is one of your ploys where you try to put him in a bad light, it's not working on me, and it never will."

There was silence at the table.

I took deep breaths. I felt like Devin would lash out, but now he wouldn't. He didn't have the authority to do it, and I wasn't scared.

I saw Castle's lip twitch upward in a smirk.

My little speech had been a blow to Devin's ego. He'd expected me to be scandalized by what he'd told me, expected me to lash out. Nothing was going to surprise me anymore.

I'd lived through the worst. My legs were broken, and I was locked in the cellar, accused of being a gold-digger, my nails wrenched out, jumped out of a moving car and emotionally broken, and all this only in a matter of a few months.

I could handle some bitter truths.

"It's not just the murder of our parents, Millie. There are other things you have no clue about."

"I'm sure whatever it is, it wouldn't be anything that I can't handle," I said, climbing to my feet. "Now, if you'll excuse me."

Just before I could leave the table, a hand grasped mine and stopped me.

I whirled around to see Castle holding my hand. His touch burned into an inferno. "Winston will get your anklet off, darling. You should find him first."

The endearing word set a flight of butterflies into my stomach, "Um...yeah...of course, sure. Thank you."

Way to go Millie! You're a blubbering mess.

He chuckled; his laugh was pleasing to my ears. I could have him record an audiobook and keep listening to it and never tire of it. "Don't thank me. It's the least I could do. This isn't a prison, Millicent, it's your home." He kissed my hand, which sent desire shooting through my body.

I was falling deeper in love with him.

I knew the old Castle accepted me and loved me, but having this one say that I belonged here was a validation that I needed to hear.

I nodded and left the room to find Winston.

It was gone. The tracker was no longer attached to my ankle. It was my first step towards freedom, the freedom that had only been possible because Castle had regained his memories.

When the time to go back to my room arrived, I felt a little on edge.

What would happen now?

Would it be awkward to share a bed? Would he expect me to move my stuff to another room? Castle had been kind to me so far, and although he had admitted to remembering everything slowly, it still felt like we were strangers.

I didn't know what to expect. I climbed the stairs slowly, and when I reached the door, I took a few deep breaths.

When I opened the door, he wasn't in the room. I heaved a sigh.

Disappointment settled within me.

He hadn't asked me to leave, so I had no reason to move out. We were married, and while I didn't know the sleeping habits of rich folks, I would still prefer sleeping with my husband.

I changed into my nightgown, choosing a champagne gold colored one that was lacy, sexy but wasn't over the top. Although I would say it was enticing.

I looked at myself in the mirror, raking my fingers through my hair. Did I look desperate for his attention?

Was I forgetting that Devin had literally called my husband a murderer? And now I was just pretending like I hadn't heard that particular fact.

It's not that I wasn't scared, it meant I trusted Castle.

I started reading a book in bed, waiting to hear his footsteps stirring from the slightest noise coming from outside, but he never came. I pulled on my robe and went out of the room to check on him.

I found him in his study. His unruly dark sable hair was out of place, but it worked for him. He was wearing a t-shirt that encased his biceps deliciously, and he was sporting a five o'clock shadow that I would have loved to feel scrapping between my thighs.

Stop it, Millie!

I tried to push away the lustful cloud. He was hunched over a set of files, going through the papers, when he looked up at me. "Darling."

I don't know if I was ever going to stop blushing like a teen girl whenever he called me that.

"I just came here to check on you," I said.

"There's a shit ton of work for me to look at. Why don't you go to sleep? This is going to take me a while."

"Okay," I was about to leave, but stopped mid-way and turned to face him again.

He regarded me with amusement dancing in his eyes and, to my surprise; he shut the file that he was looking at, giving me his full attention. "I believe you have some questions for me."

I closed the door of the study.

"Did you kill your parents?"

"Parent. Singular. Lorna, who was also known as Lorna Montgomery, wasn't my mother, but yes, I killed both my father and his wife. Devin wasn't lying to you about that." He said casually.

"There has to be a good reason for what you did. I know you wouldn't kill someone just for the heck of it."

"It was revenge for what they did to my mother. It was a chain of events. I killed them, and in turn, Devin tried to kill me. He has his reasons, and I wouldn't fault him for trying." He chuckled, "Failed to get me killed twice. Pulling a Houdini is a specialty of mine."

"So where is your mother, Aster?"

"She is where no one can harm her anymore." He said it with a sad undertone.

"I'm sorry." I said, "they hurt her, didn't they?"

There was a distant look in Castle's eyes. His expressions were dark and unreadable. "I apologize, Millicent. I don't think I'm ready to talk about my mother yet or the things she suffered."

I closed the distance between us and took his hand in mine. "I understand completely, and please know that I'm here if you want to talk. Not just as your wife, but as your friend, too."

He gave me a warm smile. "That means a lot."

"Also..." I started saying without thinking twice, "If our sleeping arrangement bothers you, you can let me know and I'll move out of your bedroom. I understand that you probably wouldn't be very comfortable sharing a bed—

"Come here, Millicent."

A few seconds passed, and I stood there awkwardly, staring at him before I went near him.

"Lose that robe."

I disrobed, but I was wearing the thin camisole nightgown. His hand snaked around my waist as he pulled me towards him. I went to sit directly in his lap sideways, my lips were in direct contact with his cheek. I didn't know what to do with my hands, so I let them remain at my sides.

"Have I given you the impression that I wasn't interested in sharing a bed with you?"

My entire body tingled with awareness as his large hand on my waist pressed me to him.

"Not really."

"But you thought I wasn't interested because I never came to your bed tonight."

"A little."

Castle's gaze narrowed, his long lashes staring at my lips. His thumb traced my bottom lip, which I kissed and, captured his face in both my hands. My nose was touching his and his stubble was grazing my palms, shooting desire to my core. Feeling daring, I gave him a quick peck on his lips.

"You're strong and smart. And beautiful." He rasped, "Any husband who wouldn't want you as their wife is fucking stupid, and I'm everything but that." His fingers dug into my hair as he leaned in and captured my mouth in his. The kiss was soul-searing, and I parted my lips, letting his tongue do the exploration. His lips moved softly at first and then it was wild, but he had finesse. He was working his magic over me, and I felt spellbound.

Castle's hands drifted towards my waist and then to my ass, and the backup. His fingers reached the hem of my cami top and touched my skin. He held me like I was precious. His hand cupped one breast, his eyes had turned a shade darker. He tweaked my nipple mercilessly while his lips continued to assault my mouth. I gasped, partly mortified that I was so completely turned on, and partly just wanting to tell him to keep touching me.

"Castle..."

"This should put your doubts at rest." He whispered, giving me that charming smile again. "I don't think I can get any work done at this point, but I have a feeling that I scare you, and maybe it's because of what you heard from Devin."

"No, you don't scare me," I said and then blushed because he could read my mind.

"I don't have a violent streak, and I didn't lash out at them. I killed them for reasons that I will tell you when I'm comfortable enough to open up. I will never hurt you, and I'm not sure how I could prove that to you." He said sincerely. "Let's do something, Millicent. We'll take it slow, okay?"

I nodded. "Okay."

I climbed out of his lap. "Can I ask you something else?"

"Go ahead."

"What is your best memory of us together?" I asked, "before you remembered your past."

"That would be when we took our walks, went out shopping, and when I took you out to dinners at restaurants. Any time spent with you has always been a delight. I don't think I can choose."

"I see." I smiled and then turned to leave, but then I froze in place.

He'd gone back to looking through his workload. "Anything else I can do for you, Mrs. Montgomery?"

"You said you enjoyed taking me out to dinners at restaurants," I said, my breaths coming out rapidly.

"Yes?"

"You never took me out to dinners, Castle. Devin did not allow it." My voice broke into a whisper.

He stared at me, realizing his mistake. A slip-up.

"Millicent..."

"You don't remember any of it, do you?" I asked, "You don't remember me and you've been pretending. It was all a lie!"

Chapter 38

Seconds ticked by as I waited for Castle to respond, to come up with an excuse and tell me I was wrong, but he didn't. Whatever he'd been saying to me was a lie. He didn't remember me; he didn't remember the Millie that he loved.

"I don't even know who you are anymore," I said, on the verge of tears, before walking out of the room.

I couldn't embarrass myself any further. He'd played me, and he'd done it well. He made me believe he knew me, and I'd been a fool to trust his words. I should have gone with my instincts, the instincts that told me the first time around that the old Castle was gone for good.

"Millicent, listen to me!" He was right behind me, hot on his heels.

I had stepped out when he grabbed me by my waist and pulled me back inside his study. He closed the door behind him, turned the lock, and blocked it with his enormous body so I couldn't go out.

"Look at me," he said.

I stared at the floor, so he held my chin and tilted my face upward to meet his gaze.

"Is this another one of your ploys? Am I just a pawn to you in this game, like the rest of your family? Because all you had to do was tell me the truth, Castle, and I would have supported you, anyway." I said, letting the tears fall freely. "I asked you if you remembered me and you lied to my face!"

"I had to do what I thought was right at the time! Please understand." His hands reached up to hold my shoulders, his whiskey-colored burning intensely. "I woke up confused in the hospital. I didn't lie about that. I remembered you, but just not the way you think I do. I recalled faces, names, flashes of certain incidents, but I was clueless."

He appeared to be worried. It looked like he wanted me to trust him again.

I refused to say anything. I hadn't gotten the answer I was looking for, and he realized it.

"Imagine this. I almost drowned, and then I wake up in my car sitting next to this beautiful woman who looked troubled and ready to flee. She held my hand throughout the car ride like she was trying to draw energy from me. I didn't know who you were, but I had visions of you. It was like looking at these pictures in my head."

"What visions?"

"Visions of you under the sun smiling at me, you trapped in the woods, crying for help." He continued, "I saw you as my bride. I saw you helping me regain my memories and protecting me from my brother. I saw you asking me to jump from the car. I was confused as hell because I didn't remember marrying you. I assumed it was part of Devin's plan, and I didn't know if I could trust you. Then I saw the ring on your finger."

"How did you know my name if you remembered nothing before the car ride?" I was playing twenty questions with him and I didn't care. I needed to see him pause or get stuck on his words, and I'd know he was lying.

He seemed genuine.

"I had a ring on my finger too. I checked the engraving inside. Your name is on it. I thought of testing it when I followed you into our room and called your name. You responded, and I knew you were my wife"

"So if you knew all this, then why did you lie to me? You could have just told me the truth from the very beginning."

"Because I knew it would break your heart. I could see it, clear as day that you expected me to remember you, and I don't know...I just didn't want to disappoint you, I guess."

I stepped away from him, folding my hands across my chest. "How do I know you're not lying to me right now?"

"You'll just have to take my word for it." He said.

I looked away from him. "I don't want you to play these games with me."

"I swear to you, Millicent, I'm not using you for any ulterior motive, believe me."

I could play one more card.

"I need more than that. I have to know fully that I can trust you. What happened to your mother? I read the second journal she wrote and in there it states that she left, but I don't believe what's written. How could she leave two of her kids to a woman she didn't trust? And if she did, why hasn't she gotten in touch with you yet?"

Castle's eyes cut through mine. His expressions were lethal. "You know about that journal?"

"Yes."

"I want to see it."

"It's in our bedroom."

Castle followed me to the bedroom and watched as I removed it from its hiding space. After reading it, I had forgotten to give it back to Theo, and he hadn't asked.

Castle took the journal from me and flipped the pages. "Do you have the first one?"

I shook my head. "Theo has it."

"Wait here," Castle told me as he disappeared from the room and then appeared a few minutes later with a file.

He put the file in front of me and opened the journal. "Look at it carefully." He pointed at it.

I looked at what was in front of me. "I don't understand."

"This journal is fake." He declared.

My heart pounded with that information. "What?"

"My mother did not write this one." To prove his theory, he pointed at the letter 'c' in the journal and the 'c' in the file where Aster had written some things. "Look, the letter 'C' is written differently in both."

Castle was right.

"Do you know what this means, Millicent?" He looked at me, pain etched in his features, "it means Chris and his wife wrote this journal to make it look like my mom packed and left. They even got it written by some professional copycat who wrote this in an identical hand. My mom would never leave us. She was murdered."

"Oh god!" I slumped onto the bed.

"Do you also want to know how I found her?"

The question was, though, did I want to put Castle through the trauma again? Could I stomach the gruesome details of the murder? From the looks of it, whatever that had happened wasn't pretty, and I didn't think I had the guts to learn.

"I'm so sorry. I didn't know what they had done. I suspected it but...how could someone be so vicious?!"

"My family." He answered, "Listen, about the divorce. The offer still stands."

"You think I want a divorce?"

"I will take them down, with or without you." His voice became a murmur, "It's going to get dirty and I wouldn't hold anything against you if you want out."

"I want to see this end. I'm not leaving."

Castle was busy in the next few days. I would hardly see him because he would go to the company in the morning and when he returned, he would be in his study and I didn't go there because I didn't want to disturb him.

I was curled up on the single leather couch under the blanket with a book in my hand. I was reading it but my mind kept going to Castle. I would always fall asleep before he made it home. Today, I was adamant about not sleeping. I was going to wait for my husband.

There was a knock on the door. Why was he knocking?

I placed the book aside. "Come in."

I was giddy at the thought of seeing him.

Until Dayana walked in.

She looked shaken. "Millie."

She never so much as paid attention to me, and she'd always gotten sadistic pleasure from seeing me get hurt, so I was not buying into her cry-baby demeanor.

I placed the book aside. "What do you want?"

She shut the door behind her and closed the distance between us. "Millie, I know you hate me and you have good reason to but please, you have to listen to me."

I remained silent.

"You need to speak to Castle; he can put an end to this. Tell him to talk it out with Devin. We are no longer enemies. We can co-exist in this house. I will make Devin understand."

My anger was ricocheting through these walls. This evil incarnate was acting like a victim.

"Dayana, I don't know what weed you've been smoking to think I'm going to be moved by your tears, but it's not working. Devin almost got us killed, remember? We survived an attempted murder. Castle and I were lying on the ground with no one to help us for miles. You put us in that situation knowing we wouldn't make it out alive, and you want me to forgive you?"

"I know what we did, and it's understandable, Millie. I'm so, so sorry for everything."

Hadn't I wanted this before?

Yes, I had imagined Dayana begging for forgiveness multiple times, but never knew it would actually happen.

"We did it because Castle killed our parents in front of us. Do you know how traumatic that was? He took everything..." She reached out to take my hands. "Please Millie, talk to him, or they might end up killing each other."

I snatched my hand away. "It's none of my business. Now, please leave me alone."

I had never seen Dayana so heartbroken, and part of me knew she was planning something. Devin was probably on this too, but I was smarter than to trust either of the siblings. They wanted Castle to have his guard down so they could strike again.

Sometime after midnight, the bedroom door opened, and Castle walked inside.

"Hey." I smiled at him sleepily.

"Hey, darling." He greeted, kissing my forehead. "I thought you would be asleep."

"I was waiting for you."

He was shirtless as he collapsed on the bed and beckoned for me to come to him. I giggled and joined him in bed. He kissed me slowly, sensuously, his tongue working the magic as usual. With his other hand, he pulled out a wrapped box and handed it to me.

"What's this?" I asked.

"Look for yourself."

I tore the wrapper and inside there was a beautiful maroon satin gown. "It's lovely."

"I want you to wear this right now."

I laughed, "Right now?"

"Yeah."

I disrobed and pulled on the one he'd bought for me. "Thank you, baby."

"I realized I've been a major asshole and haven't given you much time..."

He was saying something more, but my eyes were drowsy, and he probably noticed that because he chuckled, "Get some sleep." He placed open-mouthed kisses over my cheek and neck. My fingers dug into his hair. "We're taking it slow, so today we spoon."

"Hmmm..." I mumbled. As much as I wanted Castle to keep doing what he was doing, I was also dead tired from having a lack of sleep.

I don't know when I fell asleep in Castle's arms. I buried my face in his chest, and inhaled his ocean body-wash scent, grazing the light trail of hair on his stomach, and tracing his chiseled abs. I was drugged with this feeling. He was mine and I would happily die for this man.

The old grandfather clock downstairs chimed.

And then I heard the sound of a gun cocking.

I looked up in time to see a barrel of a handgun poised towards us in the darkness.

In the silver moonlight streaming from the window, I noticed the triumph look on Devin's handsome face.

"It ends here." He said in a deadly whisper.

Chapter 39

I blinked my eyes, trying to adjust my vision in the dark.

I was wide awake by now, and Devin stood there, hovering over us, aiming the gun at me and Castle, "Stop harboring any illusions that I won't shoot because I will."

"Why are you doing this?!" I asked.

Before I could comprehend what was happening, he grabbed my arm and forced me out of bed, pulling me taut against him. I yelped and flailed, but he had a chokehold on me, the gun now digging into my jaw.

You couldn't tell what Castle was thinking. His face was blank. He looked resigned and tired. Calmly, he said, "put the gun down, Devin, and let her go."

"What was it you said before that accident, Castle? Oh right, I remember. You said you would ruin me! Me! Devin Montgomery! You son of a bitch! How does this feel?"

"Don't be stupid." Castle said in a dangerously low voice, "If you put the gun down, I promise we can forget this twisted revenge. I'll leave town if you want. You can have all of this. Just...let her go."

"Fuck you!" Devin spat at him, and chuckled, "she's coming with me."

He pushed me towards the door by force, almost making me trip against the carpeted floor.

My heart jack-hammered against my chest.

This is it then...

This is how it's finally going to end...

He jabbed the gun against my neck. "don't try and act smart, Millie, or I'll shoot and your brains will paint these walls and I really don't want to do that. The wallpapers are fucking expensive."

"I'm walking! Stop hitting me!" I yelled at him.

A silhouette was visible on the upper level of the floor. I looked up long enough to catch a glimpse of Dayana.

"Devin! Stop!" she screamed from above. "Let her go! I've talked to—

"Dayana, stay there! Do not come down or I swear I will kill her right this very second!"

She was kneeling against the banister on the floor, staring at us with haunted green eyes. I couldn't see anything because we were going further down. "Devin, please..." she said helplessly.

Chandler had materialized on the floor wearing his bear print pajamas. He saw his brother pointing the gun at me. Fear was clear on his face. "Where are you taking Millie?" he asked in a soft voice.

"Go to bed, Chandler!" Devin said.

"Don't take her..." his voice wavered.

Was Chandler going to cry? I never thought the brat would ever cry for me.

Castle was right behind me, following Devin as he dragged us out of the mansion like a pair of kitchen rats.

I remembered everything that led up to this moment. Running away from my uncle's home, taking up the job, marrying Castle. Tears clouded my vision as I realized all was for nothing.

All that planning and Castle regaining his memories had led to Devin finally losing it.

Devin would pull us outside, shoot me first, and then Castle. Or he would shoot Castle first and then me. I didn't want to live if Castle would not survive this. It made no sense to go on living without him.

There was no Millie without Castle.

Devin brought his mouth close to my ear, his breath fanned my cheek, "if you hadn't been so taken to him, maybe I would have let you live, but I had seen it. Your fascination for Castle the second you met him. You were not supposed to fall in love, you were supposed to notice me!"

"I'm sorry, but why am I being held responsible for this? You got me married to him forcefully, didn't you? Do I have to remind you of that?"

"That was part of the plan!" he seethed. "But if you hadn't fallen for him, it would have been me by your side. Me with you! Not him!"

"So you're just going to kill me as revenge for loving your brother?"

"Shut up and keep walking!"

Finally, we made it downstairs, and he led us outside of the mansion, into the mansion gardens. Theo was nowhere in sight. He was probably sleeping, unaware of what was going on. Chandler would be confused when he learned we were dead. I felt bad for them. They would find out their oldest brother was gone and their sister-in-law slaughtered in the process.

What would happen to Theo after we were gone? Devin would no doubt make his life miserable.

We stood facing each other in the mansion gardens.

The moon remained hidden behind the tall pine trees. The gust of wind reminded me of how thin the gown's fabric was. It didn't matter what I was wearing anymore; I was going to be buried in the family cemetery on the grounds. I wouldn't be allowed outside of this property even after death. The irony was laughable and sick in equal measures.

I hated this place. It reminded me of a luxurious prison, but I had hoped with the return of Castle that it would change. I had wanted a good life for us.

Castle and I both deserved it.

I looked up at the mansion's top-floor window and noticed a dark figure against the glass. Grandpa Hugh continued to watch us as his mad step-grandson held us at gunpoint.

"Get down on your knees, both of you!" Devin commanded.

"Dev,can we talk this out, please?" Castle asked him. "I promise you no games."

A gunshot roared through the air, and I yelled loudly. A bullet was shot in the ground, "down, or the next bullet goes through her."

Reluctantly, I kneeled.

Castle kneeled with me, his hands above his head.

What was all the staff doing? Couldn't they hear the gunshot? Where was Winston?

I imagined Devin could have threatened them to ignore tonight's occurrence. It wasn't unusual for Devin to threaten people to get his way out.

I had images of our bodies on the ground next to each other. And the news headline that I'd killed him and then killed myself.

"Devin, you don't have to do this."

"Sure I do." He said, his face contorting in anger. The veins in his forehead almost popping, "this is all your fault, if you hadn't acted so smart, if you hadn't meddled in my family business, you wouldn't be here and Castle would have been dead like he should be."

"You can kill me, but let her go." Castle said.

"Not a chance." Devin snapped.

"I just need to know something. You carried out those rituals, didn't you?" Castle asked.

"So what if I did?!" Devin was breathing hard, still holding the gun to me. "Grandpa needed someone to carry out the rituals, the cult needed to move forward with a leader and I was the perfect candidate! The best!"

At this point, I wondered if Devin was not just crazy, but also delusional.

"I know what you're doing, talking to me like this. You're buying time." Devin chuckled, "it won't work. The police want nothing to do with us, Cas. You of all people, should know that. They are aware of the power we wield, and nothing that happens here tonight will make it out of these gates."

Castle and I exchanged looks. He wasn't giving me any signal, nothing that could prove that we were getting out of here alive!

Had he given up so easily? Was he only trying to gather information so he could die knowing the truth?

"What do you want, Devin? Name it and it's yours."

Devin laughed again. "You know what I want? I want you dead! I'd considered killing you since you lost your memories, but what's the fun in that? I wanted to look into your eyes and put a bullet in your head as you recalled how you ruined my family! I wanted you to remember every goddam thing!" He said, his voice dripping venom.

He had become completely deranged as he took a swing at Castle, who did not react. The hit was too hard because Castle spat blood, but he continued to regard Devin with the same coolness. "Stop this foolishness."

Devin was circling us, but he was distracted enough. He wouldn't notice...

It was a gamble.

I could get killed.

When he walked behind me, I gathered up all the force and the courage to stab my elbow into his crotch, hard.

That made him groan loudly, and he lost the grip on the gun as I watched it flying out of his hands and falling onto the tiled pathway in the gardens. I crawled away from there and got up on my feet.

"Millie! Run!" Castle shrieked.

Feeling my heart jumping out of my chest, I blindly ran into the labyrinth garden maze.

The ground was all mud, and tall trimmed shrubs surrounded by all sides with English roses blooming; pink and yellows. It was a maze, stretching on all sides, circular and huge. It looked breathtakingly beautiful in the morning.

Theo, Chandler, Castle, and I used to play here all the time. Theo would always win because he was at an expert level for finding the routes and knew all the corners. I was the only one who would always get lost.

I darted through the maze walls without looking at which way I was going.

I came to a space I thought was safe. I hid there. Running so fast had consumed my energy, I was barely left with breath.

Then I heard it, the sound of the branches crunching..."

"Ooooooh Millie..." came Devin's teasing voice. "Come out, come out..."

I heard the gun being reloaded.

"We can play this all night, if you want, but I'm not leaving until I find you."

I could hear his voice drawing closer.

I started moving away from there when something tugged my gown. I stopped to find the thorny stems of rose jutting out and tearing into it. I jerked at it angrily, tearing the fabric a bit.

And then the sound of gunfire filled the air.

My heart almost stopped completely.

Who had Devin shot?

Castle!

I sneaked out of the space desperately. He couldn't die like this! Castle wouldn't go down without a fight. I turned the corner and stopped short, gaping at the scene before me.

Dayana lay on the floor, her eyes vacant, blood pooling on the ground.

Chapter 40

No one moved as the reality of the situation sank in. The only sound heard were coming from the unknown wild animals of the night deep in the woods.

"Noooooooo..." Devin shrieked at the top of his lungs, "No. No. No...Daya...oh god..."

She lay on the floor, her eyes staring lifelessly ahead, the pink and yellow roses behind her were painted with streaks of scarlet. Truly a macabre scene.

Devin thumped the ground with his fists, wailing loudly, and pushing the gushing blood towards her as if putting it back in her body. He grabbed her body and rocked, "Daya...Dayana! Wake up!" He was bordering on hysteria.

He'd killed Dayana unknowingly.

Wait a minute...

Why was she wearing exactly the same replica of the maroon gown I was wearing?

It made sense now. Dayana probably entered the garden maze to stop Devin, and Devin knew what I was wearing. He'd mistaken her for me and shot her.

He didn't know that it was his sister!

Devin leveled his eyes towards me. Now they held a maniac glint. "It's all your fault she's dead!"

I had frozen on the spot,and then logic came to me as I realized I needed to get away from him before he killed me for real this time.

I scrambled in the opposite direction, going deeper into the maze

But his hand jutted out as he yanked me, and I crashed to the ground. A bolt of sharp pain shot through my arm. I was pretty sure I'd broken my arm by now. Ignoring the pain, I made my way out of there...

Devin reached for his gun again when Castle tackled him, sat on top of him and powerful fists came raining down on Devin. The two were wrestling against each other for dominance. Their faces were bloodied as they continued to struggle.

"I will kill you!" Devin shrieked. His visceral need for vengeance made him a dozen times more lethal. It fueled his aggression. "If I'd just killed you that day, none of this would have happened! My baby sister would still be alive..." He let out a low moan as he continued to pound his fists into Castle.

"Let him go!" I jumped into their fight to pull him off Castle, but he swung his arm so hard, I fell to the side.

Devin's hands came around Castle's neck as he tried to choke him. His teeth gritted and his face contorted like a man who'd fallen off into the dark side. Castle gasped for breath. He was fighting for his life, trying to get Devin off of him.

He was going to kill Castle!

"Stop! Please..." I cried.

I looked around for something.

Anything would work against him.

"You destroyed my family!" Devin screamed, a loud wail of frustration.

I spotted a gardening spade left there at the corner by the gardeners. I saw Devin produce a jackknife from his pocket and he was ready to plunge it into Castle.

I knew I wouldn't make it in time. It's something you realize at that crucial point of time that Castle's death was evident. I wasn't fast enough.

I picked it up and made a run towards him when another gunshot reverberated, stopping me dead in my tracks.

Who'd done that?

I spun around to look.

In the darkness surrounding the maze, I saw a small form standing at a distance, tears streaming down his face and his hands shaking visibly.

Chandler was holding a gun.

A spot of blood began spreading on Devin's shirt. He clenched it, staring at his youngest brother in bafflement. "What the fuck, Chandler?! How dare you!"

"You killed Dayana, and now you're trying to kill Castle, who gives me two thousand dollars for a monthly allowance! You gave me a hundred. I can't go back to that!" Chandler burst out.

"You little shit!" Devin swore, frustrated. "Put that gun down! Now!"

He raised the knife again to stab Castle when another bullet penetrated his body.

This time in his neck.

It was excruciating to watch a man die no matter how much you hated him.

Chandler had fallen back with the force of the gunfire, and that's when Theo appeared out of the shadows, wearing pajamas. "What's this ruckus all about?" he asked sleepily and then his eyes registered the horror in front of him. "Fuck!"

No one attempted to help Devin as he choked, spurting out blood.

We just stood there watching.

Castle pushed Devin off himself and walked to where I was standing. "Are you alright? I thought he shot you!" He said, his fingers threading through mine. He was glad I was okay. I touched his bloody face and tried to wipe the blood off it.

"Call 911." He told Theo, reaching for Chandler and taking the gun out of his hand.

Chandler, having realized what had happened, asked, "Why isn't he moving?"

Castle didn't answer, and pulled Chandler in a hug, turning his face away from the scene. "You shot him to save my life. That's what happened here."

Chandler was deathly silent.

The way I saw it, this was poetic justice.

"Hello, this is Montgomery's residence. We need help."

The funeral was held in the family's chapel by the cemetery.

Who would have thought this would happen? There were two white coffins lowered into the ground which were supposed to be for me and Castle. Chandler hadn't cried one drop. He looked like a broken doll.

Castle had injuries on his face, and people who we didn't even know were in the house paying their respects and discussing the horrific events. They looked sorry for the brother who was going to be killed by a money-hungry half-brother.

Chandler had opted out of the funeral all together. He wanted to be cooped up in his bedroom, reading comics, and Castle hadn't pushed him to attend. He'd told me to let him be. I'd seen the sadness seeping in the child's eyes and I knew he needed time to grasp everything. Devin had given him shooting training since he was ten for in cases of emergencies to defend himself. The irony of that was kind of sick.

Grandpa Hugh was also downstairs. Winston stayed close to the old man, but Hugh didn't seem to care about what was going on. He was going on and on about something. Theo and his girlfriend Madison were huddled in a corner and I'd seen him hug her close, intimately close, as she consoled him. No matter how evil Devin was, he was still his brother.

"Are sure you don't want anyone to stay here with you?" I asked when I went to Chandler's room to check on him.

He had the haunted look; the child had killed his own brother. He was trying really hard to act tough. He sniffled, "Millie, am I going to prison?"

I closed the door behind me and came to his bed, where I wrapped him in a hug. "No, of course not. It wasn't your fault, Chandler. Devin would have killed us. You saved our lives."

His large emerald eyes stared up at me, and the similarity with his brother was disturbing. He would grow up to look like Devin, but we would make sure he was a better man, one who didn't live with greed but spread love.

"You promise?" He asked with his pinky out.

I nodded, "I promise."

"Is Castle sending me to boarding school? Devin told me he was going to."

I shook my head. "I wouldn't let him."

He raised his pinky again. "You have to double pinky promise me."

I tangled my pinky with his again. "Double promise."

He hugged me again suddenly, and then a loud wail filled the silence. I held him to me until he had no tears left. He needed someone to give him a bit of maternal love and attention, and I could become that someone.

I went to look for Castle later but couldn't find him inside the mansion. Then someone told me they'd seen him walk outside.

Finally, I spotted him. He was sitting by the lake all alone, staring at the serene water ahead. He had taken off his blazer jacket, and sat wearing a dark shirt and slacks, a few buttons open at the collar and tousled hair. Even with the injuries on his face, it gave him a rugged look. It would have been inappropriate, but I had the sudden desire to kiss him.

I sat down beside him and we stared at the lake wordlessly.

He offered me a flask. "want a sip?"

I smiled, taking it from him. I took a gulp, and the alcohol burned my throat. I handed it back to him.

"I should have tried harder to help him," Castle told me.

I placed my hand over his. "he was beyond help, Castle. You can't feel guilty about this."

He nodded, taking another sip. "How's Chandler holding up?"

"He cried."

"That's good. He shouldn't bottle up his feelings. He likes to act tough."

"He was worried you'd send him to boarding school, said that Devin used to tell him about it all the time."

"Well, you should have told him he won't be attending a boarding school. He'll be going to a military school instead."

I stared at him in horror. He looked back at him and we burst out laughing. After he recovered, he said, "Devin liked to threaten him with things like that to keep him in line, and I don't think that's a very effective method of disciplining a child. Things are going to be different from now on because I'll be in charge."

"I know he was your brother, Castle, but I'm not sorry for what happened. You almost died!"

He didn't answer, and we sat in companionable silence.

"She came to me that evening."

I looked at him in question.

"Dayana." He said, "She told me Devin wouldn't make a move unless I give my word that there would be a truce. And you know what? I told her yes. I told Dayana that I didn't want violence and I was ready to let it all go if they moved out of the family mansion to another one. We co-exist no matter what, so I gave her an ultimatum, and she agreed."

"Then what happened?"

"Instinct, I guess. I knew Devin was hell-bent on killing me." He closed his eyes for a moment, as if he was trying to find the courage to speak. "I knew what Dayana was wearing. I gave you that night-gown on purpose." He turned his whiskey eyes on me. "I got my sister killed. Isn't that fucked up?"

I closed my hand around his. "You did what you had to do."

He picked up our linked hands and kissed my knuckles, tears streaked his face. "I promise you, Millie. I won't fail you again. I will love you like you deserve to be."

I inched closer to him and put my head on his shoulder. "I'm glad it's over."

"Yeah, me too. This is going to be a new beginning." He smiled warmly, "You've tolerated a lot of shit on behalf of my fucked-up family and I'm going to make up to you for the rest of my life." He sneaked a glance around to make sure no one was looking and then brought his lips down on mine.

It's as if he could read my mind.

Chapter 41

Two Years Later.

CASTLE

It's been a long time since my half-brother and sister died, and since then I've recollected most of my memories.

Saying that it was a wild ride would be an understatement of the century.

Right now, I have everything that I worked hard for, wealth, the family name, including my beautiful wife and a one-year-old son, James who was now sitting in my lap, staring at me with his golden-brown eyes, identical to my own. He gave me a mischievous smile.

To achieve all of this, I've made some sacrifices in life, gotten my hands dirty, but I guess that's part of it. If you wanted something badly, you couldn't let values, the right, and the wrong, come in the way.

You needed to own that shit, and that's what I fucking did.

We all have skeletons in our closets. Some keep them hidden under their beds. I have mine too. I kept them locked in a chest, and the chest was buried somewhere deep where no one else can find them.

My son and I were sitting in our private theater, watching one of my old tapes. Didn't understand what was going on much, but he pointed a finger at my father who was young in the tape.

"Daddy!" He said, pointing at the screen.

I laughed, "that's your late grandfather, buddy." I showed him the thirteen-year-old me. "And that's me."

Millie hadn't seen these tapes, and I hadn't shown them to her for good reason. They weren't meant to be shown to my wife.

You'll find out the reason pretty soon.

The birthday song played on the videotape on the wide screen. Devin stood in the center cutting the cake wearing some fancy designer outfit shipped from Venice. Dayana was on the side. They were laughing, their friends clapping for them.

I stood on the other side looking gangly with some loose clothes on. I was a little skinny then, and Theo was in my arms, staring glazed-eyed at the towering cake and the lavish birthday party.

That was the first time Aster Montgomery noticed us and took pity on us. Theo and I. We were born to Lorna and Christopher Gates, but of course, Aster didn't know that. She thought we were kids to a single mother at first. Devin and Dayana were heirs to this billion-dollar conglomerate.

I wasn't born a Montgomery. I stole the name.

Which was only possible because of years of patience, planning, and perseverance.

Father loved both the women. Was that his crime? I think so. He chose the rich woman over my mother, even though he was married to my mom first.

Aster fed Theo and me, she clothed us, gave us a roof over our heads, and finally we were adopted.

The journals were fake. There were no journals written by Aster or Lorna.

Theo wrote them in a similar hand to get Millie on our side, and I guess he'd succeeded. He'd woven a new story, where he and I were born into the Montgomery family. The facts were the same, only some things were different.

Aster was a home-wrecker. She destroyed my family, so I took everything from her, including her house and wealth.

Chris and Lorna were only working on this property when the entitled Aster Montgomery seduced my father on purpose and stole him from us. He remarried her with the condition that Theo and I were included in the family. Aster accepted us with open arms despite the dislike Daya and Devin showed to us at first.

And then she got jealous of my mother because Dad would always find a way to go to Lorna.

The contents in the diary weren't exactly all lies, but everything was written and presented in a way that wasn't real. My mother left us at a very tender age like exactly what was written in the diary, only it wasn't Aster, it was Lorna, and I refused to believe she had just left.

I could hear some strange sounds at night when I passed the cellar. I wanted to find out the source of the sound.

I knew something fishy was going on down there.

One night when everyone was in bed, thinking it was a burglar sneaking into the house, I snagged my baseball bat and went downstairs to investigate.

I flicked the keys from my father's room and went downstairs. The cellar was quiet that night. A small trap-door could be seen at the foot of the stairs. I had to use all my strength to open it.

A foul odor entered my nostrils. It was nasty. I remembered flicking the light on and seeing a small skeleton of a person. The woman was so frail, I couldn't recognize her to be my mother.

"Mom?" I'd called out to her.

She looked up, but she barely recognized me.

She'd spent years in this cellar with no one's knowledge.

Her teeth gone, and the place stank of urine.

"Mom?"

She blabbered something coherent, stared at me, and then raged, banging her head against the wall and causing herself harm. The blood seeped from her head wound.

It's when I knew she thought I was my father.

"Stop! Please stop!" She shrieked at the top of her lungs.

She was far gone. My mother didn't exist.

I'd gone back to my room and returned a few minutes later. I hugged her as she cried in frustration, telling me something that I didn't understand. I kissed her head. I loved her so much.

"It's okay; mom. It's okay. I'll protect you. It's over now." I sobbed.

I wanted to make them pay for this.

I pulled away from her, and although she was still trying to hurt me; I gave her a small smile. I gave her the satisfaction that she'd hurt my father. I don't think she remembered anything else. I pushed the pillow over her face and pressed hard. Her small body flailed, trying to come up for air, and I cried.

"I'm sorry, Mom. I'm so sorry." I'd told her as I'd smothered my mother, ending her sufferings.

It was quick.

Part of me had wanted to steal the gun from Chris's room and shoot him and Aster. I'd stood at the entrance of their bedroom and almost done it, but then I remembered Theo. I'd go to prison and then what would happen to him?

I'd gone to bed and pretended I hadn't done what I'd done. Killed my mother, that is.

I'd been a good kid. I'd pretended to respect Aster and father, keeping the hate and the hunger for vengeance at bay. I let them trust me enough to hand over the company. I treated them better than Devin did. I did everything my father asked of me. I covered up Devin's and Daya's fuck ups for them. I was the epitome of a dutiful son, so much that Aster nearly wished I was hers.

I waited.

For the right time.

For years I waited, and then the boating accident happened. Theo knew the accident was going to happen, and he'd helped me with it.

The Montgomery's maintained a low profile, and that meant no pictures in the tabloids, no personal information. Grandpa Hugh liked it that way, and no one had questioned his choice, and that had helped Theo and me to build up the story over the years. The lies we had weaved together to get everything that was never ours.

I'd been a good grandson to Hugh and earned his respect when he'd remembered things. Later on, he was far too affected with Alzheimer's realizing that I was his step-grandson or I'd killed his daughter, my step-mom.

"Momma..." James said, pointing at the screen again and bringing me out of memory lane.

There was another clip playing, the one with Millie and my wedding. I switched off the screen and picked him up into my arms.

"Let's go for a walk, son."

I walked out of the room and met with my gorgeous wife, who was dressed in a sea-green velvet cocktail dress. Her dark eyes were shining with adoration.

"My boys," she said lovingly, touching her cheek, "I've been looking all over for you. What were you doing here?"

"Mama..." James said, pointing at his mother.

"Just watching our old movies."

She picked James into her arms and kissed his cheek, and then quickly wiped the lipstick stain from there.

"Can I convince you to go to the charity ball with me, Castle?"

I pulled her towards me. "you know how much I hate attending those. I think James wants to sleep and guess I'll raincheck this time."

She pouted, "is it important for me to go?"

"Have a little fun, Millie," I claimed her lips with mine and I was good at drawing the kiss until she was weak in the knees. When I pulled away, she was dizzy. "You need a bit of a break from taking care of the baby. Go."

"I think I'm the luckiest woman in this world." She said, "I have to keep pinching myself to remind that this is all real."

I laughed.

"You know what? I'm the luckiest man to have you."

And I wasn't lying. She was amazing and if it weren't for Millie, Theo and I wouldn't have succeeded in what we'd started out to do. This woman, the love of my life, had helped a great deal unknowingly.

"Castle..." she said sweetly, overwhelmed.

She and I. We were similar. She wasn't aware of it, but we were born in poor conditions and we'd worked for all of this.

We deserved it!

"I'll make it up to you tonight." She said, running a finger over my jawline.

I gave her a heated look. "Go baby, or I'm tearing that pretty dress to shreds."

"Gaga...Goo-goo." James said.

"Jamie approves," I said.

Millie rolled her eyes.

I accompanied her downstairs, and then she kissed both James and me before sitting inside the car. I waited until I saw it disappear through the gates.

"Where do you think your uncle Theo is, Jamie?"

James spoke again in his baby language.

"Let's put you to bed and then I'll go look for him."

I read James his favorite book, and the kid dozed off as soon as I was done reading one page. I tried to call Theo's number, but he wasn't answering, so I looked for him.

Twenty minutes later, I'd checked mostly every place that I thought I would find him. I couldn't find him anywhere.

The door of the connecting wing was wide open, and I followed the path down to the tunnel. I went deeper using the flashlight of my phone. I'd been here countless times as a kid, but never bothered in the years that followed.

There was light emanating from a source a little farther down. I took the stairs down the spiral staircase down.

Ten people were in a circle, holding hands. Candles illuminating the place. The dark-cloaked man in the middle was chanting as the others followed him. His voice was authoritative and his actions fluid and practiced. Their faces were covered in masks, body in cloaks.

I waited until the ceremony ended.

The members kneeled, bowing to the cult leader, hanging onto his every word. When the ceremony was over, the leader walked towards me. The large pendent glinted in the dark.

He slid off the cloak's hoodie, and Theo had a grin on his face. "Didn't think you would be joining me tonight."

"Just came to check on you."

The ring in his hand glimmered. "Millie's not home?"

"Nope."

Devin thought he was running a cult, when the cult members had secretly rejected him. According to them, he did not have what it took to continue what the Montgomery ancestors had started so they let him be deluded that he was running things then, but in reality, they'd helped Theo take the position and they also played a part when I was admitted in the hospital. They were everywhere, looking out for us and protecting us.

Theo had also been the one to kill Barbara because that woman knew too much, and she'd seen Theo write the journals and would have exposed everything. The members had seen the potential in Theo, and when he'd turned eighteen, they convinced him to take the position of the new leader to continue Grandpa's legacy.

Hugh was secretly proud.

I don't know what "rituals" Theo was doing, and truthfully, I didn't care as long as he kept it on the hidden side of the mansion.

Chandler was thirteen now. I wondered what would happen if he found out the truth about Aster, his mother, and blame us for it. He might even come after us for revenge, or my James.

It would be a cycle of revenge, but I wouldn't let him find out. When he was an adult, he would realize what a loving brother I am and never let the thought of revenge cross his mind.

Maybe I'd write another story. Just for Chandler.

And he'll eat it up.

"I'm going to bed," I told him.

"Goodnight, Cas," He nodded, turning around to face the members.

Millie would never find out the truth.

I was taking all these secrets to the grave.

I started making my way back upstairs when my phone buzzed.

Millie

"Hey, darling."

"I'm so bored here. I just gobbled up dinner. I'm coming home. What were you doing?"

Oh, nothing much. Just checking out a cult ceremony hosted by your loving brother-in-law.

"I put James to sleep, Chandler's in bed too, and Theo and I were watching a movie now."

"Do not move. I'm coming home and we're watching something together."

"Sure, darling. Anything you want."

Epilogue

C ASTLE

Sundays were fun. It was also a family day out for the Montgomerys. Dad, Aster, and all my other siblings spent time together every Sunday without fail. We would have barbecues, a day out at the beach, but today we were going on a boating trip, not far away from the property.

Dad said it was a good way to communicate and bond together as a family.

I agreed with him.

This particular Sunday was different, though. For Christopher and Aster Montgomery, it was going to be Doomsday.

I sat in my study, going through the documents, making sure things were perfect.

Planning a murder is easy, executing it is not. And the execution is what I was worried about. One wrong move and things would take a different turn.

Theo knew what he was supposed to do. I had his full support, and that's all I wanted. Just my brother on my side to clean up the mess.

I watched from the French window. Devin and Daya were near the patio, helping Winston stock beverages in the icebox, laughing and joking, oblivious to the shit that was about to go down.

These were my players. The most important ones and they had no idea about it.

The door to my study opened, and Chandler walked inside. He had an annoyed expression plastered on his face.

"Do you need something, Buddy?" I asked him, checking all the documents in the file.

He folded his arms across his chest. "Mom says I have to attend this stupid fishing trip! I don't want to! All you guys do is catch fish and chit-chat!"

I grinned, "what do you want to do?"

"It's Leo's birthday. I want to attend the party. All the kids from school are going there and it's going to be super cool. Can I go there instead, Castle? I have his gift all wrapped up." Then he added, "If you explain mom, she will understand because she listens to you."

"Sure, buddy. You wanna attend your friend's party? Fine with me. I'll explain to mom."

"Yesss!" Chandler exclaimed. "You're the best older brother!"

The night still haunted me when I found my mother, Lorna, in the cellar. I couldn't forget the night even if I tried, and I'd used that night as fuel for retribution. I had kept going, marking the day, waiting for the time I could strike.

This family welcomed us even though we were outsiders, but I was going to be one of them. I deserved it.

Any person who came between this would be eliminated.

I wore a casual t-shirt and denim jeans. I liked to keep the five o'clock shadow on my face because it made me look better.

It was a beautiful day. Such a shame about what was about to go down.

Trixie wouldn't stop barking. It's as if she had a premonition of what was going to happen. I ruffled her head before boarding.

I boarded the yacht. Theo was in the back, playing music on the stereos. Dayana was texting on her phone furiously. She looked up, and when she saw me staring at her, she quickly pocketed her phone as if I would ask her who she was chatting with.

I knew she was sleeping with two of the servants, the good-looking ones. One of them was a stable boy. She was probably texting him. I gave her one look that should tell her I knew what she was doing. She looked scared.

Sis had a hard time keeping her legs closed, especially when it came to handsome men that did hard labor around the house.

I guess the Apple doesn't fall far from the tree.

How ironic that father also used to work in the stables when he met Aster. The plan had been to take enough money from the Montgomerys and leave. Aster wouldn't have even noticed, but Chrissy-boy got greedy. He wanted two women, and then he decided Aster was a better option than my mother.

Devin was at the mini-bar, downing the tequila bottle. He was always the screw-up in the family, making scandals, doing whatever the fuck he wanted, and I did the clean-up.

I was the laundry guy, always fucking cleaning the mess by Aster's children. I was the older, understanding, mature kid in the family.

I waved at Grandpa Hugh who was in a wheelchair parked on the pier. His caretaker whispered something to him.

I waited until late that night.

"Castle, honey, what are you doing there? Come here, play with us." Aster called out to me. She sat at the poker table with Dad.

"Sure." I joined them in the sitting area.

We played poker, Devin had joined the table and, as usual, he cheated. He always did.

"I win." Devin laughed, throwing his cards onto the table and collecting all the chips.

"Cheating is not winning. You knew if you hadn't cheated, Castle would have won." Theo said, laughing.

"Fuck you!"

"Language boys," Aster said, looking at us, her expressions filled with love. "I wish we could all stay like this forever, smiling and laughing."

I put an arm around Aster and kissed her head. "We will always be like this. I promise you."

She patted my cheek, and then turned to her husband, "you've been quite Chris, what's wrong?"

Dad shook his head. I looked so much like our father. I've been told that a lot of times and I hated the resemblance. I wish I hadn't looked like this vile man, but then I knew it ran inside my blood, the urge to deceive people, to take what in reality didn't belong to me.

"I'm just thinking how content I am with my children," he said, "especially you, Castle. You have made your mother proud."

I think I was grounding my teeth so hard, I might break some. Quickly, I composed myself and smiled instead, "Thank you, father."

Devin stared at us. His expressions were grim. "Let's play another round."

He was jealous. As always. He was hungry for the praise that I usually received. As for me, I didn't give a shit about what Aster or Chris thought of me.

I looked at the time. It was a little past seven p.m. I went into the kitchen and noticed that the food was all wrapped up. I found the bottles of liquor, which I poured into small glasses and pulled a glass vial from my jeans, and put a few drops in each glass. It didn't have a powerful effect, just enough to get the job done.

I took the drinks back to the sitting area, handed each member a glass, and settled down with my own.

Theo's gaze met mine before he looked back at the Rubik's cube in his hand. His concentration was on the square.

Slowly, I took a sip and waited.

THEODORE

"I'm feeling hot in here. Is the air-conditioner not working? I'll go to the upper deck to get some fresh air." Dad said, taking off his jacket.

Devin's tongue had gotten loose. "Daaaaaddddd...why do you always think Castle is the best?! Tis not true...I'm better! I'm better than him!"

"Devin, mind your tongue," Aster snapped.

"What? Did I say something wrong? I'm the fucking heir! I don't understand..." He yelled in a drunken stupor, "I'm capable of taking over. I don't know what you want me to do!"

"I'll tell you what to do." I said, smiling wickedly, "Take your drunk ass down to the cabin and sleep it off. You wouldn't remember this conversation tomorrow."

"Theo, that's not the way to speak to your older brother." Aster chided.

He's not my brother, ma'am.

"I'll come upstairs with you, Dad." Castle climbed to his feet, following our father upstairs to the open deck like an obedient son. He's played his part well while keeping the flame of revenge burning.

It was hard for me to agree to this. I'd cried, I'd hit Castle for even suggesting such a thing, but he'd convinced me it was the only way. It was kill, or be killed. And after what father and Aster had done to our mother, they deserved what was coming. Was Castle the right person to deliver justice? I wasn't sure.

I sat on the outer deck of Longue with my legs hoisted up on the railing. The red squares of the Rubik were almost complete, but the white kept messing with it.

"I don't feel that well. I think I'm going to retire for tonight."

Dad had a little more to drink, and I mixed the vial in it, which added to his drowsiness. I looked up to see Castle standing on top of the stairs, a menacing look crossing his otherwise stern features.

He looked dangerous and intimidating, all the same.

And then he gave Dad a gentle but firm push.

That's all it took for our father to tumble down the stairs violently, his body rolling on each bump, making the thump thump sound. I couldn't tear my eyes away as his head hit the railing hard and blood seeped through his forehead.

"Help me..." Dad mumbled, sitting up straighter, raising his hand towards me. "I don't know how I slipped. Theo..."

Castle walked down the stairs calmly, as if he had all the time in the world.

Devin and Daya were still inside.

Castle looked at me as if to say, Look away.

I turned my face away because even though I was included in the plan; I didn't want to see this.

I concentrated on the cube in my hand. I needed to get all the yellows in place.

"What are you doing, son?" I heard Dad asking him.

"Did she beg?" Castle asked.

"What?"

"Did mom beg you to let her go when you kept her locked in the cellar?"

"Castle...son..."

I heard the loud sound of something hard hitting the railing many times.

"What have you done?!" Shrieked Aster as she walked onto the deck and stared at the scene in front of us in horror.

I recalled Castle's words from yesterday.

Pretend like you're not part of this. You were not involved in getting them murdered. Do you understand what I'm saying, Theo? If something goes wrong, if I die, you will finish what we started.

I let out a loud sob and mustered up the acting I'd learned during drama period, "What the fuck have you done, Castle?! Why did you hit Dad?!"

Fresh bloods smeared the railing which dripped down onto the expensive flooring. Aster screamed and wailed, but I hugged her from behind. Castle ignored Aster and helped Dad stand up, only to shove him over the ledge and into the water.

"Christopher!" Aster came unhinged as she ran to the railing. "Somebody save him!"

One had to be blind not to notice that he was beyond saving. The metal blades had been running. The water colored a deep red.

She was shaking when she turned to face Castle. Betrayal was clearly spelled there. She clenched the railing hard and murmured, "Why?"

Castle turned his cool gaze towards Aster, and he looked very much like a man who'd walked out of the ninth circle of hell.

Devin walked to the deck just in time to see it.

Castle hugged Aster, "No hard feelings, Mom. It's just payback." He kissed her head like any loving son would, "But I promise you..." he whispered, "Devin and Daya will join you shortly."

Devin had no time to react. Castle picked her up over the railing and threw her legs up so she dropped into the water.

Aster had a fear of water; she didn't even know swimming and Castle knew that.

It was a cruel death.

The alcohol in Devin's system had made him weaker. I was yelling at Castle and asking him why he had done that. Dayana was crying too and talking something non-stop but also maintain her distance from Castle. She thought we were next.

I think it stunned everyone.

"Mom! Where's Mom? Why isn't she calling out to us?... Devin..." Dayana ran to the railing to stare into the dark water and then ran back inside, "We need to call someone for help!" Dayana rushed towards the cockpit to call for help.

"You murderer!"

It happened so fast.

Devin had tackled Castle to the floor and was delivering blows after blows, powerful punches and Castle only raised his hands to stop the hits. The alcohol had made Devin angrier and delirious as he dragged Castle to the gate and pushed his head underwater.

It is dangerous when a man is angry and under the influence of alcohol.

"Stop this!" I gave out an anguished wail.

Frustrated, I tried to pry Devin away from Castle, but he continued to push his head into the water. I watched Castle's head trying to bob to the surface, fighting to come up, but Devin had the up-per-hand. Castle's body thrashed for dominance, but it was of no use.

And then there was silence. Only the serene sound of the water lapping against the boat.

That's when I knew Castle was dead. In a sudden act of madness, Devin had done justice to his mother.

Three members of my family were dead.

Devin turned his bloodshot eyes towards me.

I was yelling and crying, acting as if I wasn't part of this fucked up plan.

Castle left me alone in this, and I was angry about it. I didn't want to be the one in the position to do all the planning. I wanted him alive so I could kill him all over again.

"Did you know what he planned?" Devin asked me.

My life depended on that answer and the award-winning perfor-mance.

"Fuck, no. Of course, I didn't. Why would I want Dad or Mom to be killed? Why the fuck would you even suggest something like that?" I did more yelling while sobbing helplessly.

"The motherfucker planned all of it alone." Devin said and then a helpless moan escaped his lips, "He...he killed them..." in a wild rage he began thrashing the furniture in the lounge.

Dayana had asked the captain to dive into the lake, but when he went underwater, he couldn't find the bodies.

The bodies were found a day later by a search party. Aster's body was bruised, blotted and there was what little remained of Chris Montgomery. His body came in pieces and Devin had been close to moving into the insane asylum after what he'd witnessed.

Castle's body was not found.

The postmortem had showed that Chris and Aster were both intoxicated and what happened to them proved to be a boating accident. Castle had jumped in to rescue them, but had drowned in the process. Devin had not clarified to the police that Castle had gone on the murder-spree.

Justice was done, and that's all that mattered to Devin. The police wanted nothing to do with the Montgomerys. When Hugh was young and kicking, there were cases of high-rank police officers dying in accidents. Now they preferred to look the other way, no matter how heinous the crimes were.

A day after Aster and Dad's funeral, Devin arranged for Castle's memorial. It was all for show.

It was the same morning I found an anklet tracker fitted into my leg.

"What the hell is this?"

"I want to make sure you know your place, Theodore. Mom and dad's dead, Castle's dead too, no one's on your side and I'm taking over. You will obey me."

"Fuck off," I said in my usual tone of defiance.

Devin was enjoying this. He had always dreamed of being in charge of everything, and Castle had given him that.

I was wearing a black suit, sitting in the chapel, my fingers entwined with Madison's as I tried to come up with a plan.

Castle's picture was right at the front. He was smiling in it.

"Fuck you, Castle!" I mumbled. "For leaving me alone...how dare you?"

Devin will tolerate me for as long as I was seventeen. When I was legal enough to get my share, he'd have me assassinated.

Think Theodore!

Devin was on the podium, reciting a bullshit ecology, when the door burst open.

Castle stood there in raggedy clothes that weren't even fitting him. A timid man stood behind him.

A deadly hush fell upon the entire chapel, for it was the only time that a dead or missing person had turned up at his own funeral.

Everyone stared.

The memorial had to stop.

He hadn't died that night. He'd hit his head hard against something, and then a fisherman had rescued him. He'd recognized Castle as a Montgomery and brought him home.

When we were alone eventually, I asked him, "You better be ready for what's coming for you. Devin is about to throw you to the vultures and you're about to be fodder. He will have you arrested."

I should have noticed the strange look on his face, and the confusing way he continued to stare at me.

"I...I don't understand." He said.

"The boating accident." I clarified. The word 'murder' was prohibited in this house.

"What happened?" Castle asked, and his breathing labored, and he began rocking back and forth, "I don't remember...Theo...where's mom and dad? Why was Devin...angry?"

"You've lost your memories," I concluded, collapsing into the chair.

Castle's words before the accident came back to me. If something goes wrong, you will finish what we started.

I had to take control of the situation.

That was the start.